Imperfect Justice

Cowboy Justice Association
Book Six

By Olivia Jaymes

www.OliviaJaymes.com

IMPERFECT JUSTICE

Print Edition

Cover art by Sloan Winters

eBook ISBN: 978-0-9907996-6-5
Print ISBN: 978-0-9861029-1-2

Dedication

For my amazing and wonderful editor Mary. Thank you.

Chapter One

Sheriff Jared Monroe was a man who could handle his whiskey. He rarely got drunk even in high school. He had good memories of when he and his friends would sneak six-packs from their parents. Partying out in the middle of nowhere, drinking beer and sitting on the tailgates of their trucks on a Friday night after the big game.

He'd never had a hangover in his entire thirty-nine years.

But he probably would tomorrow morning.

He was sitting in Larry's Beer and Barbecue, known to the locals of Fielding as the B&B. The bar was a typical honky tonk dive with a scarred oak dance floor, a jukebox, and neon signs. The delicious aroma of smoked meat kept the place from smelling like beer and sweat which was a plus as far as he was concerned. It was also the only bar in Fielding, which naturally made it the hangout for those over twenty-one who weren't into the fancy coffees served at the shop on the corner of Main and Maple.

Jared had been drinking for the last few hours and generally feeling like hell. For someone who prided himself on keeping his life on an even kilter and controlling the chaos he'd done a piss-poor job of things lately.

"Another, Sheriff?" Larry the owner and sometime bartender held up the whiskey bottle, the golden-brown liquid already half empty.

Jared lifted his glass and slapped it on the worn and scratched wooden bar. "Yes, another. The night is still young, Larry."

The older man nodded in sympathy and re-filled Jared's highball glass. "I heard about your dad. Someone said he had an accident. Is he okay now? Tough thing to have happen so soon after your mom."

Jared's mother had unexpectedly passed away from a heart attack not quite two months ago and the pain of losing her was still acute. She'd been the anchor of the Monroe family with her easy-going manner and common sense. She'd certainly been the only person that had ever been able to handle Jared's father.

Gerald Rhinehart Monroe, the patriarch of the Monroe family and owner of one of the largest ranches in Montana or Wyoming was something of a legend in these parts. People either loved or hated Gerald Monroe. Jared had vacillated between the two emotions through the years but mostly he loved his father.

But he always respected the man.

Tougher than nails with the temperament of a rattler, Gerald Monroe had left the Army but the Army had never left Gerald. He'd raised all four of his children with two things in mind.

Discipline and control.

Those two things had been conspicuously absent in Gerald since his beloved Rita had passed. He'd taken her death hard and his behavior had become increasingly erratic in the last several weeks culminating in the accident that had landed him in the hospital.

"He wrenched his back when he overturned the ATV. He's got a few bumps and bruises too. He's resting comfortably the doctor says. Of course Dad is screaming to come home. Hates being in the hospital. Says they're trying to kill him."

Gerald had said it loudly as he'd tried to understand why he was in the hospital with only minor injuries. The hospital staff had been forced to sedate the seventy year old man while the doctor had explained to Jared that there was more wrong with his father than a bad back and a few contusions.

These outbursts had become more and more common in a man that had always been known for his icy control. Rita Monroe, Jared, and his siblings had begged his father to see a doctor but Gerald had snorted in derision at the mere idea. He'd only been sick a few times in his whole damn life.

Now this doctor was telling Jared that Gerald Monroe, the larger than life man that had raised him and built a ranching empire, had Alzheimer's.

Larry chuckled and wiped down the bar. "Don't blame old Gerald. Don't much like hospitals myself. Seems like a depressing place to put sick people. When's he coming home?"

Jared knocked back the double-shot of whiskey and savored the burn all the way to his belly before placing the glass in front of Larry again. Larry re-filled the glass and then returned to cleaning the bar. The room tilted slightly and then spun before righting itself but Jared didn't give a shit. Right now he didn't want to feel or think and the bottom of a bottle of alcohol seemed a good place to start.

"In a few days. The doctor told him he needs to take it easy for awhile. He also suggested that Dad should lose a few pounds. Cut back on butter and meat. Stuff like that."

"Damn," Larry sputtered. "Poor man. I don't think I'd want to live that way. I bet your old man feels the same. Doctors don't know shit anyway. They tell you one thing is bad for you and then later say it's okay. My grandpa ate eggs, bacon, and toast with butter every damn morning of his life and lived to be ninety-five so don't tell me that doctors know what's best. Your old man is so stubborn, hell, he'll outlive us all."

It didn't look like that would be the case.

People came in and out of the bar, some slapping Jared on the back, joining him for a drink, and asking about the old man. Some warily kept their distance either because of something illegal they'd done or because they were thinking of doing something illegal. Tonight Jared was off duty and didn't give a shit as the time ticked away. By the time the whiskey bottle was almost empty, Larry was pointing to the clock.

"It's late, Sheriff and I think you've had enough. Want me to call Royce or Ty?"

Jared had no idea where his older brother Royce was and his younger brother Ty had gone into Bozeman earlier and wasn't expected until morning. Digging into his pocket, he tossed a wad of bills on the bar, enough to cover the booze plus a nice tip. Larry had been decent company this evening, not asking too many questions about why the normally sober, upstanding sheriff was getting sloppy drunk.

"Just call me a cab." Jared carefully got to his feet, ignoring the dizzy feeling in his head, and shrugged on his coat. "I could use some air. I'll wait outside."

Larry was already reaching for the phone as Jared pushed open the front door. The bitter cold of a Montana winter slapped him in the face but he'd drunk too much to sober up from a blast of wind. He stumbled to the bench in front of the bar and sat down, staring at the deserted streets of Fielding.

Pretty much everyone who had any sense was in bed or at least in their own homes, warm and protected. Not that Jared minded the solitude. Normally he enjoyed the quiet when he could let his mind rest and think about things. But tonight he didn't want to think about anything. That's why he'd been drinking, hoping to blank his memory if only for a few hours.

It hadn't worked and he wouldn't try it again.

For now he'd wait for his taxi and try not to think about all the things he had to do tomorrow, like tell his family that his father's accident was the least of his problems. That life would never be the same for any of them.

It seemed that it didn't matter what a man did or didn't do, right or wrong, evil or good.

✧ ✧ ✧ ✧

Misty Foster turned down the car radio as she drove past the "Welcome to Fielding" sign that sat at the outskirts of the little town. She'd been driving for hours in a vehicle that had seen better days, coming home from a gallery showing in Seattle. She was exhausted after several busy days and all she wanted was to crawl between the sheets of her bed and sleep for the next twenty-four hours straight. It had taken an extra couple of hours due to the crappy weather but the sky had cleared as she'd neared her destination. Now the issue was the rapidly dropping temperature. It was going to be another cold Montana night.

Swinging onto the main drag through town, she slowed her vehicle down to the posted twenty-five miles per hour. She didn't think anyone would be out in cold like this but she'd seen a stray dog or deer run across the street more than once.

Squinting and craning her neck to get a better look, Misty spied a figure who sat slumped on the bench in front of the B&B, not moving and possibly frozen to death. The flashing sign on the bank across the street said it was twelve-fifteen in the morning and six degrees. It wouldn't take long for some poor drunk to get frostbite or hypothermia or whatever people got when it was this darn cold.

Groaning, she gingerly stepped on the brake, inwardly wondering at the wisdom of stopping, and pulled the vehicle into the parking lot of the B&B. She'd never be able to get to sleep until she knew this person was warm and safe so there was no point in driving on.

Shoving open the car door the bitter cold hit her immediately. She grabbed her gloves from her pockets and pulled them on after buttoning up her coat all the way to her neck. Her knitted hat had fallen somewhere in the back seat and she didn't have time to look for it. Hopefully she wouldn't be out in the cold air long.

Misty carefully navigated the icy parking lot and approached the figure who was now clearly a large man who had his hat pulled down over his face to protect it from the wind. She reached out her hand and touched his shoulder.

"Um, sir? Are you okay? It's too cold to be sitting outside." A gloved hand reached up for the brim of his hat, pushing it away from his face. The cheeks were red from the cold but she recognized the handsome man instantly. Sheriff Jared Monroe. "Sheriff, are you sick?"

A quick glance over her shoulder told her his SUV was in the parking lot. Had he been on his way to the vehicle and perhaps fallen on the ice and injured himself?

"I'm fine." The sheriff's voice sounded sure and strong but her sensitive nose detected the smell of whiskey on his breath. It was an aroma she knew all too well, although she was more than a little shocked to find it circling a man who as far as she knew never drank to excess. "I'm waiting for a taxi."

At least he'd had the sense not to drive, but then he was the sheriff. Unfortunately he wasn't thinking straight about the temperature.

"You can't wait out in the cold. You'll freeze to death. How long have you been out here anyway?"

His broad shoulders lifted inside his heavy wool coat. "I'm not sure. Ten minutes? What are you doing out this time of night?"

"Driving back from Seattle," Misty replied impatiently, scanning the deserted street. "There's no sign of a cab and it would have been here by now. Why don't I give you a ride home?"

She thought he was going to turn her down but a huge gust of wind blew ice cold air into their faces, taking their breath away. He nodded and stood, pulling his hat down again. "That sounds like a good idea. Thank you."

Instinctively she reached out her hand to steady him but he was already shaking off her help with a brusque, "I'm fine. Let's get out of the wind."

Fine. If he wanted to fall on the ice and bust his ass then he could go right ahead. Misty had only been trying to help and Lord knew she'd had plenty of practice with her own mother.

"The door's unlocked."

He didn't reply and he didn't walk around to the passenger side. Instead he walked to the driver's door and for a moment she thought he was going to try and get behind the wheel before she realized he was holding open her door.

Like a gentleman.

She didn't get much of that behavior in this town. Not because of who the men were but because of who she was.

"Thanks."

She slid into the vehicle, closing the door against the wind. He joined her seconds later and she fired up the engine and turned the heat on full blast. The car was already warm from her long drive and the hot air streamed from the vents onto her numbed flesh. The sheriff pulled off his gloves and held his hands out as she backed out of the parking lot and onto the main thoroughfare.

She'd just extended her night by at least a half hour by the time she drove him to his house and then reversed directions and drove back. But it was a small price to pay so he wouldn't wake up dead in the morning, frozen and stuck to the bench in front of the B&B.

"What were you doing in Seattle?" he asked once they were on the road and thawed out. "Wait, that isn't any of my business."

Misty peeked at his profile and inwardly winced. She knew what the townsfolk said about her trips out of town. She'd heard the gossip of big city lovers and clandestine meetings in seedy motels near the airport. She didn't help things by not discussing the more private parts of her life, but then she doubted they would be believed. People rarely changed their minds about things.

"I went for business. I'm moving there as soon as my lease is up here."

That day couldn't come soon enough. She was finally getting out of Fielding. For good. No looking back and no regrets.

He turned to her and scowled as if what she said didn't make any sense. "Leaving? Why?"

Misty sighed and drove down the dark, deserted road as fast as she dared with the head lawman sitting next to her. Sheriff Jared Monroe wasn't a stupid man by any stretch of the imagination but the troubles of a single young woman probably hadn't been high on his radar.

Instead of giving him an honest answer she re-directed. "Lots of people leave small towns for larger cities. I'm certainly not the first."

"That's true," he conceded, his expression brooding. He was an incredibly handsome man with his square jaw, dark hair, and piercing blue eyes. She'd had a crush on him when she was a teenager, but then pretty much every female in Fielding did at one time or another. It was practically a rite of passage. Last she'd heard he was dating Alexa Dorning, a young divorcee from the next county over. Misty had never seen the woman but the gossips had been busy extolling the woman's beauty and wondering if she'd finally be the one to lasso Jared Monroe. "I guess I'm just not a big fan of cities. Too many people in a small space. I like having some elbow room."

Fielding probably looked a hell of a lot different from his perch far above it. He was the crown prince of one of the leading families in this area while Misty was the daughter of the town tramp. Her experiences as a child with the closed-minded citizens had led her to dream of leaving since she was old enough to know that staying wasn't a requirement.

"I'm looking forward to it. Something new and different."

Relieved he didn't respond, she turned onto the private drive of the Double M ranch. The gravel road was dark and there wasn't a street light for miles. She slowed the car to a crawl and turned on her high beams.

"The road is going to fork here in a minute so veer to the right."

She was concentrating so intently his voice made her jump. "I thought the house was near the lake."

"I don't live at the main house. I have my own."

Just as he said the road forked and she stayed to the right, holding the steering wheel with a death grip to keep the wind from knocking the car around. It had really picked up in the last few minutes. When a house appeared in her high beams she almost screamed with relief. She brought the car to a halt and turned to the sheriff.

"Home safe and sound. Let me know if you need a ride into town tomorrow to get your truck."

She almost smacked herself upside the head as she heard herself offering to help. Yet again. She had a bad habit of that, always trying to make things easier for people even if it made things difficult for her.

"I'll find a ride," he assured her. "Drive careful and thank you again."

"You're welcome."

He pushed open the door, letting in another burst of cold air that made her shiver. The temperature was definitely dropping. He got to his feet and managed to get about a yard but the wind seemed to be playing havoc with his compromised balance. The sheriff wasn't falling down drunk but he'd had a few too many.

Sighing in resignation, Misty turned off the engine and exited the vehicle determined that he wasn't going to fall in the ice and snow on her watch. She hated this worry-wart-caretaker side of herself but there was nothing she could do about it now. She'd make sure he got in the house safe and sound and then be on her way.

But she couldn't help but wonder…what would the good citizens of Fielding think about Misty Foster being in Sheriff Jared Monroe's house? Even if only for a few minutes?

No one could ever know she'd been there.

Chapter Two

Catching up to him easily, she wound her arm around his waist to steady him although his large frame overwhelmed her. If he went down he was taking the two of them.

"I don't need any help." The sheriff's voice was gruff but she didn't pay his stubborn self any mind.

"Apparently you do."

They managed to stagger up the porch steps despite the strong gusts. When they arrived at the front door she expected him to unlock it but he simply wrapped his hand around the knob and gave it a twist, the door falling open.

"You should lock your doors. There are a lot of crazy people in this world."

They both entered the house and he shut the door behind them. "Crazy enough to break into the sheriff's house? I don't think so. We've never had any problems on the ranch. If someone is lurking around here they're more interested in the cattle than my flatscreen."

He shrugged out of his coat and tossed it on the back of a chair. "Thank you for the ride home. I may sound ungrateful but you don't have to babysit me. I'm fine."

"You don't look fine," she shot back. "You look like you need some strong coffee and a couple of aspirin."

Instead of denying it he nodded in agreement. "I think you're right but the only thing I'm good for is lying down and sleeping."

How many times had Misty fixed a pot of coffee in the middle of the night? If she had a nickel for every one she would have had the money to move to Seattle a long time ago.

"Lie down while I make you some coffee." She shed her coat and was already heading to the kitchen, not bothering to listen to any of his protests. It was obvious he lived alone and he didn't have anyone to take care of him.

The house was comfortable but definitely that of a bachelor with its brown and blue color scheme and spare decorations. There were no knickknacks on the shelves or matching dishtowels in the kitchen. Instead one wall was taken up with a gigantic entertainment center with a large television and shelves of books.

The kitchen was spotless as if it wasn't used very often. The coffee pot sat on the counter and thank goodness it was a basic drip model, nothing complicated. The sheriff was still standing at the door as she pulled open cabinets. Finally he shook his head and dropped down onto the couch with a groan.

"Where do you keep your aspirin?" she called out as the coffee brewed, the smell beginning to waft around her. She loved the aroma of coffee but couldn't stand the taste. She'd never understood the allure no matter how much sugar and cream she added.

"Drawer next to the silverware." His arm was thrown over his eyes as he laid back on the couch, his boots still on and dripping on the crocheted afghan.

"You should take your boots off. You're getting your couch wet and dirty," she said as she filled a glass with water and found the correct drawer, shaking out two tablets. "You need to take these and drink this entire glass of water so you won't be dehydrated in the morning."

She stood over his reclining form and he pulled his arm away from his eyes and grunted.

"Damn, you're bossy. I'm the one who usually gives the orders around here."

He didn't sound too put out about it though, not that she would have backed down. He was worse for drink and she was an expert on how to care for that.

"By tomorrow you'll be ordering around the washing machine and telling the oven who's boss, but right now you need to swallow these pills and drink this entire glass of water."

Chuckling, his face split into a grin. "You're brave—I'll give you that. Most people wouldn't dare talk to me that way."

"Most people wouldn't have offered to drive you home. They would have let you sit there as the temperature dropped and you turned into an icicle. A dead one. It's hard to give orders with frozen lips."

She held her hand out flat with the two tablets nestled there and the glass of water in her other hand. He reached for the pills, his fingers brushing her palm and her pulse leaped in response. She couldn't remember the last time anyone had touched her bare skin. Months? No, probably years. College, when she'd had a steady boyfriend, except she'd never reacted so strongly when he'd touched her. Her skin still tingled where the sheriff had rubbed against it.

Balling up her hand into a fist she shoved it behind her back, determined to ignore the ricochet of pleasure a simple touch had evoked. The sheriff tossed back the tablets and gulped down the water until the glass was empty. He slapped it down on the coffee table.

"Happy?" he asked, an eyebrow quirked in question.

"I'm not unhappy. You're the one that would be suffering tomorrow if you didn't do it. I'll go get your coffee."

She turned but he caught her arm and gently tugged until she was sitting next to him on the couch. He'd propped himself up on a few pillows so they were almost eye to eye. A smile played around his mouth as if he found her amusing.

"Relax for a minute. You're strung awful tight, woman. Are you always this prickly?"

Her hip was pressed close to his own and the warmth easily penetrated the heavy denim of her jeans. He hadn't let go of her hand and she was having a hard time catching her breath as his thumb brushed back and forth over a sensitive spot on her wrist.

"I need to get your coffee," she said, a note of desperation in her voice that she didn't like hearing. Was she such a pushover with a handsome man that his mere nearness was affecting her this way?

"It can wait." His eyes narrowed as his gaze swept to her feet and back up again, a flush covering her body at his bold inspection. He didn't bother to hide that he was looking at her. Assessing her. "You'd be a pretty thing if it weren't for those clothes. They've got to be at least two sizes too big."

Misty knew she wasn't beautiful. She had a mirror in the bathroom and looked at herself every day while she was combing her hair or brushing her teeth. At most she was cute. Maybe. Her features were tiny to go along with her stature and she carried too much on top and on her hips to be fashionable. Misty had always thought her best feature was her pale blonde hair which she wore long, almost to her waist.

But none of that added up to pretty.

She tried her best to give him a cold look. "I don't think my appearance is any of your business. Will you let me go now?"

His fingers were still wrapped around her wrist but he wasn't hurting her, unless you counted how the heat simmered under his palm and sent bolts of electricity to her extremities.

"You're right—it's not." He nodded, but instead of letting her go he curled his arm around her waist and pulled her even closer, his face inches away. "You have the prettiest pink lips. So full and sensuous. I can't help but wonder what they taste like. I bet they taste like sugar."

"They don't taste like anything." She shook her head but something in his hot gaze kept her rooted to the spot. Knowing she should move away and doing it were two very different things. She'd never had a man look at her…that way.

"I bet they do. I bet they taste sweet, Misty Foster. Let me thank you for saving me from freezing to death."

He gave her plenty of time to pull away but she didn't. She simply sat there as he moved closer, his lips tenderly brushing her own and sending shivers up her spine before claiming her mouth as if he owned it. She'd been kissed before of course, although probably less than most other women her age. Nothing had prepared her for this. His hand cupped the back of her head, his fingers twining into her hair while his mouth plundered and his tongue played. He tasted like whiskey and she should have found it disgusting, but the warm mellow flavor was instead intoxicating. By the time he lifted his head, she was a quivering mass of confused arousal.

She couldn't let this happen. Hadn't she learned anything by now? He was no different than all the others here in Fielding.

Jumping up from the sofa, her face on fire, she smoothed down her thick sweater with shaky hands. "I think that's enough, Sheriff."

She tried to sound stern but she only sounded squeaky and unsure. She took a few breaths as her tumbling stomach settled in her abdomen, nauseated by her own behavior. She was better than this.

She wasn't her mother.

"I'm not sure I'd ever get enough, Misty. Are you sure you don't want to come back here and continue?"

Jared Monroe had that cock-of-the-walk grin on his face and for good reason. Misty doubted he'd been turned down by women very often. If ever. Of course he would be arrogant enough to think that kissing her would be some sort of payment for a job well done.

So this was going to be a shock. *Good.*

"I think when you're completely sober you'll be second guessing your behavior here tonight. I need to go. There's coffee in the kitchen."

Lifting her chin, she marched toward the door hoping he didn't follow her. She tugged on her coat and fumbled in her pocket for her keys, peeking behind her. He was still half lying on the couch and for some reason she was disappointed that he hadn't tried to stop her from going. Clearly she needed to get some rest. She was becoming delirious.

"Well, good night," she said awkwardly as she opened the front door.

The sheriff swung his legs onto the floor and winced a little, his hand rubbing his head which was probably starting to throb. Hopefully the aspirin would kick in soon.

"Good night, Misty." He had a big smile on his face. "Thank you for the ride home. And the kiss."

"Don't talk about that kiss," she replied crossly. He really was the most arrogant, smug man.

"It was just a kiss. No big deal," he said, folding his arms behind his head. "Drive careful, Misty."

She didn't bother to respond again since he wouldn't understand. Turning swiftly on her booted heel, she fled from the house and down the front porch stairs, almost sliding on the ice but catching herself at the last minute.

From now until she left Fielding she'd make sure to stay far away from Sheriff Jared Monroe.

Chapter Three

Jared groaned and twisted on the couch. He ought to get up and climb into bed but he was mentally and physically wrung out. After Misty had left he'd laid here and dozed on and off, listening to the wind outside and worrying about everything from how he was going to tell his family about his dad to whether Misty had made it home okay. It didn't make for peaceful rest.

Levering up from the cushions, he pulled off his boots and padded in stocking feet to the kitchen. One touch of his finger on the coffee pot told him it was ice cold. He poured out the liquid and made another pot, pressing the start button before heading back into the living room to check the thermostat. Misty had said something about the falling temperature and it appeared she'd been correct.

He hiked the thermostat up a few degrees and pushed the entryway rug against the bottom of the front door to seal out the chilly air. The glass of the window was cold under his palm and he took a moment to be grateful that Misty had been out driving tonight. Had the cab ever shown up? In his inebriated state he could have frozen to death out there. The whole drinking to get drunk thing had simply been a stupid as hell idea.

At least he was sobering up now. He didn't enjoy the feeling of being out of control when he was drinking but he'd wanted to stop thinking about everything.

It had been what could only be described as a spectacular failure.

In addition he'd managed to honk off Misty Foster while he was at it. He didn't think she'd liked the kiss near as much as he had, which was something he wasn't used to. Most females were eager to kiss him. And more. Misty on the other hand had looked at him as if he were something…less than desirable. She'd been like an angry spitting kitten being given a bath instead of some affection. What would make her purr?

Shaking his head, he made a mental note to apologize next time he saw her in town. It might have been a harmless kiss, but she hadn't asked for it and he wasn't a man that condoned harassment of women in any form. He'd be humble and apologetic no matter how soft her lips had been under his.

And they had been silky soft.

He was enjoying that first cup of coffee and trying to not think about Misty Foster when he heard a banging on the door. Swearing under his breath, he knew it could only be one of his brothers at this ungodly hour. His bet was on Royce, who had been noticeably absent at the hospital all damn day.

"Come in, Royce. It's open."

"How'd you know it was me?" Jared's older brother Royce ambled into the kitchen and didn't bother taking off his coat before rummaging in the refrigerator. He smelled like cigarettes, booze, and sour sweat. Jared didn't even want to think about what Royce had been doing for the last twenty-four hours.

"Because we've been looking for you all damn day. Where the hell have you been?" Jared pointed to the coffeemaker. "There's not a lot of food but the coffee is fresh."

Somehow Royce found a couple of store bought cookies and then poured himself a cup of coffee. Months of the good life had left its mark on Jared's older brother. He looked tired and drawn, dark circles under his eyes – the same blue as Jared's own. Normally fit and trim, Royce was sporting extra weight around his middle courtesy of too many beers and not enough hard work on the ranch. Ty, Jared's younger brother and ranch foreman, said that Royce only showed up one or two days a week and then barely did anything at all. Mostly he drank black coffee and nursed a hangover.

"How did you know I was awake?" Jared asked, eyeing his brother suspiciously. Royce only showed up around here when he wanted something from Jared. "I could have been asleep or on patrol."

Royce jerked his thumb toward the front of the house. "Well, for one thing, your lights are on. That was a pretty good indication that you were home. As for knowing that you were awake? One of my buddies said he saw you at the B&B tonight tying one on. Since when do you get drunk?"

One couldn't underestimate the speed of gossip in Fielding. "I wouldn't describe myself as drunk but yes, I had a few too many. So now that we know where I've been, where the hell have you been? Your absence was noticed, bro. Dad asked about you."

After a fashion. Jared's dad had asked if Royce was in school as if they were all still teenagers or something. The drugs they were pumping into him was a large part of it, but unfortunately there was more to it than that.

A pained expression flitted across Royce's face but was quickly replaced with a mask of bland indifference. He'd always had a complicated relationship with their father. Royce had been

Gerald Monroe's favorite so he had been pushed and spoiled in equal measures.

"What did the old man want? I called the doctor this morning and Dad's doing fine."

Jared had to rein in his impatience with his brother. He'd always been like this, acting like he didn't give a shit about anything. Grades. Girls. Sports. Gerald Monroe had pushed his sons to achieve – especially his oldest son – and Royce had spent the better part of forty years giving the old man the virtual finger.

"He is but he wanted you there."

Royce threw back his head and laughed. "Bullshit. He had you, didn't he? Daddy's golden boy. The smartest kid. The best athlete. The greatest sheriff. Mister Fucking Perfect." He leaned forward, a grin on his face. "Dad has never needed me, Jared. He only needed someone to carry on in his image. Congratulations, bro. You were stupid enough to do it. Me? I'm living my own life and having a great time doing it. I highly recommend it, by the way. Try it. Do something Dad doesn't approve of. Just once."

Royce had been singing this same song since they were kids. He thought doing the right thing was the same as knuckling under to their dad while Jared thought doing the right thing...was...hell...the right thing to do. For its own sake. He'd never felt the need to rebel like Royce did and had often wondered why. Of course Gerald Monroe had been filled with plans for his oldest son, so perhaps he had felt the pressure more keenly than Jared.

"I'm not going around with you again about this, big brother. Stop blaming Dad for everything and look at the choices you've made. And he did ask about you today and you weren't there."

Royce leaned against the kitchen counter, a coffee cup in one hand and a smirk on his face. "I was busy."

Jared slammed his mug onto the table. "Busy? Doing what?"

"The better question is who, little bro. The cutest little redhead in the county. Didn't catch her name but we emptied a bottle of tequila between us before getting down to…business."

Jared was exhausted and pissed off and his brother's little speech hadn't improved matters at all. Acid-like bile rose in his throat and something snapped inside. Before he could think it through he was up out of the chair. Grabbing Royce by his shirt, Jared pushed him against the wall so they were face to face. There was no way his brother was going to miss a word of what Jared had to say.

"Listen and listen good. The party is fucking over, do you hear me? I'm sick of your shit. All the whining and bitching about Dad and how he ruined your life. Tough. Dad is sick, Mom is gone, and Ty and I are not going to deal with this all by ourselves. So you better fucking sober up, keep your dick in your pants, and grow the hell up. Do you hear me?"

Royce's face had gone white, his lips pressed together in anger. "I hear you." He shoved at Jared but was too out of shape to budge him. "The doctor said Dad's injuries were mild."

Loosening his grip on Royce's shirt, Jared stepped back and swallowed the lump that had formed in his throat simply thinking about his conversation with the doctors this afternoon.

"They were mild. That's not the problem." There was only one way to say it. Straight out. "Dad has Alzheimer's, bro. It's already started. You've seen how he is…always angry. Getting confused. Forgetting things and blaming it on others. It's started. There are medications that can help but he needs to start taking them now not later."

Royce's throat bobbed as he turned to gaze out of the window into the darkness. "Does he know?"

"No. But he's going to find out. You and I are the only ones who know so far."

Royce's eyes widened in surprise. "Ty doesn't know yet? What about Becky?"

Jared shook his head, his chest tight and aching. "The doctor pulled me aside just as we were leaving." He punched a finger into Royce's chest. "You should have been there with me."

Nodding, Royce slumped down into a chair. "Shit, I'm sorry. Jesus, I can't even imagine Dad…I mean, he's always been a tough son of a bitch, ya know?"

Jared sat back down and placed his hand on his brother's shoulder. "I know. We've got to stick together so we can all get through this."

"That's why you were drinking tonight," Royce stated, knowledge in his eyes.

"It didn't help." Jared sat back in the chair with a groan. "The only thing I've done is give myself a pounding headache and an upset stomach."

Royce laughed and slapped Jared on the back. "The secret to never getting a hangover is to not stop drinking."

"Not an option." Jared gave his brother a hard look. "I mean it, bro. You need to straighten up and fly right. With Dad sick we can't trust him to make decisions for the ranch and holdings any more. Ty's going to need help on the ranch. If all four of us pull together we'll be okay."

"You always sound so sure of yourself, little brother. You really believe what you're saying at all times, don't you?"

It wasn't that Jared believed what he was saying was true, it was more that he hoped it was. He'd do whatever he needed to do to hold his family together.

✧ ✧ ✧ ✧

Misty dumped her suitcase inside the door of her tiny apartment and stripped out of her coat, boots, and gloves. The temperature on her dash had read a numbing five below zero and she was darn glad to be in her own home. A home that wasn't much warmer than outside.

Rubbing her arms, she turned up the thermostat several degrees but also flipped on the space heater she used to supplement the ancient heating unit. She'd turned the thermostat down when she'd left for Seattle but then it had been a balmy thirty degrees outside. Anyone who lived in weather like this knew thirty felt much warmer than zero.

The apartment was small but it was all hers. She didn't have to worry about anyone else but herself and that alone was wonderful. It was really only one large room plus a bathroom, but she'd taken the time to decorate it in the bright colors she loved so much. The daybed, covered in a mound of pillows, called to her tired and aching body. She'd been on the road for hours and she needed rest to clear her muddled mind.

Although her confusion might be more from Jared Monroe's kiss than lack of sleep.

She wasn't a woman that went around kissing people. And to be honest, she didn't think the sheriff was either. He'd always seemed serious about his work, not a party boy like his older brother. Perhaps she'd overreacted and made it more of a big deal than it really was.

The sheriff had a few too many drinks.

He'd kissed and teased her.

He hadn't groped her or propositioned her or anything gross.

He'd probably forgotten all about it by now. She was the one turning this molehill into a mountain.

The best thing she could do is go to bed and forget the whole thing ever happened. Except that it *had* happened and she couldn't put it out of her mind. There was only one thing to do. Misty picked up her phone and quickly typed out a text.

R u awake?

Misty held her breath and waited, hoping that Rayne was having another bout of insomnia. Her best friend lived right across the hall and she'd become the sister Misty had never had. They often spent late nights watching movies and talking until they both finally fell asleep.

Yes. R u home?

Yes.

B there in 2.

Misty sighed in relief and went straight to the kitchen to start heating some milk for hot chocolate. She would tell the one person in the world she trusted what had happened tonight over a cup of steaming cocoa.

"Come here and give me a hug, girl. I've missed you."

Rayne knew how to make an entrance. A pretty brunette, she seemed to vibrate with energy twenty-four hours a day and this occasion was no different. She burst through the front door wearing ratty sweats and a huge smile, arms open. Rayne was in the same boat as Misty as far as the town of Fielding was concerned. She'd moved here to be close to her sister who had married a local, but her dark hair streaked with purple, multiple piercings, and tattoo-covered body put off most people.

But Rayne had a heart of gold. She'd quickly seen how lonely and solitary Misty's life was and made it her mission to be the best friend ever.

Misty gave Rayne a hug, feeling better than she had all night. Just talking about things would calm her and enable her to sleep. She would miss Rayne's easy-going friendship when she moved to Seattle.

"Relax and have a seat. I'm making hot chocolate."

Rayne sprawled on the couch with a smile. "Double marshmallows for me. So how was your trip? Tell me every detail, although I should say don't tell me anything. I can't believe you're leaving me and moving. I'm going to miss you so much."

"I'm going to miss you too. I wish you would come with me. I'm sure you could get a job in any tattoo shop in the city. You have real talent."

"Thank you, but my sister…" Rayne's sister was pregnant and she wanted to be close by.

"I know. You'll just have to come visit me, that's all. And as for the trip, it was fine. I sold some paintings and made some money. All good. It was when I arrived in Fielding that something happened."

Rayne's brow went up. "Something happened in Fielding? I guess there's a first time for everything. Sit down and tell me."

Misty poured out two large mugs of hot chocolate, dumped in some marshmallows, and settled down on the other end of the sofa. Handing a cup to Rayne, Misty wasn't sure where to begin.

"I was driving home," she began. "Coming down Main Street."

Rayne blew on the steaming liquid and then took an experimental sip. "This is good. I was up reading since I couldn't sleep and I was out of marshmallows. Go on."

"There was a man sitting in front of the B&B and I was worried because I thought he might have frozen to death or something. So I pulled over to check on him."

Rayne set the mug down on the coffee table. "Let me get this straight. You stopped in the middle of the night in front of a bar to check on some guy who might or might not be dead but could have been drunk and packing a gun or knife? Have you lost your mind? You could have been killed. I know you go overboard caring for people but this was dangerous."

Misty shook her head. "No, no, no. It wasn't like that. It was the sheriff."

That statement seemed to take Rayne aback. "The sheriff? You have my attention. Was he okay?"

"He'd had a few too many and was waiting for a cab. I was afraid to leave him in case they didn't show so I offered him a ride home."

"I swear you are the original Girl Scout. Did he accept? Damn, he is one fine man. I wouldn't mind having to give him a ride home one day. Maybe I could convince him that he was lonely and needed some company."

"He did accept. So I drove him home…and it was really windy…"

"And?" Rayne prompted. "Did you have trouble with your car? You should shoot that thing and put it out of its misery."

"No," Misty said slowly. Now that the time had come to tell Rayne about the kiss Misty was wondering if maybe she shouldn't say anything at all. Rayne had made her opinions of Misty's love life – or lack thereof – very plain. "He was a little unsteady on his feet so I helped him into the house. I made him some coffee and found some aspirin."

"That was sweet and certainly above and beyond the call of duty. I hope he was sufficiently grateful."

Misty felt the heat rise in her cheeks and her heart rate pick up. "He did thank me…with…a kiss."

Rayne's eyes went wide with astonishment. "A kiss, huh? I knew the sheriff was hot. How was it? You didn't have a case of the vapors and faint on him, did you?"

"I did not." Misty's tone was indignant. "I–I kissed him back."

"Now that is good news," Rayne approved with a grin. "Now answer my question. How was it? Is he as good as he looks? That man is sex on a stick."

"It was good. I guess. All we did was kiss and then I jumped up from the couch and left. The only reason he did it was because he'd had too much to drink."

Now she was feeling like an idiot.

"Good? Then you ran away?" Rayne groaned and rolled her eyes. "What am I going to do with you? The hottest guy in Fielding – maybe in Montana – kisses you and you run for the hills. What were you thinking?"

That was the problem. Misty hadn't been thinking at all – only feeling. It had been overwhelming.

"I was thinking that I didn't want to be a casual piece of ass to some drunk guy." Misty slapped her mug down on the coffee table. "Are you saying you think I should have slept with Sheriff Jared Monroe?"

"What I am saying is that you should sleep with someone," Rayne shot back. "You could certainly do worse than the sheriff. Everyone says he's a good man and you never hear a peep of a complaint from his ex-girlfriends. Geez, you dress like a nun, Misty. You might as well be one. Repressing your sexuality isn't healthy. Like, at all."

Misty's hand went reflexively to the collar of the shirt – buttoned all the way to the top – underneath her sweater. "Just because I don't show a bunch of skin–"

"You don't show any skin," Rayne interjected, a fierce tone in her voice. "It could be ninety degrees outside and you're covered head to toe. You're an attractive woman and the way you hide away from men and life is sad."

Misty's lips trembled with the wave of emotion that ran through her. She and Rayne had discussed this so many times and it never seemed to get any easier. "You know why."

Rayne's expression softened and she patted Misty's hand. "You don't want to be like your mom. But can't you see? You already aren't like her. She let booze and men run her life, although from what you said she didn't regret a day of it. She lived life to the fullest in her own way. Going to bed with a sexy man and – dare I say enjoying it – doesn't make you your mom. It just makes you human. Believe me you don't want to miss out on one of life's greatest pleasures."

"I've had sex and I think you exaggerate."

"Tell me again how many times you've had sex."

Misty had a cringe-worthy image of her college boyfriend standing next to the bed with a disgusted look on his face. She'd been mortified as he'd pulled his clothes back on and explained that he simply couldn't date a girl who was frigid.

"You know I've only had sex three times with Steve."

Rayne snorted. "It could hardly even be called sex from what you told me. He got on top of you and pumped away and then blamed you when you didn't swoon over his technique. Ass-hole."

Misty pressed a hand to her hot cheek and winced at Rayne's bald but true statement. "He was an asshole but maybe I am frigid. I didn't really enjoy it at all. I just wanted it to be over."

Rayne took a sip of her cocoa. "How did you feel when the sheriff kissed you? Did you just want that to be over too?"

"No," Misty confessed softly. "It felt…"

She didn't even have the words for how it had felt except that her body hadn't even seemed like her own anymore. She'd spent so many years stomping away any semblance of sexual desire and he'd managed to blow a hole in her defenses with one kiss.

"Yep," Rayne nodded in satisfaction. "You were kissed by a real man. A man who knows what he's doing. I bet if you'd gone to bed with him you wouldn't be talking about all this frigid crap. You'd be smiling. A lot."

Misty picked up her cooled mug and took a drink, taking a moment to gather her scattered thoughts. The night had thrown her carefully curated world onto its ear.

"Well, I didn't and I doubt I'll see him again before I leave so it's over and done with. Besides, starting a relationship with someone when I'm leaving for Seattle doesn't seem like a smart thing to do."

That made Rayne laugh. "A relationship? Honey, I'm not talking about a relationship. I'm talking about a night of passion with a man that knows his way around a woman's body. Forget the gossips and busybodies in this town and have some fun. What does it matter? You'll be long gone and people can talk about you all they want. Believe me they'll lose interest when someone else does something even more juicy."

"I'm not going to drive back there and offer myself to him. I guess I'll have to find another candidate for this night of passion you speak of."

"The world is filled with them."

That might be true but she'd only come alive with one man.

Sheriff Jared Monroe.

Chapter Four

"Can you fix it?" Misty anxiously asked the garage attendant as he peered under the hood of her car. It had seen better days but for the most part it was reliable transportation. Until today. This afternoon she'd wanted to go to the store but the car wouldn't start. She'd been forced to call a tow truck and now here she was with the repairman who could make or break her day.

"Of course I can fix it." The man gave her a reassuring smile but it did little to bolster her spirits. She was getting ready to start a new life in Seattle and it was much more expensive to live there. Although she was making good money with her paintings, she'd been poor too long to take anything for granted. "It's probably nothing big. Maybe the alternator or the fuel pump."

Misty knew nothing about cars and even less about the internal combustion engine. Was an alternator worse or better than a fuel pump? She hated feeling helpless in any situation but this repairman could rip her off and she'd never know it.

"Trouble?"

That deep voice that had been running through her mind was suddenly right behind her. Misty had gone out of her way the last ten days to neither see nor speak to Jared Monroe and so far she'd been successful. He'd been haunting Misty's dreams every single night since she'd helped him home. Her sleep was punctuated with images of the two of them doing things she'd never pondered until…that kiss.

She stiffened her spine and turned to face him. He was so tall she had to look up into his handsome face. "Just a little car trouble, Sheriff. No big deal."

"That's good." The sheriff gave the mechanic a sidelong glance. "And please call me Jared. Sheriff seems too formal."

"Fine. Jared," she said stiffly, wanting him to leave her alone. Her knees were going weak and her heart had sped up to an alarming rate. That couldn't be healthy.

The repairman was watching them both, his gaze finally resting on Jared. "Hey, Sheriff. I've got the oil changed in your SUV. It's all ready for you and parked out back. Keys are hung up in the usual spot and we'll send the bill along at the end of the week."

"Thanks, Ray. I appreciate the quick service."

"Any time, Sheriff. Day or night."

Jared shoved his hat back on his head and strode over to the front office a few feet away.

The repairman's gaze swung back to Misty. "So we'll need to get your car up on the lift to really see what's wrong. I'll call you tomorrow with an estimate."

"Tomorrow?" Misty echoed with alarm. "You can't fix it today? I can wait."

The man shook his head and nodded to the clock on the wall. "It's already after two and we have a full day's work and then some. Tomorrow morning is the best I can do."

He tried to sound regretful but he had to know she was in a fix. She wasn't going to have the car towed anywhere else.

"I'd take it as a personal favor if you would take a look at Miss Foster's car first thing in the morning, Ray."

Misty opened her mouth to object to Jared asking on her behalf but then remembered that she really wanted her only means of transportation back. His words seemed to have a magic effect on the mechanic. The man's expression grew serious and he scratched a few more things on the clipboard in his hand.

"I didn't realize Miss Foster was a friend of yours, Sheriff. I'll make sure her car is first up in the rotation tomorrow morning."

"He's not my friend." Her protest came tumbling past her lips before she could censor it. It sounded mean and a little desperate. Her cheeks flamed and she had to take a few deep breaths before speaking again. "What I mean is, Sheriff Monroe is everyone's friend of course, but I don't want any special favors."

The mechanic looked at her strangely, his bushy dark brows pulled down in question. "It's no trouble. I'm happy to do the sheriff a favor."

"Thank you, Ray. I appreciate it," Jared interjected smoothly before turning back to Misty, his keys dangling from his fingers. "Looks like you need a ride. I'm going off shift in a few minutes so I can run you home."

Misty wanted more than anything to object but the fact was she did need a ride. She just didn't want it to be with Jared Monroe. She could always get a cab.

"Um, thank you," she replied awkwardly. "But I really need to stop at the grocery store. That's what I was coming into town for."

"That's fine. I need to finish some end of shift paperwork. How about I pick you up in front of the store in about half an hour?"

He'd swept away her objections so easily she didn't have any choice. Numbly she nodded and turned to the mechanic who was watching them with great interest.

Dammit, this would be all over town by dinnertime. She didn't need this in her life.

Wait…I'm moving to Seattle.

The small-minded people of Fielding weren't her problem any longer, but of course Jared would have to deal with them.

He looked more than capable.

She signed the paper that the repairman shoved in front of her before following Jared out to the sidewalk in front of the garage. Fumbling in her pockets for her gloves, she carefully avoided his gaze.

"Is half an hour enough?" Jared asked.

"Plenty of time. I'll be out front."

As far away from the large windows as I can be. I don't want everyone to see this.

"See you then."

Jared ambled down the block to the sheriff's office and Misty stood there watching his large, powerful frame until he turned the corner and was out of sight. She'd vowed to stay away from him and now he was giving her a ride home.

In front of the whole town.

Once again…nothing good could come from this.

✧ ✧ ✧ ✧

Senior deputy and second in command, Knox Owens was waving a piece of paper in the air when Jared walked into the station. Sighing, Jared snagged it from the man's hand as he walked by. This was going to keep him from getting his paperwork done tonight, he could just feel it. Knox had a grim expression which wasn't the norm for the usually easygoing deputy.

Jared patted his empty breast pocket looking for the glasses he needed to read these days. Not yet forty, he'd decided growing older officially sucked when he'd found himself holding paper at arms' length simply to be able to make out the small type. They were missing as usual so he slapped the paper back on Knox's desk.

"Just read it to me."

"It's Boyd Hicks. He got parole."

"Shit," Jared said softly. Boyd Hicks had always been a dangerous man. Now he was a dangerous man with little to lose. It was a recipe for very bad things. "When?"

"A few days ago," Knox answered flatly as Chris Marks, another deputy and the son of one of Jared's best friends, joined them. He was on second shift today. "Think he's on his way here?"

"Who is Boyd Hicks?" Chris asked, settling his hat on his head.

Knox handed the paper to the junior deputy who perused the contents. Jared leaned against a desk and rubbed his suddenly throbbing temples. This was bad news.

"Boyd Hicks is a career criminal that we put away about five years ago," Jared replied, already thinking about what Hicks might be planning. The safety of his men and town were uppermost in his mind. "He swore vengeance on us the day they sentenced him and dragged him out of the courtroom. Revenge is sort of a hobby for him."

"If he's a career criminal why was this time any different?" Chris asked. "It couldn't have been too serious of a charge if he got parole in five years."

"This time was different because during his sentence his wife OD'd and lost custody of their baby daughter. It was different because Hicks swore up and down he didn't rob that liquor store. Said he'd been set up."

"Who would bother to set up a petty criminal?" Chris queried.

"His brother Dale," Knox answered with a grim smile. "That family is something else."

"Like the Manson family," Jared muttered. "But we found no evidence of him being framed. Everything pointed to Boyd."

"So Boyd thinks he did time for his brother, lost his wife and daughter," Chris surmised. "And he blames…Fielding's finest?"

"Correct," answered Jared. "Welcome to the club."

"I wish it was a little more exclusive," Chris joked. "Maybe he's not pissed at me. I'm new."

"Boyd Hicks is pissed at the world. He once stabbed his uncle in the arm because the man smoked Boyd's last cigarette. I wouldn't say he was a think first, shoot later kind of guy."

"So what do you want us to do?" Knox swung his legs down from where they were propped up on the desk. "I could go talk to his wife. See if she's heard from him."

"Ex-wife," Jared corrected. "She divorced him a couple of years ago. I heard she got clean and is married to a guy who works on a nearby ranch. But that's a good idea. We need to talk to her, Dale, and any of Boyd's former associates, assuming we can find them. Also, make sure all the deputies have a picture of Boyd and are keeping an eye out for him. Everyone should consider him armed and dangerous. No one should try and bring him in alone. Call for backup. Hell, call me at home if you have to. This guy would love to put a couple of slugs in a cop. Let's not give him a chance."

"Amen to that," Knox declared, already printing out photos of Boyd Hicks for the staff. Jared spoke with Chris for a moment and then headed to his office. He still had a few minutes to try and get some of that paperwork done and off his desk.

Twenty minutes later Jared gave up and stacked the file folders in a neat pile for tomorrow morning. They'd have to wait one more day which wasn't out of the ordinary. There was always plenty of administrative work to keep a lawman busy at his desk instead of out on patrol where he'd rather be.

Shrugging on his coat, he grabbed his keys from his pocket and made his way to the front door. "Call me if you need me."

"It's all good. See you tomorrow," Knox called out. The senior deputy wouldn't call Jared unless the shit really hit the fan, which was more than he could say about the last guy that had the job. He'd woken Jared up almost every damn night with one thing or another. A good night's sleep sounded like heaven right about now.

But first he had some groveling to do.

✧ ✧ ✧ ✧

Misty was sitting next to Jared as stiff as the statue of the local war hero in the park. He'd picked her up in front of the grocery store where she'd refused to let him help with her two heavy bags. Now she was sitting next to him in his truck chewing on those pillowy soft lips and staring straight ahead.

Time to man up and apologize.

"Listen, I wanted to say that I'm sorry about how I acted the other night. Obviously I'd had a few too many. I hope we can put it all behind us and still be friends."

For a moment he thought she wasn't going to say anything, but then she nodded stiffly but still didn't meet his gaze. "I think it's best if we never speak of it again."

Jesus, Mary, and Joseph, had the kiss been that bad? He'd never had any complaints before.

"It's clear that I upset you."

This time she did look at him, her dark blue eyes almost gray with some troubled emotion. "I thought we weren't going to talk about it."

"We won't. After this. What I'm trying to say is that I'm sorry that I acted like a horse's ass. It certainly wasn't my intention. You probably saved my life, after all. I could have frozen to death on that bench."

Misty gave him a long-suffering sigh. "I wasn't upset. Being kissed by a half-inebriated man, however, does not excite me. Now can we drop the subject?"

For some reason Misty wanted to pretend she hadn't been affected by the kiss, even though that was complete hogwash. He wasn't a virgin. He'd felt the way her body trembled and the sweetness of her tongue's tentative explorations. If that was what she was like when she was uninterested, he'd love to be with her when she was all in.

"Sure. We'll drop the subject." For some perverse reason he couldn't leave it alone. "I just don't want things to be awkward between us now."

She was chewing on her lower lip again. "Does it matter? I'm leaving for Seattle in a month. We'll probably never see each other again."

"Won't you come visit your friends and family?"

"I don't have any family and I only have one real friend. She'll come visit me."

The thought of never seeing her again bothered him and he had no idea why. He'd called them friends but they really weren't. Before the other night, they'd said five words to each other in the last five years. He was much older than she was and they didn't socialize in the same crowd.

"I'm sure you have more friends than that."

Misty shook her head and looked out of the window. "No. Just Rayne."

That seemed like an awfully lonely life. Jared was constantly surrounded by family and friends almost to the point that it drove him crazy. He couldn't fathom being alone most of the time.

Jared tried a new subject since it was clear she didn't want to discuss their kiss. "So you're looking forward to Seattle? Do you have a place to live yet?"

That question seemed to perk her up. She smiled and her gaze swung from the scenery back to him. "I signed a lease the last time I was there. It's the cutest little one bedroom that overlooks a park and is near public transportation."

Misty Foster was a beautiful woman when she was animated like this. Her eyes sparkled and her cheeks were pink from excitement. It made him want to reach out and trace her smile with his finger, and then maybe run his fingers through that mass of long blonde hair.

Whoa. That train of thought needed to derail immediately. She was too young, and even if she was older she obviously thought he was slime. He needed to remember that to keep his mind moving in other more productive directions. Like Boyd Hicks and what the fuck Jared was going to do about him for starters.

"That sounds real nice. We'll miss you around here though."

Jared pulled into the driveway in front of Misty's apartment just in time to hear her snort in derision.

"Miss me? Sheriff, Fielding is going to throw a party when I leave. No one," she said icily, "is going to miss me. I've been *persona non grata* my entire life. Let's face it, my mother and I offended the delicate sensibilities of the good citizens of this fine town."

There was nothing but scorn in Misty's tone and Jared didn't blame her a bit. He'd grown up in this town and he knew the good…and the bad. How they'd treated the Fosters wasn't a shining moment in Fielding history.

No wonder Misty couldn't wait to leave.

✧ ✧ ✧ ✧

Misty shouldn't have said what she did but she hadn't been able to help herself. People always acted like they didn't notice how the town treated her but she knew the looks and whispers all too well. She couldn't wait to put Fielding in the rearview mirror and be someplace where no one knew her history. It would be the fresh start she so badly needed.

Despite her protests Jared insisted on helping her with the grocery bags. The wind and snow had really picked up during the drive and she was glad to be in the warmth of her own home. Once he'd placed her sacks on the kitchen counter she was ready for him to leave. Anyone driving by could see his truck parked out front although they might think he was visiting a neighbor.

"Well, thank you. I appreciate the ride home and the helping hand with the bags."

"It was the least I could do after you saved my life the other night." Jared looked around the room appreciatively. "This is very nice. I like the colors. I never know how to decorate things so I stick to beige and blue."

"Your home looks nice." Misty pulled back one of the curtains and peeked out. "The weather is getting worse—you should probably get on the road."

Jared's smile widened. "I get the hint, Misty. Sort of a 'here's your hat and what's your hurry' kind of thing. Can I ask you a question before I leave? Was it just the other night when I kissed you that made you not like me or have you disliked me all along?"

She liked him too much, but how did she explain she couldn't afford that luxury?

"I don't dislike you," she explained carefully. "It's just not a good idea for anyone to know you're here."

"Why not?" He looked genuinely puzzled which only fueled her frustration. Was he being deliberately obtuse or had the cold damaged his brain cells?

"We both know why not."

"Apparently we both don't because I haven't the foggiest idea what you're talking about," he retorted. "Will you let me in on the secret?"

"If the good people of Fielding find out that you spent even five minutes inside the home of the town whore's daughter they'll never let it go. You'll hear about it until your dying day. I, on the other hand, will be in Seattle so really Jared, I'm thinking of you here."

She'd shocked him. His eyebrows shot up in surprise but then a funny thing happened. He smiled.

"I don't think this is very funny, Sheriff."

"On the contrary, it is. Just so we're clear here…I don't give a shit what the people of Fielding think about me. I really have no idea what their opinion is and I don't spend any time wondering about it. Now will you relax?"

Misty pressed her lips together, her face warm. "What about your family? What will your brothers and sister think? Or your father?"

His smile fell away and a grim expression took its place. "I can handle them. Honestly I think this is more about you than me. I think you don't want me here."

The set of his shoulders told her he was serious. And he had a point. This had a great deal to do with her insecurities about how she was perceived by the people of Fielding. Since she was soon leaving perhaps it was time to shake off their preconceived notions and simply live her life. After all, it was only polite to offer him a hot chocolate or something. It would give the old biddies at the hair salon something to talk about for months.

"Fine," she said smartly. "You're the one that's going to have to deal with it. But don't say I didn't warn you. Would you like to sit down while I make us a hot chocolate?"

Jared smiled and spread his arms wide. "Misty, I'd love some."

It was a dangerous thing to have a man this handsome up close and personal. But Rayne's words echoed in her ears.

It was time to live life on her own terms. It was time to live. Period.

Chapter Five

"Take off your coat and throw it over the chair there."

Jared shrugged out of his coat and gloves, shoving them into the pockets before draping the jacket over the kitchen chair. There was a chill in the air and she was fiddling with a space heater that was supposed to look like a fireplace.

The heat was welcome as he settled onto a comfortable chair, careful to navigate away from the daybed against the long wall. From the looks of things she slept there and it would give him way too many ideas that would not be welcomed.

"Marshmallows?" she asked, bustling around her tiny kitchen. The apartment was really one large room so she was never far away no matter where she was. It was quite a contrast to the rambling house he'd grown up in, but then they'd needed the space for four rambunctious kids.

"I'd love some, thank you. But you know you really don't have to make me anything. I was just giving you a hard time a few minutes ago. I don't want to upset you."

Misty had floored him with her statement about the town gossiping, although she wasn't far wrong. Fielding had some terrible gossips and Jared knew that they'd been pretty hard on Misty's mother Annette. From what he'd heard – and it was gossip, after all – she'd loved to party. Men and booze had been her passions, which left her young daughter to pretty much fend for herself.

She barely looked old enough to take care of herself although she was probably somewhere in her early twenties. A tiny thing, barely reaching his shoulder, she had elfin features that were too cute to be called beautiful or gorgeous but pleasing enough that a man could look at her all day long and never get tired of it. Her long pale blonde hair was pulled back in an untidy braid and her eyes were so blue they were almost violet.

"I'm not upset. Not really. I was just thinking how Fielding must look like to you."

"Probably better than it does to you. But people don't still give you trouble, do they? I mean, we're all grown up now."

Misty poured the hot chocolate into two mugs and dropped a handful of marshmallows in each before handing him one. Settling herself on a large cushion on the floor near the heater, she wrapped her hands around the cup, her forehead furrowed in thought.

"You think only little kids can be mean? All through school from kindergarten to my senior year the other kids made fun of me. I had old clothes that were bought from thrift shops or given to us by the local church. I remember one girl pointing out that I was wearing one of her shirts that she'd thrown away. It was humiliating. No one wanted to be my friend. I didn't have any friends, really. Even the other outcasts didn't want to be tainted by me."

Jared shifted uncomfortably in his chair. He hadn't been in school with Misty but he'd done his share of acting like an ass when he was kid. He sure as hell wasn't very proud of it and right now he was deeply ashamed.

"It didn't get better when you got older?"

"You mean high school? I got asked out once. His name was John Reeves. Turns out he only took me on a date because he thought I would be *easy* like my mom. He said that to me before ripping my shirt. I had to kick him in the balls to get him off of me. I ended up walking home that night. So no, it didn't get better as I got older. I couldn't wait to leave for college. Since I didn't have any friends I had a lot of time to study. Got a full-ride scholarship to art school in Denver. I wanted to stay there after graduation but then Mom got sick. Since I've been back I've made one friend. Rayne."

He knew John Reeves and the grown man wasn't any less a punk than the teenager had been. Jared made a mental note not to cut that guy any slack next time he got in a bar fight or did something else equally as dumb. In fact, he might just punch the guy on principle for being a total asshole. All those incidents in her past had to have inflicted wound after wound on someone as sweet as Misty. She needed someone to protect her from the world.

"If it's any consolation John Reeves turned out to be a big loser."

Misty sipped her hot chocolate and shrugged as if she didn't care but he could tell she did. Very much.

"The whole town thinks I'm a loser. Or a tramp. I hear their whispers behind my back. They think I have boyfriends or someone out of town and that when I travel I'm shacked up in some cheap motel with one of them."

Jared had heard the gossip but hadn't paid it any mind. He was of the live and let live variety and had always been bothered about the double-standards in society. It didn't make sense for only men to enjoy sex.

"Misty, you must have the self-control of Ghandi. Why haven't you told those old biddies off?" Jared wondered. "Really let them have it."

"I tried fighting back once when I was eight. Punched some kid in the stomach. Made him puke up his peanut butter sandwich. Nothing changed. His mother called me and Mom a few names next time we were in town. Mom said that I needed to turn the other cheek, that words couldn't hurt me. Stuff like that didn't bother her. She was all about living life to its fullest. At least that's what she would say."

Misty had a sad smile on her face as she remembered her mother. Anger at what she'd had to endure all these years balled in his gut making it hard to drink his cocoa. He would have punched all those other cheeks but then nothing like that would have happened to him. His father was a respected member of Fielding and so by extension were his sons.

Even the fuckups.

"Your mother sounds like a nice lady."

Clearly he couldn't trust anything he'd heard about her from the town gossips.

Misty straightened and took a long drink of her hot chocolate. "She was but she had flaws like everyone else. I know she loved me as much as she was capable of. Can we change the subject? I don't like talking about myself this much. In fact, I have no idea why I told you what I did. I never tell anyone anything."

Jared gave her a smile wanting to lighten the mood. "It's my charm. People love to tell me all sorts of things."

"That must come in handy being a cop," she observed. "But I don't think that's the reason I told you that. I've only told Rayne."

Misty wouldn't want anyone to feel sorry for her. She was a strong, stoic woman. He had deputies that could take some lessons from her.

"Maybe you just wanted to tell someone."

She looked down into her cup for a long time and then finally looked up at him. "Maybe. Maybe I'm just looking back as I get ready to leave here."

Jared looked around the apartment. It was clean and tidy but there wasn't one moving box in sight.

"It doesn't look like you're moving."

"It won't take long to pack up my things. The furniture is staying here so it's just my personal belongings. I don't like having clutter around me so I'll put off packing until the last minute."

"I don't like it either. I like things to be organized."

"My friend Rayne complains that men are slobs."

That hadn't been an option in the Monroe household, although Jared had relaxed a little since his college roommate was happy to marinate in his own filth. Heaven help the woman he'd ended up with.

"I'm definitely not a slob. I can clean up after myself, cook for myself, all that stuff."

Misty giggled and it sounded like the tinkling of his mother's expensive crystal bells she'd hung on the Christmas tree every year. "You say that so proudly. A woman is expected to do those things but a man gets brownie points for it."

"Brownie points, huh?" She wasn't wrong, but the world wasn't going to change simply because Jared thought it was unfair. "My parents – my father really – ran a tight ship growing up. He was ex-military and he liked the household to run efficiently."

"And did it?"

Jared considered her question as his childhood flashed in front of him. There were images of his mother handing out brownies and hugs after school, helping with homework, and basically holding the family together with meatloaf and fried chicken.

His father had been the iron-fisted, straight-talking patriarch of the Monroe clan. He'd pushed his sons and his daughter to work harder, to strive and achieve more than anyone else. He was the reason Jared had played and excelled at sports, academics, and eventually the military. Making his father proud had been goal number one for most of Jared's life.

Now that man was slowly withering away.

"For the most part. There's always a little chaos when you have four kids. But there was a schedule for everything and we stuck to it. I think it did make things easier in the long run."

Misty was frowning at him. "A schedule? What do you mean?"

"You know, breakfast at seven, dinner at six, lights out at a certain time depending on our age. The usual stuff."

From the look on Misty's face she had no idea what he was talking about. "I guess we were a little more casual. We ate when we were hungry and we slept when we were tired."

When she said it like that it didn't sound so bad. But…

"Did you eat when you were hungry? You said there wasn't much money growing up."

It was a deeply personal question but the thought of this sweet woman going to bed without dinner bugged the hell out of him.

"There was food." Misty shrugged, back to chewing on her lower lip. "I didn't starve. We just didn't have extra food. But I never went hungry."

Jared thought about the dinner table growing up and how it had been practically bowed from the weight of the food. Feeding four ravenous, growing kids had been a gargantuan task and the refrigerator had always been stuffed with leftovers and snacks.

"You know what I like about you, Misty Foster?" He leaned forward and looked her right in the eye. "You sure as hell aren't a whiner. I think you have a backbone of steel. A *tiny* backbone of steel because you're just a little slip of a thing but I can see that you're a strong person. I admire that."

In law enforcement he met people every day who bemoaned their victim status, wallowing in excuses for how their life had turned out. Not this woman. She sure as hell didn't feel sorry for herself.

"Thank you," she said quietly. "You can thank my mother for that. She always said crying and complaining didn't change things. She was right. I had to take control of my own destiny."

"And how have you done that?"

A delicate shoulder lifted. "Art school. And now my painting. I make my living that way and now I earn enough to leave Fielding. Finally."

"From what I've heard it's not easy to make a living in the art world. You must be good."

Misty smiled and drained the last of her hot chocolate. "Art is subjective. Some people think I'm good and some think I paint garbage. They're both right."

"And the people that don't like what you paint – that doesn't bother you?"

"After living in Fielding for most of my twenty-five years I think I've built up a thick skin. At least art critics have the decency to say I suck right to my face."

Laughing, Jared nodded in agreement. "There is something to that. I've had people call me every name in the book. Basically cursed the day I was born. But at least they're honest about it."

"Do you have a lot of enemies?"

Right now the only one he needed to worry about was Boyd Hicks, and as long as Jared watched his back he should be fine.

"A few, but I'm always open to making a few more as I do my duty. This isn't a job for someone who needs to be liked."

"Do you like your job? Don't your brothers work on the ranch?"

She didn't realize she'd brought up a complex subject that was still discussed in the Monroe household to this day. Gerald Monroe hadn't been a happy man when his middle son had announced he wanted a career in law enforcement.

"I do," he replied, keeping his answer simple. "I help Royce and Ty as much as I can when I have time. Hard work is the best antidote for stress."

He'd finished his hot chocolate and ought to be leaving, although he found he could talk to her for hours. She had a nonjudgmental way about her that made her easy to be with.

He held up his empty mug. "I guess I should be on my way. Thank you for the hospitality."

"You're welcome. It's nice to have company." She stood and took their cups over to sink and rinsed them under the faucet, her movements quick and efficient. He found himself trying to see beneath the thick layers of oversized clothes to the woman beneath. Was she slim and boyish with small breasts that would just fit his hand? Or was her figure lush and curvy with a body he could press himself against?

Pushing away the disturbing images, he got to his feet and reached for his coat. Misty Foster was leaving Fielding and she definitely didn't seem the fling type. Neither was he if the truth be known. He'd had a series of long-term girlfriends since high school, although none had piqued his interest enough to make it permanent.

Now standing, he could easily see out of the front windows of Misty's apartment and the sight made him almost groan with frustration. The storm that had been worsening when on the way here had already dumped a load of snow outside with a nasty wind that was blowing it all over the road. He couldn't even see his SUV from the windows that were only ten feet away. Anyone driving in this – unless forced – was insane. He should know. He spent way too much of his time rescuing people from their cars in the middle of winter.

"Well, have a good night," he said, palming his car keys in his pocket. This was his own damn fault. If he hadn't teased her earlier about spending time here he'd already be home and off the road.

"You can't drive in that," she stated, waving her hand at the picture window. "It's a blizzard out there."

"I'll make it. I'm the cops, remember? That's why I have a four-wheel drive SUV."

"If anyone could drive in this it would be you, but it wouldn't be smart. You can stay here until it blows over," she offered.

"I can't put you out like that. I've already imposed on your time."

"It's not imposing," she protested. "I made some dough earlier. I can make us a pizza and we can wait for the storm to pass. It's no trouble really."

Misty smiled encouragingly and Jared felt himself weakening. She was quite pretty when she smiled, although she'd be a hell of a lot more attractive if she wasn't buttoned up like a nun. Her jeans were baggy and practically hung off her small frame while her sweater swamped her torso, covering too much bare skin.

Jared couldn't stop his mind from picturing her in something less…enrobed. A purple satin bra and panty set that matched her eyes for starters. Of course he had no idea if the images he conjured up were even close to reality. And he couldn't believe how much he wanted to find out what lay underneath. He couldn't be more fascinated than if she'd worn a sheer negligee or tight blue jeans and a t-shirt. His personal favorite.

"Are you okay?" Misty was looking at him strangely, her head cocked to the side.

Jared scraped his hand down his face and stifled a groan. She must think he was…horny? Strange? Not very bright? All three combined?

"I'm fine, just tired. It's been a long day."

"Then why don't you just relax while I fix dinner. What do you like on your pizza?"

He peeled his coat off once more before sinking into the comfortable chair. He didn't mind driving in bad weather but he was also smart enough not to want to do it unless he had to. Besides, he was man enough to admit that he was enjoying himself.

"I'll eat anything. Surprise me."

Why not? This entire encounter with Misty had been a surprise. One he wasn't eager to see end.

✧ ✧ ✧ ✧

Dinner hadn't been the ordeal Misty had envisioned.

When she'd stood up and looked out the large picture window of her apartment she'd known she couldn't let him drive home in that storm. She couldn't even see his truck with the swirling snow that was coming down fast. So she'd asked him to stay for dinner.

And more?

Rayne's words were running through Misty's mind over and over again, barely allowing her to relax in his pleasant company. Jared was an intelligent man with a quick wit and a charming personality. Instead of relaxing he'd leaned against the kitchen counter while she made the pizza, asking her about art, books, and film. He liked Tom Clancy novels and superhero movies. He'd been shocked when she confessed she hadn't seen any of the Marvel Comics films. In fact, the last movie she'd seen had been a chick flick whose mere title made him wince.

Now they were stretched out in front of her faux gas fireplace and lounging on a pile of cushions. Misty had made more hot chocolate and they were both sipping at the sweet, rich liquid. A question had been niggling at the back of her mind over dinner. It was a personal question, but then he'd somehow managed to get her to open up.

"Can I ask you something?" She paused but he didn't say no. "Why were you drinking at the B&B the other night? From everything I've heard about you it seems out of character."

"I'd had a bad day. Bad news. And you're right—it's not my usual *modus operandi.* I don't think it's behavior I'll be repeating any time soon."

As a rule Misty didn't drink, so she couldn't imagine anything bad enough to make her start. "You can tell me about it. I'm a good listener. I won't tell anyone else what you say. I promise."

With her fingers Misty crossed her chest like she was still in grade school and he rewarded her with a smile.

"Listen, I appreciate your offer to hear about my problems but I'm not one to talk about things."

"Sometimes it helps. You never know. It can't hurt anything. I'd like to help."

His hands were wrapped around the mug but his gaze was far away. "I don't think there's anything you can do." He took a sip and then seemed to come back from wherever he'd gone. "Let's just say I got some bad news on top of other bad news. The kind of news that changes everything. I had to tell my family the next day."

She studied him for long moment. "I'm sorry. How did they take it?"

"They were shocked of course. Everyone was. We still haven't told my father."

Jared's expression was dark and tortured. Whatever the news, it clearly wasn't anything good or happy.

"Are you going to?"

His gaze swung to her and his blue eyes were almost gray with pain. "I have to. My father was diagnosed with Alzheimer's."

Misty sucked in a breath at the anguish in Jared's tone. She didn't know what to say so she placed her hand over his. He wound their fingers together, his larger and rough from work and hers much smaller and softer.

"I'm so sorry. So you're waiting to tell your father?"

Somehow they'd moved closer to one another, their faces only inches apart and their hands clasped together. Her skin tingled where they touched and her stomach fluttered in her abdomen at his nearness.

"No. The doctor wants to wait until Dad is a little stronger before we tell him. Maybe in a week or so. He's recovering quickly but he's so damn stubborn about resting and taking his pills. If Mom were alive he'd listen to her."

His callused thumb brushed the spot on her wrist where her pulse pounded madly, making it difficult to talk. "At least you have each other. You know, family to help each other through this."

His fingers scraped through his short, dark hair. "My family can be as much hindrance as help. Royce has spent most of his waking hours partying with random women. Becky is only thirty-three but she has two ex-husbands and is engaged for a third time, God help the poor bastard. Dad spoiled her to such a degree I don't think there's a guy on the planet that could make her happy. Ty, thank heaven, is mostly normal and is running the ranch, which just makes him a target for Dad who likes things done a certain way. He's been giving Ty shit all week and my little brother has about had it. He's ready to turn things over to Royce, who as I said earlier doesn't have the best work ethic."

An outsider would never see the dysfunction in the Monroe family. Everyone thought of them as the royal family of Fielding and Jared was the prince. They had such a facade of perfection it was startling to see a crack in the foundation.

"What about you? Where do you fall in all this?"

Jared turned her hand over and traced a line on her palm with his callused finger. Her body trembled and the blood roared in her ears. "Me? I'm simply trying to hold the whole damn thing together."

"Your father must be very grateful."

Smiling, Jared shook his head. "Dad doesn't do gratitude. He still hasn't quite forgiven me for taking the sheriff's job instead of working on the ranch. I knew it would make him angry but I did it anyway."

"Why did you do it then?"

Jared rested his chin in his hand. "I wanted something of my own. Mom understood and she encouraged me to follow my own path. Dad wanted Royce to run the ranch. I've known that since I was in diapers. I wanted to be more independent than taking orders from my older brother day in and day out."

Misty smiled and squeezed his hand. "You wanted to give the orders?"

Jared chuckled, his lips turned up at the corners. "Damn straight. If you haven't guessed yet I like to be the boss."

"It shows."

His chuckle turned into a hearty laugh. "I like you, Misty. Anyone else would tiptoe around me, afraid to make me mad. You? You just tell it like it is."

"I like you too." She sort of strangled on the words and they came out choked and barely audible.

His warm hand slid up her arm and over her shoulder so his fingers could tip up her chin. Their gazes met and she saw a heat in his eyes that was echoed in her thundering heart.

"I want to kiss you, Misty Foster. But not like last time. This time I want you to want it as much as I do. Should I walk out the door or should I lean in and kiss your pretty pink lips? It's your choice."

Her breathing shallow, Misty was lightheaded and dizzy. She did want Jared to kiss her. So much. But did she want more? She could feel the attraction simmering between them growing stronger each and every minute they spent together. A kiss would only be the beginning. If she said yes it wasn't going to stop there. He would want it all. Was she ready to do something out of the ordinary? She was leaving Fielding in about a month so he wouldn't be around to remind her if this turned into a fiasco. But something inside was tugging her toward him…pulling her inexorably…

She wanted to feel everything. More. She wasn't her mother but she was a woman full of passion and desire. For this one man. For one night.

"Kiss me."

Chapter Six

Misty's lips were soft and trembling, tasting of sweet chocolate and something undefinable that only she had. His fingers curled around the nape of her neck and tangled in the long silky strands of her pale blonde hair. He rubbed a tendril between his fingers – like satin against his rough skin – his body tightening at the contrast between them. Man. Woman. Her innate femininity made him feel infinitely more…masculine.

Yet protective. Her smaller frame was so delicate he needed to be supremely gentle tonight. He could feel her surrender but her nervousness too. He'd take this as slow as possible, allowing her inhibitions to fall away.

Reaching up to the daybed he yanked away a blanket and laid it on the rug, never letting his lips move far from hers. He pressed her back so they were both lying on the soft flannel throw as his lips explored the hollow of her throat were the pulse beat madly. Her hands moved restlessly on his back and his cock tightened painfully behind the fly of his jeans. He couldn't remember the last time he'd wanted a woman this badly. She called to more than his base instincts. Her sweet and gentle nature called to his soul.

"Jared," she sighed as he nipped at her earlobe and then soothed the tiny hurt with his tongue. She was squirming underneath him and his only thought was to strip the layers of clothing between them as quickly as humanly possible.

His fingers closed around the hem of her sweater but he paused, needing to be absolutely sure this was what she wanted. Her skin was warm and soft under his palms and he itched to delve deeper, exploring all the secrets she'd hidden under heavy clothing.

"I can stop if you want me to."

Although it was clear from his tone he sure as hell didn't want to. But then he wasn't trying to hide how much he wanted her. Considering the hard ridge in his jeans it would have been a waste of time.

Her fingers gripped his shoulders and he felt a shudder run through her body. "No. No, I want this. You. I–I just don't have much experience."

He froze, the full import of her words smacking him between the eyes. "You're a…virgin?"

He said the last word in a hushed voice as if someone was listening in, but they were the only two in the room.

Misty shifted underneath him restlessly and a blush crawled up her skin. "Well, not technically."

"Technically? I need a little more to go on here, honey," he said almost desperately. He wanted her fiercely, and to his dismay her innocence only fueled that fire when it should have turned him off.

"I–I've had sex three times," she admitted, her teeth sinking into her lush lower lip. "I wouldn't say it went well. In fact all three times were a bust. He said I was frigid. Maybe I am. I don't know."

"I'm absolutely sure you're not frigid, honey."

"Why?" she asked, struggling to her elbows. "Because I'm the daughter of Annette Foster, the town floozy? If my mother loved sex that much then I must too?"

Jared wasn't the most sensitive of men but even he knew his answer to her question was important and he couldn't fuck it up. He laid his palm on her shoulder and gently pressed her back onto the blanket.

"Your mother has nothing to do with this. The reason I know you're not frigid is by how you've responded to me. No frigid woman heats up like that after a kiss. As for your would-be lover, he may want to check a book or two out of the library about sex. I think he needs to learn a few things. Maybe a lot more."

He must have said the right thing because her pupils had turned a deep purple and her breath was becoming more shallow. His little Misty was definitely aroused.

"He seemed to know a lot about…you know…sex. What would he need to learn?"

Such an innocent question but the perfect opening to showing her all the pleasure her body could give and receive. Jared made a mental note to punch that asshole boyfriend of hers if they ever met up. That made two of her former men he was looking to put a hurt on. Jared couldn't think of any other woman who brought out the Neanderthal in him like Misty did. He wanted to drag her off to his cave for the next week and make love to her over and over until she was convinced beyond a shadow of a doubt she wasn't frigid.

He balanced his weight on his elbows and dropped kisses on the skin just above her collar, enjoying the sigh of pleasure that fell from her lips. "For one thing, he needs to learn that a woman takes a little longer to get warmed up and he should go at her speed. Take his time."

"What–what else?" she asked, a sexy breathless quality to her voice that made the blood pump in his veins a little harder. Her innocence was so goddamn sexy it hurt.

"A man needs to learn how to undress a woman, for example. Kiss every inch of skin as he exposes it. Tell her how incredibly beautiful and sexy she is and how much she turns you on. A woman wants to be romanced and seduced."

Her eyes were wide with amazement now and he had to hide his chuckle of amusement. She was glued to his every word.

"A man should make sure the woman has an orgasm first, and if possible has at least two. That's job number one. If she isn't satisfied and exhausted from your lovemaking then you're half-assing it." Hadn't Gerald Monroe always told Jared that any job worth doing was worth doing well? He'd taken his father's words to heart. "Maybe we should get these clothes out of the way."

His hands slid under her sweater, inching it up until her midriff was on display. He pressed kisses from her waistband up her belly until the cotton of her bra halted him. Wanting to make this last for her, he dragged his tongue down her rib cage and then around to her belly button. Misty giggled and wriggled underneath him, brushing his denim-covered cock and taking his breath away.

Her skin was creamy and velvet-soft, and he had to deliberately slow himself down as he gently tugged the knitted monstrosity over her head while his lips and tongue traveled up the sweet scented valley between her breasts and then under the lace edge of her bra. He tossed the sweater to the side and continued to rain kisses across her shoulders all the way down to her delicate artist's fingertips, loving the groans and sighs she emitted with each tender touch.

Jared nuzzled her neck while his fingers grazed her stomach on the way to the button on her jeans. He slid them open and tugged the zipper down slowly, letting his lips create a path down the middle of her torso all the way to the elastic of her white cotton panties.

He had to close his eyes and concentrate on his breathing so he could keep up this slow and steady pace. She didn't need him coming on too strong and ravishing her like a caveman. He would treat tonight as if this was her first time. In a way it was…this was the first time she'd know true passion. He'd make sure of it.

Working the thick denim down her legs, her baggy jeans joined the sweater in a pile on the floor. He knelt beside her and let his gaze run up and down this woman who was looking up at him so trustingly.

What he saw took his breath away.

She looked like an angel.

An angel with hourglass perfect curves that he couldn't wait to worship and praise. In fact, he was going to start right now.

"You're gorgeous, Misty. So fucking beautiful. I don't even have the words to describe how amazing you are. I wish I did but you take my breath away." He lifted her hand and pressed her fingers to his hard cock pushing for release from the confines of the denim. He bit back his groan of frustration as her palm pressed and rubbed against his fly. "This is what you do to me. I swear I could pound nails with my dick, I'm so hard. I've never wanted anyone as much as I want you right now, right here."

His compliments had turned her already pink cheeks a bright red and it spread all the way down to the curve of her luscious breasts. Her arm was crossed over her chest but it only served to push them up temptingly. If he didn't make love to her soon his cock and balls were going to explode in a burst of flames.

"I'm too heavy," she whispered, her gaze darting everywhere, unable to look him in the eye.

"Are you kidding? You're perfect. Why do you cover up this gorgeous body with those clothes that are two sizes too big? You should be showing it off and making us men drool on our chins."

She looked up at him through her lashes. "I didn't want people to think…"

Her voice trailed away but he got the idea. She didn't want anyone to think she was like her mother. Somewhere along the line she'd taken it to the extreme, suppressing her own healthy sexual appetite. But tonight he hoped she would throw away all that baggage.

And let herself go.

✧ ✧ ✧ ✧

Nothing had prepared Misty for Jared's assault to her senses. She felt wonderfully alive as if for the first time. Every nerve ending in her skin tingled, her breath came in rasps, and heat swept from her toes all the way up to her forehead. This was nothing like the fumbling attempts she'd had before. Jared seemed to know all the places to touch and kiss.

She felt helpless to resist.

But shouldn't she? Would he think she was easy or trampy if she went up in flames so easily? She was acting so different from her usual reserved self it unnerved her. She wasn't sure how she was supposed to feel about it.

Jared didn't give her a chance to ponder the question.

His tongue traced the straps of her bra as he reached behind her and unclipped the fastenings. The garment seemed to slide away of its own volition along with her panties moments later, leaving her bare to his heated gaze.

Bending his head to her breast, he teased an already hard nipple with his tongue until it was painfully tight. She closed her eyes and gritted her teeth to try and get some sort of semblance of control over the arousal and heat that fizzed through her veins. A man's touch had never affected her like this before.

He lifted up and paused his ministrations. "Relax, honey. There's nothing wrong with what we're doing here. If it feels good it's okay."

His soft assurances made her realize she was holding herself stiff and immobile in his arms, trying to think about anything but how he made her feel.

"It's just–I've never felt…" Completely inarticulate at this moment, she simply shook her head. "It almost feels…too good."

That made him grin and chuckle, his warm breath like a caress on the sensitive peaks of her breasts.

"You're good for my ego, honey. But there's no such thing as too good. I feel the same when you touch me."

The thought that her hands and lips could make him feel this amazing piqued her curiosity. She'd never had anyone say she aroused them but Jared's words intimated that very thing. And she wanted to make him as wonderful as she did. She slid her palms down his chest over his flat abdomen, tearing a groan from his lips and making her smile.

Plucking at the buttons on his shirt, she parted the material and let her fingers explore the muscles underneath the fabric. His eyes closed and his breath became more ragged as she tentatively explored the ridges of his stomach. A surge of feminine power ran through her, hiking up her own arousal tenfold.

"Do you like how I feel, Misty? I love how silky soft your skin is." Jared nuzzled the underside of a breast, running his tongue down her belly and pushing her legs apart. Reflexively her hands when to cover her already drenched slit. Her reaction caused him to stop but there was determination gleaming in his eyes. "There's nothing to be ashamed of. You're beautiful all over. Let me show you."

His tone was soft and cajoling and the battle inside of her intensified. She didn't want all this sparkling pleasure to stop and she desperately wanted to feel his tongue do all manner of naughty things to her. With a determination she didn't know she had she lifted her hands away, exposing all of herself.

"Ah, beautiful. All pink and wet, just for me."

Jared ran a finger through her pussy, drawing a scream of pleasure from her lips. He chuckled and bent his head to lap at her now swollen clit and she almost came off the blanket, the feelings so intense. So good, so wonderful. Lights danced behind her lids and lightning zipped to her extremities. A coil of arousal tightened in her abdomen with each movement of his tongue, now running through every fold and crevice.

Her body was completely under his control now. She felt herself moving toward orgasm, her entire being up in flames. When his mouth closed over her clit and sucked she was lost. Crying out his name, her muscles tightened as the pleasure intensified. Wave after wave rolled through her leaving her breathless and wrung out. When she finally came down from the clouds he was whispering sweet words in her ear and stroking her hair.

He didn't say anything for a long time, letting her luxuriate in what she'd experienced. She'd had orgasms before but never with someone else. It was more intense and exciting – more pleasurable than she'd ever imagined.

He pressed his lips to her temple and then her cheekbone.

"Can I ask you a question?" She nodded, still wrapped in her cocoon of wonderment. "Is Misty a nickname or short for something else? It's pretty but so unusual. I've never met one before."

She smiled at his question. This was one of her favorite memories from childhood. "It's from the book *Misty of Chincoteague*. That was my mother's favorite book and she said she was like the mom horse in the book – Phantom. Phantom wanted to run wild and free. Kind of like my mom."

"What do you want?" She could feel his words against her skin and it sent vibrations to every part of her body. How could she still be aroused after coming so hard?

"I don't need to be wild but I can't wait to be free. I'll be free in Seattle."

"Free from what, honey?"

Jared's fingers were already doing magic things as he stroked her skin, tickling the base of her spine.

"Free from the expectations of this town. Free from their judgment."

"You need to stop caring what they think, honey. You need to stop giving them so much power over your life and how you live it."

He wasn't wrong but she didn't want to dwell on that now. She wanted to feel more of what he'd given her a taste of.

Exquisite pleasure.

Pushing open his shirt, she pressed kisses to his muscular chest, the skin warm and firm under her lips. Her fingers tugged at his clothes and he finally chuckled and began to help her, the shirt coming off to reveal wide shoulders and a lean waist. His boots came next, then his jeans and boxers. His male beauty was a sight to behold and she wanted to explore every inch of his body – so different from her own.

Her gaze zeroed in on his hard cock – large and jutting proudly from a nest of dark hair. The head was reddish-purple and the slit had a few shiny drops of fluid on it, while the shaft was painted with a web of red and blue veins. She tentatively reached out and traced one with a finger but snatched it back when she heard his sharply indrawn breath.

"Easy, honey. You can touch me all you want but just remember you're going to get a reaction. But I want you to touch me."

This time she started her exploration at his shoulders, her hands gliding down his arms and then to his abdomen. Her fingers explored each ridge and plane before finally traveling back to his cock – her fist surrounding him. It seemed to swell even larger under her palm and she bent over to swipe her tongue on the head just as he'd done to her earlier. He jerked and swore but didn't pull away and it gave her confidence to delve further, running her tongue around the head until he groaned and shuddered.

"I can't take much more, honey. My balls are pulled up so tight it's painful. I want you but I don't want to rush. Are you ready for me? Do you want more?"

She wanted it all. Nodding, she lay back down on the blanket and held out her arms beckoning him to lie on top of her. His large body pressed hers into the floor and his cock nudged her entrance. She tensed for a moment having known only discomfort previously, but his soft butterfly kisses on her shoulder took away any trepidation she might have. He'd been so gentle up to this point there was no reason to think that would end.

He began to press forward but then pulled back quickly, an expletive on his lips. Leaving her for a moment, he grabbed his pants from a pile close by and her heart sank. He was going to get dressed and leave. She'd done something to turn him off. He didn't want her anymore.

Her breathing returned to normal when he pulled a condom packet from his pocket. "Damn, you scramble my brains, honey. I almost forgot this."

Tearing open the square with his teeth, he quickly rolled the protection on and came back down on top of her, the heat from his body warming her own. Arousal was already bubbling through her veins like the champagne she'd drank at New Year's Eve and she clung to Jared like a rock in a storm.

This time when he entered her she spread her legs in readiness, not wanting him to think she didn't want this or that she was unsure. He pressed forward slowly and gently a few inches then stopped, letting her get used to the invasion before pushing forward again, each easy thrust gaining more purchase. Her honey eased his way and when he was into the hilt he paused and let his forehead drop onto her own.

Their breathing was ragged and labored and his body was covered with a sheen of sweat. She wasn't so naïve not to know it was from the immense control he was keeping over himself. He'd taken his time and given her all the gentleness and patience she could have asked for but it had taken its toll on him. His expression was tortured, his jaw tight with the effort.

He waited there, not moving and she realized he was waiting for a sign from her. She dug her fingers into the hard muscles of his back and lifted her hips, slightly letting them sway right and then left. Shivers of pleasure ran straight to her clit and she repeated the motion, drawing a moan from her own lips.

This was what people read and talked about.

Jared began to move, slowly at first and then faster as her sighs and moans urged him on. Pleasure rushed through her like a waterfall with every stroke and thrust of his cock. He grunted and buried his head in the crook of her neck, his teeth nibbling the flesh there. The combination of pleasure and pain was too much and Misty tumbled over the edge, her body tightening on his.

He growled her name as he too climaxed, and she closed her eyes as the room tilted and swirled around her. Nothing could come close to how she felt with him at the moment. She'd given control of her body over to him and had no regrets. She wouldn't have missed this – him – for anything. Maybe she'd never feel this again but she would always know what was possible.

"Are you okay?" His lips brushed the top of her head. "That was amazing."

She nodded, her cheek rubbing his chest where she could feel the steady thud of his heart. "I'm okay…exhausted. Isn't that what you said I should be?"

He chuckled and she felt it rumble under her ear. "That is what I said. Why don't you close your eyes and get some rest? We can talk about this later."

Her lids floating closed, she didn't argue. Her limbs felt heavy and she just needed a little sleep. Just a few hours.

And then she'd want to do this all over again.

✧ ✧ ✧ ✧

Misty hadn't known how to act the next morning. She'd expected it to be awkward between her and Jared but he'd gone out of his way to make her feel at ease. It was hard to put aside the intimate things they'd done to one another only hours before. He'd encouraged her to explore her sexual curiosity and the results had been mind-bending. She'd been suppressing her sensual hunger for years but with Jared it felt safe to give way to those urges.

Now it was almost morning, the sky a charcoal gray waiting for the sun to rise and paint it with vivid colors of daylight. Jared was in her bathroom getting dressed and she was brewing a pot of strong tea. She poured the hot dark liquid into two mugs and added lemon and sugar to hers. Tightening the tie on her flannel robe, she leaned against the counter and sipped her tea in the silence.

A click and the bathroom door was open, Jared stepping into the main room. He wore last night's clothes and his jaw was covered with dark stubble, but he'd tamed his hair that had been disheveled from her fingers winding through it as his tongue had done naughty things to very private places.

"I guess I should be going."

Jared picked up his coat and shrugged it on, his expression giving nothing away. Was he happy to leave or did he wish he could stay? She was confused herself so she wouldn't blame him if he didn't know. Part of her wanted him to leave so she could be alone with her thoughts but another part of her wanted him to stay and continue the sensual exploration they'd started the night before.

"I made tea." She pointed to the mug but he shook his head. "Sorry I don't have any coffee."

"I need to get on the road. I have to get back to my place, shower, and change for work today." He paused and smiled. "Listen, I hope you don't regret what we did. I know I don't. But you're still planning to leave, right?"

She placed the mug on the counter. "Yes, that hasn't changed. I guess our timing sucks."

"Yeah, it kind of does, doesn't it? If you weren't leaving…"

"But I am," she said quickly. Making love to him was amazing but she wouldn't be deterred from her plans. "So you know more about this than I do. What happens now?"

"Usually one night stands don't end well because one of the parties wants more. But this is different." He held out his hand. "How about we shake and be friends? I like you, Misty, whether we sleep together or not. I think you're a good person. I'd like to be able to call you my friend."

She placed her hand in his larger one, the skin warm and comforting. "I'd like that. I think you're a good person too. So we're friends now?"

His hand fell away and she felt a sense of loss. "We are. If you ever need anything you just let me know."

"You too," she replied as he stuck his hat on his head and fished in his pocket for car keys. "Drive careful."

"I will. Let me know if you need a ride back to the garage."

It was sweet of him to offer but it was better if she didn't see much of him from here on out. He made her normally logical thoughts fuzzy. She'd ask Rayne for a ride.

"I'll be fine. Thank you. I mean…for the ride home last night."

He smiled a little wider at her stammer. She didn't want him to think she was thanking him for the terrific sex although she probably should. He'd shown her a side of herself she hadn't even known existed.

Or maybe she did and that's why she'd worked so hard to suppress it.

He leaned forward and dropped a kiss on her forehead. His male scent surrounded her and she had to force her arms to stay at her side instead of wrapping around his waist.

"Take care, Misty."

"Bye, Jared."

Then he was gone. She watched from the window as he drove away, his taillights finally disappearing in the distance. Sitting down on the rumpled bed that still smelled like sex she lifted a pillow to her nose and breathed in deeply of the woodsy citrus scent that would always remind her of Jared. She wrapped her arms around it and pulled it close to her chest.

It was one night and it was over. She needed to concentrate on her future. Outside of Fielding. And away from Jared Monroe.

Chapter Seven

"Are you coming down with something?" Rayne asked Misty as they sat in the diner. Misty had been busy with preparations for moving – packing, turning utilities on in Seattle, among other things.

She and Jared had kept to their bargain. Neither of them had called the other since that night. She'd seen him once at the pizza place but they'd simply smiled and nodded. Just as casual friends might.

Misty didn't want to think about how she'd reacted. Her pulse had sped up and her palms started to sweat. Even her stomach had gone fluttery when he was near.

She couldn't get their night together out of her mind. She thought about it constantly, torturing herself in the middle of the night. She needed to move on and packing her apartment was a good start.

"I think I might be," Misty admitted. "All I do in the evenings is lie on the recliner and fall asleep in front of the television."

Rayne wrinkled her nose. "Is your throat sore? That's usually how it starts. Body aches? Fever? Stuffy nose?"

Misty shook her head. "Just tired. Maybe it's stress from the move or something."

Rayne sighed, her mouth turned down. "I'm going to miss you so much. I swear you're the only person around here I can talk to. You know, really talk to."

"What about your sister?"

"I love my sister but she and I are different people. I want to be there for her now that she's pregnant but she's not making it easy. Her hormones must be on the rampage because she's been having these tantrums. When she wants something she wants it now, and she expects all of us to drop whatever we're doing and run and it get for her while she sits back like Jabba the Hutt. Even Mike has about had it and he's in love with her."

"What does your mom say?" Misty asked. Rayne was close to her mother even though she lived in Florida.

"My mom says Camy is using her pregnancy as an excuse to act like a bitch and that we all need to take a stand or she'll be even worse when the baby comes. She mentioned doing some sort of dance in the moonlight for the Goddess." Rayne rolled her eyes and groaned. Rayne's mother could only be described as eccentric. "I can't imagine her getting worse but Mom might have a point. I'm not too worried about it though. She's planning to fly up here when Camy has the baby, and if you know my mom you know she'll put my sister in her place within five minutes. I can't wait to see it."

Misty had never met Rayne's mom but she sounded like a formidable woman despite her mystical air.

"It sounds like you'll be too busy with your sister to miss me but we can Skype. I hope you'll come visit soon too. Maybe in the summer. That's supposed to be a nice time of year in Seattle."

Rayne waved to get the attention of the waitress. "I'm already tired of the cold and snow. Every winter seems longer than the last. That reminds me. How's your car doing since you got it out of the shop? No problems?"

Did everything have to remind Misty of Jared? If her car hadn't broken down he wouldn't have given her a ride home. And if he hadn't given her a ride home…

"No problems, although I'm glad I won't be needing it so much after I move. Eventually I'll have to save for a new one."

The waitress finally made it to their table, pad and pencil in hand. "Anything else or just the check?"

"Refills for both of us," Rayne replied. "And maybe a slice of that apple pie with ice cream on top."

The woman scribbled something down and smiled. "I'll have that right out to you. Good choice, by the way. The pie was freshly made this morning and smells wonderful. How about some caramel sauce on top?"

"Perfect," Rayne agreed, mirroring the woman's smile. "I love apple and caramel."

The waitress bustled back to the kitchen and Misty's gaze went to the front windows and Main Street. The sheriff's station was only a block down. It was Saturday but Jared might be working. Misty didn't know much about law enforcement but she'd heard they worked strange hours.

Just stop.

She was doing it again. Daydreaming about Jared when she should be doing something else. Anything else.

"You know, you've been acting weird lately. Is there anything you want to talk about? Are you second-guessing your decision to move?"

Misty hadn't told Rayne about her night with Jared. She didn't know what to say or how to explain what made her do it.

And she sure as hell didn't know how she felt about him now. Until she was clear in her mind she didn't know how to talk about it.

"No," Misty said firmly. "I've been waiting for years to leave. This is absolutely the right thing to do. And I haven't been acting weird. I've just been preoccupied with all the things I need to get done before I leave. I have a bunch of packing still to do."

"I'll help you with that. We'll have it done in no time."

The waitress slid the slab of caramel apple pie in between them. Two scoops of vanilla ice cream melted on top leaving a milky pool on the plate. The strong aroma of apples and cinnamon wafted around Misty's nose and her stomach heaved in her abdomen. Eyes watering, she tried to pretend she wasn't bothered.

She failed.

"Holy crap, are you okay? You look positively green." Rayne looked down at the plate of apple pie and ice cream. "Since when does apple pie make you sick?"

"It's not," Misty denied, although she couldn't even look at the plate. The ice cream had melted even more and was mixing with the caramel into some sort of milk soup that turned her stomach until bile was in the back of her throat. "I'm fine."

"You're not fine. You're the color of a Martian from outer space." Rayne's gaze never wavered from Misty's face. "You really are sick, aren't you? I think we need to get you home and into bed. The sooner you start resting up the sooner you'll get better." Rayne signaled for the check and began to gather her purse and gloves. "Let's head home and I'll make you a nice cup of herbal tea. That should settle your stomach. You must be coming down with the flu."

A feeling of dread settled in Misty's chest. She'd been staring at her calendar every single day since that night with Jared. Waiting.

"Can we make a stop first?" Misty asked, her voice quavering with emotion.

"Sure, where do you want to go?" Rayne paid the bill – it was her turn – and pulled car keys from her purse.

"A drug store. Preferably one out of town where no one knows me."

Rayne's brows were furrowed but then understanding crossed her features. "Oh God. Are you sure?"

"No." Misty shook her head, feeling miserable but not from the smells any longer. "It's just a hunch. It's early yet. But apple and cinnamon has never made me nauseous before."

"The sooner you find out for sure the better. Let's go," Rayne said brusquely. "Everything is going to be alright."

If Misty's suspicions were true, nothing would ever be the same again.

✧ ✧ ✧ ✧

Lindsey Hicks looked completely different from the woman Jared had seen in the courtroom five years ago. Then her hair had been long and lifeless, her body stick thin, and her face pale and gray. She'd had a perpetually sullen look that had struck Jared as almost petulant as she'd sat there during Boyd's trial. When the verdict had come down, she'd walked out of the courtroom without a look back at her husband.

The woman before Jared today didn't have much in common with the former female. Dark hair was trimmed and styled so it curled around her chin. Her face was carefully and skillfully made up and her body was no longer emaciated. In khaki pants and an argyle sweater she looked every inch the happy housewife in a middle-class suburban neighborhood.

Lindsey sat across from Jared in the comfortable living room decorated in green and gold. There were pictures of a small young girl on the mantle which he knew from his research was the daughter Tilly who was currently in foster care. He'd also learned that Lindsey had a court date coming up to try and regain custody of her daughter. Currently she was only allowed supervised visits.

"So how can I help you, Sheriff?"

"I appreciate you talking with me, Mrs. Hicks. As you know I'm here to talk about your ex-husband Boyd."

"Jackson," she corrected, her posture going stiff. "It's Lindsey Jackson now. And as I told you on the phone, I'm not sure how I can help you. I haven't seen Boyd in years – not since his sentencing."

Jared pulled out a small notebook and a pen. "You didn't talk to him on the phone or visit him?"

"No, by the time Boyd was sentenced I knew I needed to get clean. I knew I couldn't do that if I was still married to him."

She certainly seemed to have turned her life around. No one would ever need to know about her less than pristine past. Jared had seen very few people overcome addiction and he had a great respect for this woman for doing just that.

"But you almost died from an OD several months later," he reminded her. "And you didn't file for divorce from Boyd for another six months after that."

Her hand fluttered to her throat and her composure slipped for a moment. "I'm not sure I can explain how time feels when you are…under the influence."

"You don't have to," he assured her. "I'm just trying to understand the events of the last five years."

"The only thing that is important to me is my daughter. I just want to make sure that Boyd stays away from her. Can you keep him from seeing her?"

Lindsey's tone was urgent and she'd leaned forward, her eyes pleading.

"Do you have any reason to believe that Boyd knows where your daughter is residing?"

Jared could find out where Tilly was living, but unless there was some credible threat to her life he couldn't really do anything except warn the foster parents not to let the young girl out alone where Boyd might be able to kidnap her.

"Well…no. But I don't want him to have access to her."

Jared scratched down a note to check on whether Boyd had inquired about visiting his daughter.

"I'll check on whether he's tried to see her. Do you think he would hurt her, Mrs. Jackson? Harm her in some way?"

The woman's cheeks had turned red and those hands that had fluttered uselessly before were balled into fists. "Just being around her would be awful. He'll lead her down a bad path just as he led me. My addiction is all his fault and I won't let that happen to Tilly."

He didn't want to upset her any longer so he changed the subject.

"What can you tell me about Dale Hicks and his relationship with Boyd?"

Lindsey's mouth twisted and her gaze dropped. "That's complicated."

"What do you mean by that?"

She looked back up at Jared. "Dale and Boyd are very competitive."

Jared felt the phone in his shirt pocket vibrate but he'd let the call go to voicemail. This was too important to allow interruptions.

"Boyd said Dale framed him for the robbery. Why would he do that?"

"They were always angry with each other for some slight, real or imagined. Both of them have a mean streak to boot. If Dale had twenty dollars Boyd wanted twenty dollars too. Plus Dale's twenty. And vice versa."

That sounded like what Jared knew of the two men. Citizens of the year they were not.

"Do you think Dale actually framed Boyd?"

"Why would I know anything about that? I'm just as in the dark as you." She stood, obviously agitated, and walked over to the fireplace where pictures of her daughter sat. "I'm just worried about Tilly. You don't think they'll let him see her, do you?"

He had to be honest. "I honestly don't know, Mrs. Jackson. I'm not really involved in that type of law."

Her fingers glided over a few picture frames lovingly. "I just want to put my past behind me. Are we done?"

"I do have one last question. When he was sentenced, Boyd threatened the Fielding sheriff's department because he felt we had helped convict him wrongly. Did he ever talk to you about that?"

Shaking her head, she walked to the windows that overlooked the front yard. "My husband is home so I'm afraid I'll have to ask you to go now. He doesn't like reminders of my past. For obvious reasons."

"So he did or didn't say anything about it?" Jared didn't want to leave without the answer.

Lindsey opened the front door letting in a blast of cold air. "He didn't say anything. Now can you please go? I don't want my husband upset."

Jared stood to leave. "Thank you for your time. I do appreciate it." He pulled a business card from his pocket and handed it to her. "If Boyd, Dale, or anyone from the Hicks family tries to contact you, please let me know."

She nodded and Jared pulled on his coat and exited the house. A large muscular man was getting out of a black pick up truck in the driveway – the kind with oversized tires and fancy multi-colored pin striping on the side and tailgate.

"Honey, is everything okay?" the man asked, his gaze darting back and forth between his wife and Jared.

"It's nothing. Come in out of the cold and I'll tell you all about it." Lindsey slid her arm through her husband's and tugged him toward the front door but the man wouldn't be hurried. Jared stuck out his hand and introduced himself.

"I'm Sheriff Jared Monroe of Fielding."

With one arm draped protectively around his wife's shoulders, the husband shook Jared's hand. "Dave Jackson. Are you here about Boyd Hicks? We heard he was out."

"I am. I just had a few questions. I do appreciate your wife's time. If you hear from him please let me know."

"Will do." Dave Jackson nodded, his expression solemn. "I don't want him anywhere near Lindsey."

"That makes two of us. Thank you again."

"Thank you for stopping by, Officer."

The couple walked into the house and closed the door behind them while Jared headed to his vehicle. Swinging into his SUV, he pulled out his phone to see who had called earlier. He cursed a blue streak as he listened to the voicemail. As was becoming the norm, the shit had hit the fan at home and he needed to go put it right before things got worse.

Right now Jared needed to have a serious talk with his father.

Chapter Eight

"Don't treat me like a child, boy." Gerald Monroe's voice held a tone of warning but Jared had come too far to heed it now.

"Then stop acting like one," Jared retorted. He didn't have time for this shit. Gerald Monroe was a grown man who knew better than to act like this. "You had a doctor's appointment today. An appointment you apparently decided not to go to, so when you didn't show up they called me. Why didn't you go?"

Gerald scowled and sat up straight in the rocking chair. With the sunlight streaming through the living room windows, the older man still looked pale and drawn from his time in the hospital. He needed to get out and about but stubbornly stayed in the house and watched television.

"Didn't want to. All those doctors do is poke and prod at a body, then write them a prescription. Well, I've got plenty of medicines already. Don't need no more. Besides, they're all full of crap anyway. I'm fine. Don't you have criminals to catch or something?"

Jared could be doing several "or somethings" right now, every one of them more pleasant than arguing with his father but here he was doing it anyway. Since finding out about his Alzheimer's Gerald had taken to sitting in his rocking chair and staring out the large front windows of the house. He didn't want to talk. He didn't want to tell Ty how to run the ranch. He didn't want to do anything.

And that worried Jared most of all.

Gerald Monroe had always been a man full of energy and purpose. Not so anymore.

"We're still talking about you. You can't just decide not to go to doctor's appointments. Mrs. Gaston was supposed to drive you. Where is she?"

Gerald's face turned red but his chin lifted in defiance. "I fired her. She was always fussing and she's the worst cook ever. Can't a man be left in peace in his old age?"

Jared made a mental note to call the nurse after this discussion and beg the woman to come back. They needed someone here at the house to make sure his father took his medications on time, ate his meals, and all those other things they'd always taken for granted before.

"Then I'll just call and rehire her, Dad. You can't be here all day by yourself. You forget to take your medicine."

"Medicine is for sick people," Gerald snorted. "I'm just getting old. When did that become a disease?"

That was a good question. His father was getting older, seventy on his next birthday. Still strong and fit, his hair was silver and his face lined. You couldn't tell by just looking at him that he sometimes became confused and disoriented.

"Dad," Jared began carefully, knowing how stubborn his father could be when he wanted to be. "Maybe Royce can take you to the doctor."

Royce seemed to be the only one who could get a smile or laugh out of the old man these days. Gerald might not approve of his older son's exploits but that didn't stop him from enjoying Royce's company.

Gerald shifted in the chair, a wool throw over his knees. "That'd be a sight better than that woman. She's always nattering on about things. At least Royce knows when to keep his mouth shut."

"Fine. I'll talk to Royce. I rescheduled your appointment for Tuesday at two."

Jared could simply add talking to his brother to his ever-growing list of crap he needed to do that no one else wanted to. And that's if he could find Royce. He had a way of disappearing whenever work needed to be done.

Gerald grumbled under his breath but didn't – to Jared's relief – object. That was one issue taken care of today.

"I need to get back to the station. Becky's around here somewhere if you need anything."

She was probably on the back porch with her cell phone glued to her ear. She seemed to spend almost every moment of every day on that thing.

"You worry like a woman. Get out of here and get back to work," Gerald growled, his face still red and scowling.

Jared didn't take his father's bait and continue to argue. Instead he turned and headed out the door and into his truck. He had a mountain of work waiting for him and this side trip hadn't helped his schedule in the least.

As he drove he mentally ticked through his list as to whether it was something he needed to do personally or if he could delegate. By the time he entered Fielding and was driving down Main Street, he'd managed to move a few to-do items elsewhere.

Passing the diner, he saw Misty get into a car with another woman. He hadn't seen her for over a week, the last time at the pizza place on Maple. They'd agreed to just be friends after the one night of passion they'd shared but his libido hadn't received the message. One glimpse of her pale blonde hair and he was imagining how her bare skin had looked in the low light. In fact, he'd been visited by those images pretty much every damn night. There was something about her that he couldn't seem to get over. Maybe it was her shy smile or the way her fingers had touched him – tentatively at first, and then bolder as her confidence grew. Whatever it was, she'd burrowed into his subconscious and damn if she wasn't impossible to shake.

And she was leaving.

There was no future in mooning over a woman who wanted nothing to do with Fielding. This was his home and he couldn't imagine any circumstances that would compel him to leave. Misty Foster would have to be one of those women who left a pleasant memory in their wake. Nothing more.

Pulling in front of the station, he parked the truck and headed inside. Despite the load of work ahead of him he felt himself relax, his shoulders loosening. With everything going on at the ranch these days the station held less stress and hassle. Here he knew what and how things needed to be done. Everyone had a job and he expected his deputies to pull their weight.

"Talk to me," Jared said to Knox before heading straight to the coffeemaker. "What did I miss?"

"That's a good question. I'm trying to figure that out right now."

Jared didn't like the sound of that. "Maybe I can help."

Knox leaned back in his chair while Jared settled on the edge of the desk with a hot cup of coffee. "Right after you left we got a flurry of calls. Domestic violence. Vandalism. Possible break-in. Suspected drunk driver." Knox scratched his chin. "Funny thing. None of them turned out to be true. Everyone was running all over the place like chickens with their heads cut off.

All for nothing. In the meantime, real reports had to wait in line."

"Tell me about the real crime first." Jared's brain was already whirring with possibilities, although one seemed more likely than the others.

"A house burglarized just east of town. Perp took the television, a laptop, a cell phone, and two hundred in cash." Knox peered at another piece of paper on his desk. "And this one completely unrelated. A woman's purse was snatched but not in town. It happened in her own driveway as she was getting out of the car. Weird."

Jared gulped at the hot coffee, angry that he'd missed so much. "Do we have deputies on those scenes now?"

Knox nodded. "We do. They'll be filing their report before they go off-duty."

Too antsy to stay still, Jared stood and paced the small area between the desks. "Are you sure the other reports were fake?"

"Positive." Knox smacked the top of his desk in obvious frustration. "I had deputies spread to every corner of our jurisdiction and nothing. When they got there…not a damn thing. Maybe a bunch of kids were playing pranks on us."

Shaking his head, Jared sank into the chair behind his desk. "I don't think so. I think this might just be the first shot fired by Boyd Hicks. He's telling us that he can scatter and control us. He likes to play games and this would be right up his alley. Get in touch with the 911 operator and get the originating phone numbers for those calls. Also, I'll want to see the addresses the deputies were sent to. If it's Boyd, he'll want to make sure we know it's him."

Knox handed Jared a stack of papers. "I'll get those phone numbers right now."

"Good. I'll see if there's any connection between these addresses and Boyd Hicks. I have a feeling this was no kiddie prank."

Jared had caught Hicks once, and if he needed to he would do it again. No one was going to terrorize the town of Fielding while he was in charge.

He couldn't fix the situation with his dad or Royce or even Misty. But there was one thing he could do – keep his town safe.

✧ ✧ ✧ ✧

Misty grabbed the instructions, her tense fingers crumpling the paper. She couldn't see straight and the room was spinning. This simply couldn't be right.

"Two blue lines," Rayne pronounced, plucking the stick from Misty's nerveless fingers. "Positive."

Somehow Misty managed to sit on her daybed, the lunch she'd had hours ago churning in her stomach. They'd used a condom. People didn't get pregnant with condoms. Or did they? She had to admit she knew little about birth control. It had never been a factor in her life before.

Until today, that is.

"I can't be." Still in denial, Misty shook her head. "It must be a mistake."

Rayne sat down next to her and patted her knee. "Is there something you want to tell me? It appears that you are pregnant, Mist, and unless this is something miraculous I think you need to start talking."

Misty buried her head in her hands, panicked beyond rational thought. She'd made her plans so carefully. "We used a condom. I cannot be pregnant. This thing is wrong."

"Okay. Now we're getting somewhere. You said *we*, which means there is a man, then. I don't have to alert the media about a virgin birth or anything."

Groaning and falling back on the bed, Misty wrapped her arms around her torso as if in comfort. "I had a one night stand. I thought it would be okay. Just one night and then I'd be off to Seattle, just like you said. This has to be wrong," she repeated, but she had an idea it wasn't. She simply hadn't been feeling like herself these last three weeks.

"You had a one night stand. Maybe I should alert the media after all. I never thought that would happen."

Misty lifted one hand from her eyes and glared at her best friend. The same friend who had encouraged her to let loose a little. Now look what had happened.

"You're not helping, Rayne."

"I'm sorry, you're right. Listen, people do get pregnant even when using a condom. They're not a hundred percent."

Misty slapped her hands down on the mattress, feeling helpless and not liking it in the least. "They ought to tell people that then. Oh God, how am I going to tell him?"

Rolling over, she buried her head in the comforter. She had no idea how she was going to tell Jared. What would he say? Would he want the baby? Did she?

Yes. Yes, she did.

Already she was feeling protective of the life deep inside of her. If Jared didn't want it, she would love it enough for both of them.

"And whom might you be telling about this pregnancy?" Rayne queried.

Misty levered up to her elbows and sighed. "You want to know who the father is, don't you?"

"That would be a helpful tidbit of information. Are you going to tell me?"

Rayne fell silent leaving the decision in Misty's lap. She'd already kept so much from Rayne so couldn't keep this from her any longer.

Burying her face again, Misty braced herself for Rayne's reaction. "Jared Monroe is the father."

Rayne's mouth gaped open, her brows almost to her hairline in astonishment. "Sheriff Jared Monroe? The town hunk? Christ on a unicycle, you don't do anything halfway, do you? Holy shit."

Misty nodded miserably. She had no idea what she was supposed to do now.

"And you're going to tell him, right?" Rayne prompted. "He deserves to know."

"I'll tell him. I'm just not sure how or when," Misty admitted, still reeling from the news herself. She needed time to get used to it before talking to Jared. "After that one time we said we would just be friends."

"About that one time…I need details, girl. I can't believe you kept this a secret. There's no way I could have kept something like this under wraps."

Misty leaned back against the pillows, grabbing one to hug to her middle. "I'll give you details but I'm kind of in the middle of a crisis here, you know? Rayne, I'm pregnant."

Just saying the words shook her to the core. She was going to be a mother. The only thing she knew at this moment was that she wanted to be the very best mother she possibly could.

Rayne threw her arm around Misty and pulled her into a fierce hug. "It will all be okay. I'm your friend and I'm here for you. Always. If Sheriff Gorgeous doesn't want this baby, I'll be right by your side. I promise."

Sniffling, Misty wiped a few stray tears of gratitude that had trickled down her cheeks. She might not have had friends growing up but she'd hit the jackpot with Rayne.

"I think I'm going to need all the help I can get. I don't know a thing about babies."

"We'll learn together. I'll steal some of my sister's pregnancy books." Rayne pressed her forehead to Misty's. "You'll be okay. You're going to be a great mom."

Misty could only hope and pray that was true.

Chapter Nine

Jared tipped his hat to the lady behind the counter of the Springwood diner when she told him to take any table he liked. Driving here today, he'd been intrigued by the call from Misty. She wanted to talk to him, which was good in and of itself. He hadn't been able to get her out of his mind since that night weeks ago. Maybe she'd changed her mind about leaving Fielding.

Of course her request to meet out of town had caught him by surprise, although it shouldn't have. Misty had some scars from the gossips in town, and somehow they'd both escaped being grist for that mill after the night he'd spent at her apartment.

Settling into a booth back in a corner, he ordered a coffee for him and a hot chocolate for her. For some reason he was nervous, which was unusual. He couldn't remember the last time a woman had made him feel like this, but then Misty was different than the women he usually dated.

Sweet. Giving but strong. And definitely more innocent.

The bell over the diner door rang and Misty entered, bundled up in her long black wool coat that made a stark contrast to the paleness of her hair. She'd left it down today and it curled at the ends, making him want to reach out and pluck at a silky strand.

Standing as she settled across from him, he took her coat and hung it on the hooks provided outside the booth. She was wearing blue jeans and another cream colored sweater that completely swamped what he now knew were the sweetest curves imaginable. It ought to be against the law to cover up a body that perfectly beautiful.

"I ordered you some hot chocolate," he said after they greeted each other. It had been slightly awkward but he'd managed a kiss on her cheek before she pulled away. "I hope that's okay."

"That's perfect, although it's not too cold today. Spring is right around the corner."

The waitress put their two mugs on the table with a smile before bustling away to help other customers.

"I think it's supposed to get to forty today," he replied, not sure what else to say. This was Misty's meeting.

Clearly out of weather conversation, she dipped her spoon into the whipped cream and licked it off. She had no idea how sensual it appeared to him and how his groin tightened in response. He cleared his throat and mustered up an easy smile.

"So you wanted to see me. And all the way out here in Springwood."

He didn't say that he'd wanted to see her as well.

Misty set her spoon down and picked up the paper napkin, scrunching it between her fingers. "I apologize for the subterfuge but I wanted to talk to you without the prying eyes of Fielding on us."

"It's not a problem. I have a buddy in town I can visit while I'm here."

It would be good to see Tanner again, although he would see him on Sunday at the meeting with all the other guys. Jared was particularly anxious to talk to all of them about the specter of Boyd Hicks.

"That's good." She was fiddling with her spoon again and staring down at the table. "How have you been?"

"I've been good. And you?"

His curiosity was getting the better of him. If she wanted them to start seeing each other again, hell, he was all for it. Maybe he should make this easier for her.

"I'm good. I've been busy packing and getting ready to move."

His stomach seemed to plunge and twist in reaction to her words. She wasn't staying. She was still leaving. So what was this about? Another night before she left for good? Was he just the boy-toy now? If this wasn't about them, he wanted to get down to business.

"So what did you want–" he began.

"I'm pregnant."

Her words were whispered but he heard them clearly. But his mind was having trouble with their meaning while the back of his neck broke into a sweat.

"Could you say that ag–"

"I'm pregnant." This time she raised her gaze from the table. Her lips were trembling as if she was about to burst into tears. Instinct made him grab her hand and squeeze the fingers comfortingly.

But who was going to comfort him? His dense brain had finally processed her statement and a surreal feeling came over him. This couldn't be right.

"I wore a condom."

Her eyes closed briefly and she shook her head. "Yeah, that was exactly my first thought. So I took a second test. It was positive too."

Positive.

He felt like a judge had just pounded a gavel and a cell door swung shut. It sucked the oxygen from his lungs, making it almost impossible to breathe.

Positive.

Misty was pregnant and he was going to be a father. At that moment she looked so young and vulnerable. Too young to be having his kid. She looked scared as well. Well, that made two of them. He wanted to run from the diner and not look back.

But he wouldn't do that.

Misty had trusted him that night to take care of her. He'd been the one with experience and he'd told her everything would be okay. He was responsible for this and by God, he'd do right by her. That's what a man did. Take responsibility for his mistakes.

"Are you okay?" he finally asked, still trying to wrap his mind around what she'd said. His head was telling him he ought to get proof or something but then realized Misty wasn't the type of person to pull something like that. From her expression she was just as devastated as he was.

"I'm tired and I don't like the smell of certain things, but I'm okay." Her fingers had twisted together and the knuckles were white. "Listen, I'm not asking anything of you, okay? I just wanted to tell you because it was the right thing to do. You can be as involved or not involved as you want. And you can come visit the baby anytime. I mean that."

"I'm the father." His voice sounded strangled but the words came out. "Of course I'm going to be involved."

His thoughts were coming into focus now and a sharp stab of fear pierced his heart. He didn't want to lose out on being this child's father. Planned or unplanned. He was going to be a dad.

A dad. As crazy as it was it was also kind of miraculous. He and Misty had made a baby.

"I'm just saying I'm not trying to put any pressure on you."

Jared tried to smile and put her at ease. Clearly she'd been terrified to tell him and he was glad she wasn't telling some other kind of guy. The kind that wouldn't be supportive or caring. He hoped he was better than that.

"I think we're both going to feel pressure for the next eighteen years or so. Raising a child is going to be a challenge, honey, but I think we're up for it. We'll figure this out together."

She smiled, obviously relieved he was taking the news so well. He congratulated himself on his calm demeanor and take charge attitude. He'd be there for her every fucking step of the way. But first things first.

"I'm glad you feel that way," Misty sighed, her fingers finally unclenching, letting the paper napkin fall unheeded to the table before taking a sip of her hot chocolate. "I feel better knowing I won't be alone."

He patted her hand. "You definitely won't be alone. We should start making some plans right away. Once I tell my family I can call the judge and we can set something up maybe next weekend. What do you think?"

Misty placed the mug back down on the table and frowned. "Judge? You want to settle custody right now? I was hoping we could work this out between us without going to court."

Why would they need a custody agreement?

"Misty," he explained impatiently, his mind already moving at light speed thinking of all the things that needed to be done. They'd need to move her belongings into his house today if possible so he could keep an eye on her, care for her. "I'm not talking about custody. I'm talking about getting married. We can have the judge come to the house next weekend and marry us. I think the sooner the better, don't you agree?"

"No."

She was shaking her head and Jared realized he was pushing. Again. He had a bad habit of that.

"I'm sorry. I guess I forgot that some women dream about their wedding and all. If you want a big ceremony that's fine, but that's even more reason to get started planning it. I'd like to be married before you start showing."

"Jared, listen to me." Her gaze captured his forcing his attention away from his plans and back to the woman in front of him. "I'm saying no. No, I won't marry you."

"No?" He couldn't believe his ears. She must not understand what he was asking.

"No."

There was finality to her tone that got through to him at last. All the women he'd dated since he was a teenager…all the women who had schemed to be Mrs. Jared Monroe…now he was offering it to this little slip of a woman.

And she'd turned him down flat.

✧ ✧ ✧ ✧

Misty could see the impatience in Jared's eyes, his entire body tense. She didn't flatter herself to think that he was hurt by her refusal to marry him but he was not happy. An alpha male like Jared made plans and expected everyone else to fall in line.

"Please let me explain. This doesn't have anything to do with you. This is about me."

His eyes narrowed. "The old – 'it's not you, it's me' – line? I thought you enjoyed our night together."

Sheesh, was it all about a man's ego? In the midst of all this he was worried about his sexual performance?

"I did. Very much, but that's hardly something to base a marriage on now, is it?" she replied reasonably. "We don't love each other, Jared."

He threw his hands into the air. "What does that matter now? We're having a baby. A baby that needs both his mother and father. Aren't you being a little selfish?"

Was she? From the moment she'd seen those two blue lines on the pregnancy stick she'd known every decision she made from that moment on would be about the child she carried. She already loved it – boy or girl. She wanted to be sure this baby felt loved and secure.

"No, I'm thinking ahead. This might work while the baby is young but eventually he or she is going to get older. Don't you think she'll notice that her parents aren't like other moms and dads? That they don't kiss or hug? How do you think that will make her feel? Eventually she might blame herself. I don't want that. I don't want that at all."

Jared shifted on the vinyl seat. "We'd kiss and hug. Just because we're not in love doesn't mean we couldn't, you know, like each other. I like you, Misty."

"I like you too. And I want it to stay that way. But what happens if you really fall in love someday? With someone else. You make it sound so simple but I don't think we have what it takes to make a marriage work." She paused, not sure she should even admit it to him. "If I ever get married, I want a husband that loves me. I want a loving home. It's what I want for my baby too."

"I'm trying to do the right thing here." Jared's voice was gruff and full of emotion and her own throat tightened in sympathy.

"I know, and I'm grateful that you're willing to step up to the plate so to speak. I think we can give this baby a good life without doing something that could only end badly. For both of us." Misty forced a laugh. "Besides, can you see the ladies of Fielding if you and I got married? They might actually have a stroke right then and there. We can't be responsible for something like that now, can we?"

Jared didn't smile but he stopped frowning. "You know I don't give a shit what people think. They're going to find out about us anyway when you start to show. I hope you don't have any thoughts about trying to keep the fact that I'm the father a secret."

"I'll be in Seattle by then," she reminded him gently. "No one here in Fielding even has to know about the baby unless you tell them. And I'll respect your decision either way on that."

Jared slapped the top of the Formica table, his face turning red. "You are not going to Seattle."

Heads all over the diner whipped around and Misty slunk down in her seat to get away from their prying eyes. She didn't know anyone here but she also didn't like Jared making a scene.

Apparently Jared thought that getting pregnant meant she had to give up on all her dreams. If anything, it meant she needed to chase them all the harder. It wasn't just about her anymore; this was about what she could give her child if she succeeded.

Misty took a deep breath to calm herself. Getting angry at him wasn't going to help the situation. "The lease on my apartment is up at the end of next week. I signed a yearlong lease on the new place and put down a large deposit which I would lose if I break the contract. The gallery I'm working with is also in Seattle. That's how I earn my living and how I'll support this baby. You're still the father no matter where I am. I said you could see the baby whenever you wanted to and I meant it. I'm not giving up my dreams to stay here in Fielding so everyone can point and whisper as I walk by."

"Now you are being selfish." Jared's tone was low and accusing. "You're taking my baby away from me. As for money, you don't need to work. I can easily support both of you."

Misty groaned and slapped her forehead. This man simply didn't get it. "That's awesome. I can be your kept woman as long as I give up everything I've ever wanted in life. What a great deal. Tell me, Jared, what do you give up?"

"My freedom," he snapped back and then seemed to think better of it. "Shit, I didn't mean that to come out that way. Dammit, Misty, you've got me all turned around here."

"Welcome to the club. Now you know how I've felt since I found out. But can't you see? We're at each other's throats already about who's making a bigger sacrifice. That's why marriage between us wouldn't work. We shouldn't be two victims making vows we really don't mean. We'll only come to resent each other eventually and believe me, our child will figure that out. Kids are smart."

The fight seemed to drain out of him at that point. "Okay, let's table the marriage discussion. For now, anyway. But I don't want you to leave town. How can I make sure you're okay if you're in Seattle? I don't want to miss a minute of the pregnancy or our baby."

Misty had to admit Jared's protective streak was kind of sweet. What he didn't seem to realize was that she'd been taking care of herself since she was eight years old. "You could call me. Or text me. Even Skype. That way you could see I was fine and healthy."

"It's not the same," he argued and he had a point.

It hadn't occurred to her that he would want to be this involved, which only underlined the fact that they didn't know each other well enough for marriage. Maybe she needed to rethink the whole Seattle thing. The city wasn't going anywhere and she could paint from here and travel back and forth as needed. She didn't want to be the kind of person who deprived a loving man of his child.

"I see that you really mean it about wanting to be involved. Can you give me a few days to think about this? If I stay here in Fielding I'll have to find another place to live since my apartment has already been leased by someone else. Plus I have to do something about the contract in Seattle. There has to be a way we can compromise."

Jared nodded, seemingly satisfied with her answer. "A fair compromise is all I ask. And as for your lease in Seattle I can buy you out of that. Just say the word."

It must be nice not to have to worry about money and if she decided to stay in Fielding, even for just the pregnancy, she'd think about taking him up on the offer. She had her pride, but otherwise she was going to lose pretty much all her life savings.

"You took the news better than I expected," she admitted, stirring the whipped cream in her hot chocolate. "I'd heard you were calm in a crisis and now I've seen it for myself."

"I wouldn't necessarily file this under a catastrophe. There are worse things in life." Jared signaled for the waitress. "Just for grins…how did you think I'd react?"

Misty laughed and shook her spoon at him playfully, glad the tension between them had dissolved. "I thought you might run screaming down the street, hop in your truck, maybe change your name."

Chuckling, Jared asked the waitress to bring them two menus and more coffee and hot chocolate. "That sounds pretty extreme. Why don't we order some lunch and maybe talk about baby names? I had an uncle named Horatio. It's kind of a family name."

Her look of horror must have amused him. "I'm kidding. Well, not about my uncle's name but about the whole family thing. I think we might want to pick something more mainstream."

Misty barely glanced at the menu. "I'm not really hungry."

Jared pushed the menu back in front of her. "You're eating for two now. How about the grilled chicken with rice and vegetables? That sounds nice and healthy."

Her stomach, already nauseous from anticipating this meeting, took the opportunity to churn in her abdomen letting her know undoubtedly that was not what she was going to be having for lunch.

She pressed a hand to her middle and shook her head. "That doesn't sound so good. Oh look, they have chicken pot pie. Now that I think I could eat."

"That's a lot of carbs." Jared was frowning at the menu as if it had done something to offend him.

"Do you want me to eat or not?" she asked sharply. Geez, he was bossy. He was going to have to learn no one ordered her around. Badge or no badge.

He cleared his throat and stuck his nose back in the menu. "I want you to eat. I just want you to eat healthy."

Reining in her swirling emotions, she sighed and pushed the menu away. "Listen, I'm tired and my stomach is queasy. I just want some comfort food for it. I promise I won't spend the next nine months eating cheeseburgers and chili fries."

Rubbing the back of his neck, he nodded but she could tell it was reluctantly. "You need to make sure you get your rest. Maybe even get in a nap if you need to."

"Trust me, I'm falling asleep at all hours of the day and night. My friend Rayne says this is normal in the beginning. I'm making a human being here. It's a lot of work," she tried to joke and was rewarded with a real smile this time.

The waitress came back with their coffee and hot chocolate and Jared ordered for both of them. Chicken pot pie and a side salad for her and a steak sandwich with extra cheese for him. It looked like he worried about her health but was relatively unconcerned about his own. She'd make him eat the darn salad since he'd ordered it. Greens would only make her tummy more upset but he didn't seem to be really hearing what she was saying.

"If this is going to work you're going to have to give me some space. You can't just horn into my life and start ordering me around. I'm not going to fall in line like one of your deputies," she warned, wanting to put them on equal footing right here at the beginning. He needed to respect her wishes and trust she wouldn't do anything to hurt their child.

"Just don't relegate me to the sidelines." Jared's blue gaze captured her own, his expression deadly serious. "I want to be involved. Hell, I *will* be involved. I know you're used to doing everything on your own, Misty, but this isn't just yours. This baby belongs to both of us. We may not have planned this, but now that it's happened I'm going to be the best damn father in Montana."

From what Misty knew about this man that was exactly what he would be. And where would that leave her? She could see now that leaving for Seattle would be a selfish move. How many times as a little girl had she wondered about her own father? No, this baby would know it was loved. By *two* parents.

Somehow she had to make this work. The question was how.

Chapter Ten

Jared didn't have much time to dwell on the shocking news Misty had delivered to him. Halfway through their lunch he'd received a call from Deputy Knox that Chris's departmental SUV was on fire at a convenience store out of town. He hated to leave her in a lurch like that but if she was going to be his wife then she would need to get used to stuff like this. And she was going to marry him. She wasn't thinking straight right now, but in a few days or weeks she'd realize it was the only sensible thing to do.

By the time Jared made it there the flames had been extinguished but the vehicle was going to be a total write off. Hays, the tow truck driver, was hitching the burned-out hull to his truck as Jared circled the SUV looking for signs of what had started the blaze.

"So you were inside talking to Billy about the shoplifters when this happened?" Jared asked Chris. The younger man looked upset and a little scared, as if he was afraid Jared was going to rip him a new one.

"Yes, sir. But Billy didn't know anything about the call. I had my back to the windows so Billy was the first to spot the flames.

I got his fire extinguisher while he called the fire department. I'm sorry, boss."

"Doubt this is your fault," Jared said briskly. "This is a gas station, after all. Perhaps someone threw a cigarette butt into some spilled fuel. Hell, the truck could have had a gas leak. We won't know until we can get a closer look."

If they ever found out. It was a fucking gas station. Flammable shit was everywhere. On television he'd even seen a car go up in flames from the static electricity spark from a damn cell phone. But one detail stood out from everything else.

Billy hadn't reported any shoplifters. Another bogus call out.

Which made Jared very suspicious about this vehicle fire. Good chance it wasn't an accident. Hopefully Billy had cameras stationed around the property because they'd had no luck with the earlier calls. All of them had been made from separate prepaid cell phones. He couldn't trace them anywhere but that was sure suspicious.

Dammit. Jared needed to have a chat with Boyd Hicks immediately. He'd had no luck as he never seemed to be "home" whenever Jared stopped by. He was sure that was by design.

"Billy, we're going to need any footage from your security cameras inside and outside."

"Sure, Sheriff." The man nodded and scuttled away. "It's in the back room."

"I'm really sorry," Chris said again. "Jesus, when I saw it…"

Jared slapped the younger man on the back. Chris was a good junior deputy and was going to make a great senior. He might even be a sheriff one day. Sharp and brave, he didn't make excuses. In other words, Jared's kind of lawman.

"Relax—I really don't think this is your fault. I think there were other forces at work here."

Chris's expression cleared. "Hicks? What's that guy's end game anyway? What does he gain from something like this?"

"Right now he's amusing himself," Jared replied. "He wants to make us look stupid and so far he's not doing a bad job of it. We need to regroup and figure out how to deal with this because knowing him – and I do know him – he's going to escalate. Ultimately this is about revenge."

After retrieving the footage from Billy, Jared gave Chris a ride back to the station. Knox was already there keeping things running smoothly as usual. Jared sent Chris to the motor garage in the back to see what extra vehicles they might have available. Jared was sure there was a decent cruiser. It wasn't as good on snow as an SUV but it was better than nothing until the insurance payout.

"We need to figure something out here," Jared said to Knox, pulling him aside. "It looks like that was another bogus call. And yes, I think Hicks is behind this."

Knox shook his head. "I don't doubt it either." He held out a slip of yellow paper. "Looks like your brother wants to talk to you."

Jared took it and picked up the phone. He'd call Seth Reilly first before Royce. It would be a good chance to bend Seth's ear about being a father so quickly after meeting Presley. All Royce was going to do was bitch about Ty, Dad, or something else just as stupid.

Jared scribbled a reminder to himself on the pad next to the computer. He needed to order a book about pregnancy and being a dad. He didn't know shit about the subject and although his own father was a fine man, Jared wasn't sure that the competitive atmosphere Gerald Monroe had raised his children in was the right thing. Look how screwed up Royce and Becky were. Hell, look how screwed up he himself was. He'd been competing for his father's approval and love his entire life. His friends told him his standards for his deputies and women were too high.

In general, he was a pain in the ass. It wasn't that he didn't know it. He did. He just couldn't seem to stop himself. Too many years of his father inspecting how straight his shoes were lined up or how he'd made his bed. Crap like that was going to leave a mark.

It made Jared want to be the best he possibly could. It also made him difficult to be around because he wanted everyone else to feel that way. And he sure as fuck didn't want to lay that burden on his child.

He had some changing to do. Luckily he had nine months to do it. If he didn't drive Misty away before then.

✧ ✧ ✧ ✧

Misty sipped the herbal tea and relaxed back onto the daybed. It had been quite a day but she'd told Jared about the baby. She'd been practically shaking like a leaf when she sat down but failure had not been an option. He needed and deserved to know.

He also deserved to be the kind of father he wanted to be. Maybe because of her upbringing, never knowing her own father, she'd assumed he wouldn't want to be that involved. Somehow she'd pictured him in the periphery – there but only on birthdays and holidays.

But Jared Monroe wanted to be hands on.

He wanted to marry her so they would be a family.

She didn't even know what that was. That was the real problem here. Yes, she wanted her husband to love her. Unlike other girls she'd never fantasized about her wedding or a white dress and flowers. She'd dreamed of getting out of Fielding, having enough money to buy new clothes that weren't from a thrift store and eating out at fancy restaurants with interesting people as her friends.

But his proposal had set off so many other warning bells inside of her. He wanted them to be a family but what if she didn't know how? She didn't want to screw this up but she only knew how mother and daughter related to one another. She'd never seen anything else except on television. And she was sure that wasn't real or anything she might want to emulate.

But Jared knew all about being part of a family. From what she could see, the Monroe family might have its issues but they were close. She'd never fit into their world. She was Misty Foster, daughter of the town harlot and Jared was practically local royalty. It would never in a million years work.

Sleepy after a long day, Misty set the cup on the end table and let her eyelids drift shut. She was too tired to make any decisions today but tomorrow she had some real thinking to do.

✧ ✧ ✧ ✧

"Let's call this meeting to order." Tanner Marks, head lawman in Springwood and Chris's father, pounded on the rickety wooden table, scarred and worn from years of abuse. It was Sunday morning and Jared and his seven sheriff friends were sitting in the roadhouse as they had every month for the last five years or so.

Wait. Make that six friends.

"Where's Reed?" Jared asked. The amiable lawman wasn't sitting in his usual chair near the window.

"Illinois with Kaylee," Logan Wright replied, popping open a soda and sliding more cans down the table. "She's got business she needs to deal with and he didn't even burn half of his accrued vacation time when he was there this fall. The mayor was happy to give him a week off."

"Actually I'm surprised to see you here," Evan Davis observed. "Have the twins been letting you and Ava get any sleep at all?"

Logan's wife Ava had given birth to a boy and a girl the last week of December. Now two months old, they were only sleeping four hours at a stretch last Jared had heard about them.

"Brianna and Colt are doing fine, and yes, they are letting us get a little sleep. Luckily Ava's mom has been lending a hand too."

"They grow up fast," Seth Reilly warned with a chuckle. "Little Ben is starting to talk back to me. His favorite word? No. He likes to throw things too if we don't listen the first time."

"Then I'd make sure I'd listen," Griffin Sawyer laughed before munching on a pretzel with what appeared to be more enthusiasm than normal. His fiancé Jazz had both of them on a clean diet or something like that from what Jared had heard. He made a mental note to look that up now that he had a pregnant woman to look after.

A part of him wanted to shout the news from the top of the building. These were his best friends in all the world and they would be happy for him. But he held back, cautious as always. He hadn't even told his family yet or talked to Misty about how to make the announcement.

"New business?" Tanner smoothly cut in, getting them back on the job.

Jared raised his hand and told them all about Boyd Hicks and the bogus callouts they'd been receiving.

"I heard about the SUV catching on fire of course from Chris. Have you had any luck talking to Hicks or his brother?" Tanner queried from the head of the table.

"They seem to be out every time we show up, which is quite convenient. For them. I'm getting damn impatient."

"I think I can help you." Dare Turner had been sitting quietly back in the corner with the usual scowl across his face. The man never seemed happy, although no one could figure out what he was mad about. Maybe just life in general. He had issues at home, that much Jared knew, including a sickly father and a little sister under eighteen.

"You'd have my gratitude if you can," declared Jared. "I need to keep this situation from getting worse."

Dare leaned forward, his fingers laced together. "Dale Hicks is dating a girl in my town. In fact, he's there most days and evenings. If you're wondering how I know, he's already had a run in with law enforcement. He likes to race his car up and down the streets at twice the legal limit and then pick fights in the local watering hole."

"Sounds charming," Griffin said grimly. "A family of career criminals. Nice."

"What they need is a cell for two from the sound of it. I think our towns would be safer with the Hicks family off the streets." Tanner tossed his empty can in the trash behind the counter.

"You're okay with me questioning Dale?" Jared asked, cracking open another soda.

"I'm fine with it but I'd like to be there." Dare had his cell out and was tapping away. "If you have time we can go right after this meeting. I'll have one of my deputies drive by and make sure Dale's truck is there before we go."

Jared was finally going to get to talk to Dale and hopefully make some progress on this case. He was sick and tired of spinning his wheels and getting nowhere.

The rest of the meeting was uneventful. Evan seemed a little out of sorts but everyone knew he was still getting used to being a small town law officer after working for the Marshal Service.

In the meantime they'd all be there to help him make the transition.

"Ready?" Dare asked him as they stood in the parking lot after the meeting broke up. "You can follow me if you like."

"Sounds good. How do you want to play this? I don't think Hicks is going to be all that happy to see me."

Dare almost smiled. Almost. "He ain't going to be giddy as a schoolgirl to see me either. I've already busted his ass for public intoxication this week. I'm guessing he'll spit on our shoes and tell us to go fuck ourselves."

Jared loved a challenge. "No one has said that to me since last night, so that's all good. Here's hoping I can be charming and persuasive."

Dare swung into the cab of his truck. "You do whatever you want. I think bad cop comes more naturally to me though."

Jared couldn't argue with the man.

Chapter Eleven

Dale didn't bother to stop and tell Jared and Dare to fuck themselves. When they'd knocked on the front door of the tired rundown house, a woman with stringy brown hair and dark circles under her eyes had answered the door.

Before they could even get a word in she was already speaking. "Dale ain't here. I don't know where he is."

Jared knew it wasn't the truth from the way her gaze darted all around and her defensive posture. He walked to the end of the porch and peered around to the back of the house. This wasn't his first day on the job but people always seemed to think cops were stupid. Today was no exception. Dale Hicks had exited the house through a back entrance and was now running across a snowy field on foot.

Well, shit. Why did they always run? And on slippery snow too.

"He's running, Dare."

He didn't look back to see if the lawman was following him. Jared leaped over the railing and down to the snow covered ground below before taking off after Dale. It was times like this he was glad he kept in shape, otherwise he'd be coughing up a lung. The icy cold air made it painful to even draw breath. To complicate matters he had to lift his knees high to be able to navigate the deep snow drifts without falling on his ass.

Clearly Dale wasn't as vigilant about his fitness as Jared was able to close the distance between them. When he was about two feet away he leaped into the air and came down on the fleeing man's back, both of them landing in the cold, wet snow. Dare must have been on Jared's heels because he was right there kneeling on the cold ground, helping subdue Dale.

"Why'd you run?" Dare asked, turning the red faced Dale over and pulling him to his feet.

"Because I saw the fucking cops," he spat out. "Don't need no other reason."

Dare marched Hicks through the snow back toward the house with Jared on the other side. When they arrived the woman rushed outside and fussed over Dale while giving Jared and Dare the evil eye. All four of them went into the living room and settled into chairs. Jared was glad to be out of the cold, his clothes damp and chilly against his skin.

"This is Sheriff Jared Monroe of Fielding." Dare jerked his thumb in Jared's direction. "He'd like to talk to you and ask a few questions."

Dale's expression turned contemptuous. "We've met. And I ain't got shit to say to him or you. Angie, get me a beer."

It was true they had met previously and Dale hadn't been any different then he was today. Jared hadn't expected it either. He knew dealing with Boyd's brother was going to be a pain in the rear.

"Relax, I'm not here about you. Not this time anyway. I'm here about Boyd. Where is he hanging out these days?"

Dale's thin lips turned up into a half-smile. "Why do you think I know?"

Angie picked up a cigarette from a pack on the table. "You don't have to tell him anything, Dale. Tell him to go to hell."

Charming wife. Or girlfriend. She was a real gangster's moll wanna-be.

"Shut up," Dale growled, barely casting a glance in her direction. "Boyd's around. That's all I know. He doesn't tell me everything. Why don't you ask Lindsey?"

This was interesting. Why did Dale think Lindsey had seen Boyd?

"We did ask her. She says she hasn't seen him since he was sentenced. Is that the truth? Has he seen Lindsey since he got out?" Jared asked, closely watching Dale's body language for any tells.

The man shrugged carelessly. "I dunno. He's got a new girlfriend now but that don't mean he hasn't seen Lindsey. They were married."

"So you're saying Lindsey's not telling the truth?"

"If you're asking if she's a damn liar the answer is yes," Angie spat, her thin features contemptuous. "Always acting like she's better than everyone else."

"Shut up and get me a goddamn beer," Dale shouted at the brunette who slunk toward the kitchen.

"Is Lindsey lying?" Jared asked again.

"If she says she hasn't seen him then she hasn't, I suppose. You're the suspicious type. Boyd's around—he just don't like cops."

When it came to keeping peace in his town, Jared was more than suspicious.

"So you have seen him? When?"

"Shit, I don't know." Dale moved restlessly on the couch. "Is he in trouble or something?"

"Or something," Jared replied, careful to keep his expression neutral. "We just need to talk to him."

Dale pulled the half-smoked cigarette from Angie's mouth when she sat back down on the couch, two beers in hand, and took a long drag. The woman scrambled for another from the pack. "Then call his probation officer. Isn't that how you cops are supposed to communicate with us former convicts?"

"I did. He's lost track of Boyd as well. Seems like your brother is flying under the radar. It could get him right back in the slammer if he's not careful."

Dale threw back his head and laughed, dropping the cigarette into an overflowing ashtray. "Boyd's never been known for being careful or smart, Sheriff. Doubt he'd start now."

Jesus, was Dale the brains in the family?

"So how can I find this girlfriend of Boyd's?"

"She's a waitress at some pancake house outside of Springwood. Her name's Beatrice or Bethany…hell, it's something with a B anyway. That's all I know. Now are we done here because I'm done talkin'."

"That depends," Dare growled from the corner of the room where he'd been silently observing. "If I call your probation officer what will he say? Have you been checking in? If he asks me to search these premises will I find anything illegal?"

"Go right ahead," Dale invited. "I've got nothing to hide."

Dare didn't take Dale up on the offer so Jared and the other sheriff took their leave and headed back out to their trucks. They paused by Jared's driver's door and Dare glanced at the house behind him.

"So what do you think?"

"I think that something's up. Normally Dale would rather shoot me than tell me anything about Boyd. So why did he give up the girlfriend so easily?"

"Maybe it's a wild goose chase," Dare suggested. "Something to keep you busy elsewhere while he and Boyd go off and do something illegal and out of sight."

"It's possible," Jared conceded. "Although I wouldn't say Dale has ever been a quick thinker. Whatever he said here today is something he's been thinking about for a long time. He didn't make her up off the cuff."

"So you're going to try and find this Beatrice-Bethany?"

"I am. Maybe she can lead me to Boyd."

"What if Boyd isn't your man? What then?" Dare asked.

"That's a damn good question and the answer is that I'm shit out of luck. Other than Hicks I've got no evidence and no suspects."

"What does your gut tell you?"

"That Dale is up to something. It could be my issue or something completely unrelated. So now I go and talk to Boyd's girlfriend. Maybe I can learn something there. Either way I appreciate your cooperation here today."

"No problem. I have a feeling I'll be running old Dale Hicks in before too long. He seems to have an issue with being law abiding. When I do I'll give you a call. Maybe he'll be more willing to talk then."

It wasn't in Dale or Boyd Hicks's nature to be cooperative with the law. Jared would have to bide his time until one or both of them were more motivated to talk. Until then, he'd follow the trail of clues.

It was all he had.

✧ ✧ ✧ ✧

"I haven't seen Boyd in about a week." The pretty blonde in the blue waitress uniform shrugged as they stood outside the restaurant. "He comes and goes as he pleases which is fine with me."

It hadn't taken much for Jared to find Boyd's girlfriend – named Bonnie, not Beatrice or Bethany. After he ordered a stack of pancakes and left a big tip the young woman seemed more than willing to talk to him.

"Where does he go when he's not with you?"

Bonnie pulled the lapels of her coat tighter around her slight figure and rubbed her hands together.

"Boyd's not much for sharing details, if you know what I mean. When I see him he has other things on his mind."

Jared sure as hell didn't want to talk about Hicks's sex life.

"What do you talk about?"

Bonnie moved closer and batted her eyelashes at Jared. "We don't talk much either."

"Does he ever talk about his daughter?"

The question clearly made the young waitress uncomfortable. "Sometimes. It wasn't fair what happened. Boyd's mother would have taken custody of the little girl since the mom was a junkie. But they put her in a foster home instead, saying the whole Hicks family was unfit. They won't even let him see her which is bullshit. He wants to go to court to find out where she is but he can't afford the lawyer."

For the first time since dealing with Hicks Jared actually felt a small bit of sympathy for the man. He wanted to see his child and was being turned away and told he wasn't good enough. Whether Boyd was a good father wasn't for Jared to judge. They had an entire family court system for that.

"Does he talk about being wrongly convicted?"

Bonnie stiffened and took a step back, her lips flat. "He's talked about that. Dale set him up."

"Why would his brother do that? What would he have to gain?"

Shoving her hands in her pockets, she shifted from foot to foot. "I don't know. Boyd said it was a family thing. That's all."

"A family thing?"

"Something like that. He said Dale took something from him that he shouldn't have. He didn't say what and I didn't ask."

A family thing. Jared needed to look further into the Hicks family.

"Has Boyd been to see Dale since he got out?"

The young woman threw her head back and smiled. "Dale would be dead if he had. At least that's what Boyd said."

Two brothers so angry they'd kill each other. What "family thing" was worth murdering over? Money? It was more interesting with every moment.

"How did you meet Boyd Hicks anyway?" Bonnie didn't look a day over twenty-two. Too young to be mixed up with a man who had sworn vengeance against his own brother.

"I got involved in one of those 'write a letter to men in prison' campaigns at my church. He was different than the other guys who answered my letter. They just wanted a picture of me naked. Boyd was interested in me."

Yeah, Hicks was a real humanitarian.

"So it doesn't bother you that Boyd wants to kill his brother?"

A shoulder lifted then dropped. "From what he said Dale would do the same. The way Boyd explained it to me it's self-defense. Can I go now? It's cold out here."

"Yes, thanks for talking to me. Can I give you some advice though? If I were you I'd stay away from Boyd Hicks. He's a dangerous man."

"He'd never hurt me," the blonde said confidently, retreating toward her vehicle. "He loves me."

Jared stood there as the woman drove away, the sound of the engine fading into the distance. It was time to sit down and try and figure out what could make two brothers turn against each other and what they would do now.

It was Jared's job to keep innocent people from getting caught in the crossfire.

✧ ✧ ✧ ✧

Misty laid her forehead on the cool porcelain edge of her bathtub. From the moment she'd set foot on the bedroom floor this morning her body had been determined to purge every single thing in her stomach, including the lining. Now she was wrung out, covered in sweat, her abdomen aching and sore and her mouth feeling like a garbage pail.

Morning sickness had shown up today with a vengeance.

The pregnancy book that Rayne had brought her said that the key to not being sick was to keep a little something bland in the stomach at all times. But she hadn't had time to put anything in her stomach before the nausea hit. She'd felt okay lying down but the minute she'd sat up…wham.

She was concentrating on breathing in and out when the bathroom door flew open, slamming against the wall. Jared stood in the doorway, his features pale and his eyes wide in panic. He took one look at her and dropped down next to her on the hard tile.

"Are you okay? Talk to me, Misty. Jesus, did you fall and hurt yourself?"

She waved her hand and shook her head. His fear was real from the tone in his voice and she needed to neutralize it. Now.

"I'm okay. Just sick. I didn't fall."

It was a lie to say that she was okay but the normally calm, cool, and in charge sheriff was clearly out of sorts. His rough palm pressed against her forehead while the other hand smoothed her hair back from her face.

"You don't feel warm." His palm moved to the side of her face and then her neck. "Do you have a thermometer? That's the best way to check for a fever."

"I don't have a fever." Remembering they were sitting on the floor, she started to get up but he pushed her back down. "I have morning sickness, Jared."

He jerked back and she heard him suck in a breath. "Oh. Are you sure? You're not supposed to have that yet."

"What do you mean I'm not supposed to have it yet? It's morning and I'm clearly sick."

She wasn't in the best of moods and she didn't want to play guessing games with him.

A line of red appeared on each cheekbone. "I bought a book about pregnancy and it said most morning sickness starts around eight weeks."

She wanted to rinse her mouth and splash cool water on her face. Then she wanted to lie down for a very long time. "Maybe the baby hasn't read that chapter yet. Can you help me up now?"

"Of course." He lifted her to her feet and hovered as if she was going to fall into a heap back on the floor. Under his watchful eye she went to the sink and rinsed her mouth and dabbed a wet washcloth on her face.

"I think I need to lie down."

The words were barely out before he swept her off her feet and into his arms, carrying her back into the main room and setting her gently on the bed. "I'll make you some tea and toast. The book said that would settle your stomach."

She lay back on the propped up pillows while he started boiling water in her tiny kitchen. "So you're an expert in pregnancy now?"

"I wouldn't say that. I haven't made it all the way through the book yet. But it brought up some interesting subjects like safety. I need to babyproof the house. You know, cabinets and outlets. Things like that."

"Jared, the baby isn't going to be able to crawl for several months so you've got about a year to worry about that."

He was rummaging in her cabinets for a teabag which he found before she could say anything. "I don't like to put things off. We also need to be thinking about names, the nursery, and putting together a birth plan."

Apparently he'd read pretty far in that book. Farther than she had. Her current plan was to give birth as painlessly as possible.

"I'm sure we have time for all that."

Jared popped two pieces of bread into the toaster while the tea steeped in the cup. She must be feeling better because she was actually looking forward to a little breakfast. Despite being sick, hunger was gnawing at her stomach.

"There are lots of decisions to make. Like whether you want a home birth or a hospital. Or whether you want drugs or want to go natural."

"A hospital." These decisions were no-brainers. "And an epidural."

She'd already been privy to the decision made by Rayne's sister for her upcoming delivery. Besides, Misty was a wimp when it came to pain. She didn't much like blood either.

Jared brought her the plate of dry toast and the tea, setting the cup on the side table. "I haven't had a chance to research epidurals yet but I think you might want to reconsider a totally natural birth. It's how it's been done for centuries."

Misty bit into the toast with a sigh. The bland bread actually tasted good. How messed up was that?

"Maybe we could get a vial of smallpox and some leeches to make it as authentic as possible."

She hadn't meant the words to come out with that smart ass tone but Jared was railroading her already and they still had eight months to go. Jared, to his credit, scraped his fingers though his hair and appeared abashed.

"I'm not trying to push. I swear. I guess I'm just excited. I want to do this right."

That wasn't the first time she'd heard him say that and it was the crux of the matter. He thought there was a right way and a wrong way to do pretty much everything. There weren't many shades of gray in Jared Monroe's life.

"I was just thinking there's been several medical advancements in the last century regarding childbirth we might want to take advantage of. Frankly? I'm terrified of pushing this baby out if you want to know the truth. Terrified."

Jared sat next to her on the day bed and patted her hand comfortingly but it made no difference. She was still scared. "I'll be with you the entire time. I promise."

She eyed him skeptically. "Can you make it not hurt?"

His smile fell and he shook his head. "Well…no."

"Then let's have someone there in addition to you and me that can do that, okay?" Misty clasped his hand in both of hers and gave him a gentle smile. "But I have to tell you that I'm overwhelmed by how eager you are to embrace the role of father. I think it's wonderful."

Jared's lips twisted. "I'm going to be pushy. I'm not sure I can help it."

Giggling, she nodded in agreement. "Yes, you are. How about I just remind you when you do that?"

"Deal." He held out his hand as he had done the morning after their night together. She placed her hand in his much larger one and felt the now familiar electric zing when he touched her. "Is there anything else I can get you?"

To her surprise she'd finished her toast and tea and felt two hundred percent better. "No, but thank you. That was exactly what I needed for the nausea. How did you know I was sick? Wait, how did you get in my apartment?"

He picked up the cup and plate and carried them to the sink. "I didn't know you were sick. We were supposed to meet for breakfast this morning, remember? When you didn't show I got worried and came here." He glanced at her front door. "As for how I got in? When you didn't answer my knocking I got even more worried so I broke the lock. Guess I'll be fixing that this morning. It really was a piece of crap. I barely had to give it a push."

Misty groaned and rubbed her temples. "I completely forgot about breakfast. The minute my feet hit the floor I had to run to the bathroom. I'm so sorry."

"Relax," Jared assured her. "Nothing bad happened except to you. We can always have lunch after I fix your door. If you're feeling up to it, of course."

Misty was actually feeling pretty human. "That sounds good but I won't keep you in suspense as to what I've decided. I'm not leaving for Seattle. At least not right now or even in the near future. I want you to have the chance to be a father and honestly, especially after this morning, I think having help at this parenthood thing would be awesome."

She'd finally done something right because Jared was grinning like she'd given him a fantastic birthday present or something.

"That's great news. Speaking of this morning…I do want to be there to help you every step of the way. Which is why I think you should move in with me. Right away. As in today." He looked around the apartment, boxes piled up everywhere. "What do you say?"

Chapter Twelve

Jared held his breath as Misty contemplated his offer. He'd been thinking about it for the last few days. It was the perfect solution really. She'd have someone to help her when she didn't feel well and they could work together on the long list of things that needed to be done.

It didn't hurt that it might ease her into the idea of marriage and making them a family.

"You want me to move in? Rayne offered to let me stay with her until I found a new place."

"If you live with me everything will be easier, don't you think? I can take you to your doctor appointments and make you tea and toast in the mornings."

She was wavering and he couldn't have that. He needed to make the case compelling enough there was no doubt what her answer would be.

"What about the town? They'll all talk if I move in with you."

So that was her issue. The citizens of Fielding and their tendency to stick their nose where it didn't belong.

"Since I don't intend to keep this baby's parentage a secret they're going to talk anyway. Why don't we really give them something to gossip about?" Jared grinned at the thought. "You and I living in sin and expecting a child out of wedlock should keep tongues wagging at least until the Fourth of July picnic and parade."

Her fingers rubbed the embroidered design on the pillowcase. "Have you told your family yet?"

"No. I wanted to talk to you first about that. I was planning to tell them at Sunday dinner but if you move in today, I'll drive by and tell them tonight if you want me to."

Misty was chewing her lower lip again. "They're going to be upset. I doubt they're going to like me."

How could he possibly explain the current family dynamics to an outsider? Hell, she wasn't going to be an outsider anymore so he might as well try. It was only fair she be aware of what she was walking into.

"These days Dad is upset with everything and everyone so no change there. Becky spends most of her time on the phone so I doubt she'll even notice that something outside herself is going on. My younger brother Ty is a great guy so he'll welcome you with open arms. Royce will too but he'll also probably try to proposition you if he's not sober at the time."

If anything she looked more troubled, her brows furrowed with worry. "I just don't want to make your life more difficult."

That was a refreshing change from everyone else he knew. "Too late. Between my family, deputies, and the town my life is already difficult. Not that I'm complaining. It's my life and I wouldn't trade it for the world, but that doesn't make it stress free."

"You really want me to move in?"

He had her, he could feel it. "I do. I think it's the answer to making everything easier, especially when the baby comes. We won't need to argue about who gets the weekends. We'll both be there all the time."

"I'm not promising to move in forever." Misty held up her hand in warning. "Let's just take this one day at a time and see how it goes. We might not like living together."

"I doubt either one of us has a habit so objectionable that the other wouldn't be able to cohabitate easily. I'm pretty easy going."

That was a big scary lie. Sort of. He'd grown up in a house that was all about discipline and many of those habits had carried over. But as of this moment on he was going to try and be more like Ty. More relaxed about dishes in the sink and the way shirts were hung up in the closet.

Stuff that didn't matter.

Misty however didn't appear to buy his bullshit. In fact, she was openly laughing at him. "That's what everyone says. Sheriff Jared Monroe is so easygoing." She giggled and his heart twisted in his chest. "*Not.*"

Even wearing a pair of baggy flannel pajamas and her hair a mess this woman was seriously cute. Living with her wasn't going to be a hardship in the least.

"Maybe I'm turning over a new leaf," he teased, enjoying the sparkle in her violet eyes and the pink color on her cheeks. "A man can change you know."

"For the worse," she snorted. "Everyone knows changing a man is useless. I won't bother trying."

"Honey, I've got mountains of change in me. You'll see."

In fact, Jared was about to surprise everyone he knew with how much he'd changed. The inveterate playboy was going to become a settled family man. He'd show everyone – especially Misty – that he could be the perfect father.

✧ ✧ ✧ ✧

"I've got your back, bro." Ty grinned with delight as Jared finished telling him about Misty, the baby, and the announcement he was planning to make during dinner. He'd dragged his brother into the kitchen of the family home while Misty was freshening up in the restroom. "And can I say congratulations? This is great news. Misty Foster is a cute one too. But I didn't even realize you were dating, you sly dog."

Jared hadn't gone into detail about his and Misty's relationship. It wasn't anyone's business but their own. He'd shared the important facts and left the rest private.

"Dad's going to have a cow when I tell him the news."

And that was something he wanted to protect Misty from. He didn't want her scared if Gerald Monroe lost his temper as he so often did these days.

"Dad has a cow every day. About something or other. I think I can help you though. I have a little news myself that might take the focus off of you. Actually two pieces of news. Truth is I've been waiting for an opportunity like this."

"I'll take any help that I can get. I don't want to send Misty running her first night with the family."

Jared had fixed her door this morning before they stopped at the diner for lunch. Their appearance had caused a small sensation with every eye in the place trained directly on them. Uncomfortable with the scrutiny, Misty had fidgeted in her chair but Jared had simply stared right back with a cocky grin.

After lunch, he'd moved her meager possessions into his house and had been appalled at what he'd seen. Unlike every woman he'd known before, she only had three pair of shoes if you didn't count her slippers. Her clothes situation wasn't much better, her wardrobe consisting of jeans and sweaters mostly. Those humongous jeans and sweaters. He wanted to replace these as soon as possible with clothes that showed off her natural beauty.

Convincing her to let him was going to take some doing however. She had more than her fair share of pride. When he'd asked for the information from the Seattle lease so he could buy it out she'd stiffly told him she had that under control. But he certainly didn't intend to let his future wife and mother of his child lose her life savings. He would have his lawyers go over the lease. He was sure they could get her out of it without losing everything.

"No better time to sit down and eat than now," declared Ty as Misty rejoined them. Their dad was sitting in the living room as usual and Becky was somewhere in the house as well.

"What about Royce?" Jared hadn't seen his brother in a couple of days. "He promised he'd straighten up and be around more."

Ty chuckled. "He's keeping his promise, don't worry." He turned to Misty and gave her a big hug. For some reason Jared didn't like seeing his little brother's arms around the mother of his child, which was ridiculous. She wasn't interested in Ty. Was she? "Welcome to the family, Misty. Dinnertime is likely to get a little rowdy but don't pay any attention to the old man, okay? He's not himself these days."

Misty licked her lips and nodded. She was clearly nervous and Jared wished he could promise her everything would be fine. "Jared told me he's ill."

"Probably you won't want to mention that," Ty replied with a grimace. "He doesn't like being reminded of it. He's used to being more active and more involved."

Jared leaned in, a quick glance at the door to the living room. "Did he take his medication today?"

"The day nurse says yes so we have that going for us." Ty slapped Jared on the back. "Relax. I won't let Dad kill you if you promise to do the same for me."

"Why would he kill you? He ought to be thanking you for straightening the ranch out."

Ty gave him a mysterious smile. "I don't think he's going to be in the mood for that after dinner tonight. Good thing we all have our own houses. Otherwise I'm pretty sure we'd be sleeping in the barn again."

Ty scuttled away to announce dinner at the top of his lungs while Misty looked up at Jared with a worried frown. "What was he talking about sleeping in the barn? What did he mean?"

"When we were being disciplined Dad felt that it was because we didn't appreciate what we had, so he would make us hike in the mountains or sleep in the barn. Stuff like that."

Her eyes went wide and her mouth fell open. "That sounds horrible. That's abuse, Jared."

He patted her shoulder and shook his head. "I swear it's not. He always made sure we were safe and healthy enough for it but he felt physical challenges were important to build character. He had rules about keeping our rooms clean and the maintenance of the house and vehicles. If we broke those rules or any others, we had to complete some sort of challenge. It really wasn't a bad way to grow up. I swear we never slept in the barn unless it was summer. Heck, it was like camping really."

Misty pressed her lips together. "I don't want our child disciplined like that. It sounds barbaric."

"Believe me we had it better than most boys my age. My friends adored my dad and wished he was theirs. He was tough on us because he wanted us to grow up and be strong men."

She tilted her head in question. "Did it work?"

"For the most part. Royce has his issues, of course."

"And your sister? Did she have to sleep in the barn too?"

"Becky? No way. Dad punished her by taking her credit card."

"Doesn't sound like much of a punishment."

"It was. Wait until you meet my sister. You'll understand. I'd say I hope the two of you become friends but I can't think of anything you have in common except me. She's–"

He couldn't finish his explanation as Ty, his dad, and Becky were all assembling at the table. Gerald gave Jared a sharp-eyed look when he saw Misty but Jared didn't say anything, content to wait for the right moment for their news. Becky, on the other hand, was still holding her phone so she barely glanced up.

Jared seated Misty to his right while his dad was at the head of the table on the left with Ty and Becky sitting across. Jared put his arm around Misty's shoulders and cleared his throat.

"Everyone, I'd like you to meet Misty Foster. Misty, this is my dad, Gerald, my sister Rebecca, and you've already met my brother Ty."

Gerald's eyes narrowed and he looked Misty up and down but she didn't shrink away from the appraisal, instead raising her elfin chin with pride.

Good for you, honey.

"Is there something to announce, son? Something we should know?"

Jared opened his mouth to answer but never got the chance. His sister had slapped her cell phone down on the hard oak surface of the table so hard the water shifted in the glasses.

"Oh my God," Becky exclaimed. "Mantrap Misty is your new girlfriend? Have you completely lost your mind?"

Misty winced at what must have been a childhood nickname but Jared tightened his hold on her shoulders and stared down his incredibly selfish and vapid sister.

"No, I have not. And I don't think I'll listen to a lecture about choosing a mate from you, sis. Your track record leaves something to be desired."

Becky's expression turned ugly but Jared was used to his sister's tantrums. They had no effect on him at this point in his life. "She's probably fucked every guy in a hundred mile radius. Is that what you're into now, big brother? Sloppy seconds?"

The table shook as Gerald Monroe pounded the oak surface. "Rebecca Jane, I will not have you using that sort of language at our dinner table. Do you understand me?"

Pressing her lips together, Becky nodded but she shot Jared a nasty look that promised more to come from her in a different venue.

"Now son, please continue." Gerald shot his daughter a look to keep her silent.

"Misty moved in with me today," Jared announced. "And we're having a baby."

Not even Gerald Monroe could keep Becky from exploding in a torrent that Jared didn't bother listening to. His father kept trying to cut her off but finally gave up and leaned forward so Jared could hear him clearly.

"When's the wedding, son? I assume you'll want to do it sooner rather than later."

Jared glanced at Ty who was grinning ear to ear. This was the difficult part – telling his father that so far there would be no wedding.

"About that, Dad. For right now anyway there isn't going to be a wedding."

His father's brows shot almost to his hairline. "What's this? Jared, when a man gets a girl in trouble he steps up and does the right thing."

Jared groaned inwardly at his father's old-fashioned thinking. They'd come a long way since a girl was "in trouble."

Misty placed her hand on Jared's arm. "Your son did offer to marry me, Mr. Monroe. I'm the one that said no."

Ty was laughing his ass off across the table at Misty's statement. Apparently getting a marriage proposal thrown back in your face was completely hilarious.

If it was happening to someone else.

Jared's father looked confused. "What do you mean you said no? You are pregnant, aren't you?"

"I am." Misty nodded, not in the least cowed by his bull-headed father.

"It belongs to my son?"

"It does."

"Then why the hell aren't you marrying him? The baby will be born a bastard."

Jared did groan out loud this time. "That's enough, Dad."

Gerald turned on Jared. "What's wrong with you that you can't convince her to marry you?"

Becky threw her napkin down on the table. "She probably doesn't want to tie herself down to one man. I'd get a DNA test if I were you, Jared."

"I'm not you," Jared shot back. He couldn't wait until Becky went back to Colorado Springs where she'd been living since her last divorce and new engagement. In fact, the sooner the better. He should call her fiancé and let him know that Becky's presence here was no longer required. She only upset their father and things would be calmer when she was gone.

"Excuse me, but I also have an announcement," Ty said in a booming voice. "Has anyone wondered where Royce is?"

As a matter of fact, Jared had been wondering that exact thing but his brother had been known to disappear for a day or two and then turn up. Usually he was shacked up with some woman in another town.

"Well, get on with it," Gerald said impatiently. "Where is he?"

Ty placed his fork next to his plate. "Your oldest son borrowed your truck, Dad, since his is in the shop from hitting that telephone pole a few weeks ago. Anyway, he had a few too many – again – and hit the storage shed out in the pasture. Ran it clean over." Ty scratched his head. "And totaled your truck, Dad."

Jared's father slammed his fist down on the table again. Royce might be his favorite son but that truck was practically a family heirloom. His dad had babied that thing for almost three hundred thousand miles.

"Where is that boy?" Gerald thundered, his face red with anger.

"I drove Royce to a rehab center in Denver two days ago. He'll be home in about a month," Ty said calmly, picking up his fork again and shoveling a mouthful of pot roast into his mouth. "One more thing I wanted to announce. I'm gay."

Sheer pandemonium.

Becky was frantically texting God-knows-what on her cell phone while Gerald pounded the table a few more times. Ty simply sat there with a smile on his face eating dinner. Despite the playful grin, Jared had a feeling Ty was being totally serious.

"What about Sally Simmons?" Gerald demanded. "You dated her for over a year and not that long ago."

Ty broke his dinner roll in half and buttered it generously. "Sally's a sweet girl but not my type. I'm actually dating her brother Kyle Simmons."

Jared snuck a glance at Misty, wondering what the hell she must be thinking about the Monroe family but she was serenely eating her dinner and watching the floor show.

Rubbing the back of his neck, Jared asked the question everyone was thinking. "Are you serious, Ty?"

His brother's smile faded and his jaw tightened as if waiting for a punch. "Yes, I am. And if you all don't want me to be part of this family I sure as shit know where the door is. As for Royce, rehab for him has been a long time coming. At least there he won't wreck anything else. Unless he tries to break out or something."

"I don't have a problem with you in this family," Jared replied quickly, wanting to put any question to rest. He loved his brother no matter what. Both of his brothers.

Becky looked up from her phone. "Me neither."

All eyes turned to the patriarch of the family.

"Can we call Royce or something?" Gerald asked, his voice now calm. His father might be ailing but he'd found his famous self-control and was displaying it now. "The boy might be lonely."

Ty nodded, his expression guarded. "He can have calls and visitors in a few weeks."

Gerald nodded and picked up his own fork. "Hope he gets straightened around. Are you sure the truck is totaled? Maybe Hays at the garage can take a look at it. We can discuss it after dinner when we go over the ranch invoices."

It was as close to an admission of support as Ty was going to get from his old-fashioned father. The fact that Gerald was talking with Ty about ranch business as if nothing had been said spoke volumes. Ty was accepted.

"Sure, Dad. More potatoes?" Ty asked, a smile playing around his lips. "Misty, how about you?"

"I'm full, thank you." Misty shook her head but Gerald reached for the large bowl and spooned out a serving.

"You're eating for two now," Gerald grunted, his eyes on his plate. "You should have more roast. Protein is good for pregnant women."

God bless Misty. She smiled and reached for the platter of meat. "You're right, Mr. Monroe. Protein is good for me."

She only took a tiny piece but she'd made miles of progress with Jared's stubborn father. Becky stood up abruptly, the legs of her chair scraping on the maple floorboards.

"I'm leaving," she announced dramatically. "If anyone cares."

"Then go," Gerald answered irritably. "No need to make a spectacle out of yourself. Your mother–"

Becky didn't wait around to hear what her mother might have thought of things. She was out the front door in seconds. Jared had a good idea where she was headed. She was going to meet her friends with the gossip scoop of the decade. Sheriff Jared Monroe had knocked up Misty Foster and she wouldn't marry him.

It was pure gold. Becky was sure to get days, if not weeks of mileage from it.

After she left the four of them ate quietly for a few minutes, tension still in the air. When dinner was over Gerald retired to the living room to watch television and the remaining three cleared the table. Jared rinsed plates while Misty stacked them in the dishwasher. Ty brought in a fresh armload from the dining room and placed them on the counter.

"How'd I do, big brother? I think I made your news sound pretty trivial compared to mine."

Ty had a smirk on his face and Jared had to chuckle in response. His little brother certainly had taken the wind out of their father's sails tonight, although it could have easily backfired on Ty. He'd taken a real chance.

"You did, but it might not have turned out so well you know."

"I know but I've been waiting for just the right time to say something. It's not often that all three Monroe boys have something to make their father crazy on the very same day. It's like the planets aligned or something."

"You should have said something to me before now. Did you think I would care?" Jared asked.

Ty scraped his fingers through his hair and gave them a sheepish smile. "I couldn't be sure. You have some stubborn ideas about how you and others should act."

Jared didn't know what to say. Ty was right and Jared needed to rethink a whole lot of things lately.

"So," Misty said brightly, obviously trying to lighten the atmosphere between the two brothers. "That Kyle Simmons is pretty handsome. Way to go."

They ended the evening laughing in the kitchen, Ty and Misty getting along like old friends and future brother and sister. Despite the fiasco of an evening she fit in just fine. He just needed to convince her that marrying him was the right thing to do.

Chapter Thirteen

Dinner hadn't been near the horrific disaster Misty had predicted. Sure, Rebecca had a hissy fit right there in the middle of the dining room and Gerald Monroe hadn't been happy they weren't getting married, but all in all she'd actually enjoyed the latter part of the evening when she, Jared, and Ty had sat around and exchanged stories about their childhoods.

At least Ty and Jared had; she hadn't wanted to bring up those early years all that much and both men seemed to understand. Ty had changed the subject to baby names and nursery decor. He wanted them to name the baby after him. Boy or girl.

He was silly and sweet and if she'd had a brother she would have wanted him to be just like Ty Monroe.

"My brother really liked you. And Dad will come around."

She and Jared were sitting in the living room of his house. She was ready for bed – pajamas and robe, face washed, teeth brushed. She'd made two mugs of hot chocolate and after giving him one she was now relaxing in front of the fire and staring into the flames. Jared had a pile of paperwork around him and looked to be settled in for a good long while.

"I liked Ty. Your dad was fine. He just wants us to get married, that's all."

She didn't mention his sister, as Misty's mother had always said not to say anything at all if one didn't have anything nice to say.

"I want that too."

"I've explained why I can't."

Although after seeing how he stood up for her at the diner at lunch and then with his family, she was beginning to think she might not be able to do any better than Jared Monroe.

But they still weren't in love. Was it too much to ask?

"And I've explained why I think we should. But I won't push it tonight."

She didn't want to be a *should.* She wanted to be a *want* and a *need.* There had to be someone out there who could love her.

Finishing her hot chocolate, she rinsed the cup in the sink and dried her hands on the dishtowel on the counter. Jared's home was comfortable and well-equipped. Decorated in masculine tones with a minimalistic flair, the living area and kitchen were one large great room. A formal dining room was off to the side but Jared admitted the only thing he used the table for was to wrap gifts on Christmas and to fold laundry. There was a large master suite with an attached bathroom that was almost as big as her entire apartment, plus two other bedrooms with one being used for workout equipment. The last one Jared had suggested as the nursery since it was closest to the master bedroom and had a nice southern exposure.

She hadn't answered at the time, still overwhelmed by all the space he had for one person. Her clothes barely took up ten percent of her side of the closet and the bed looked like something from a movie it was so huge.

And that had been another issue today.

When he'd invited her to live with him he really meant *live* with him. In his bedroom. In his bed. She'd pictured some sort of roommate arrangement where she slept in a spare room. But when he'd pointed out that the horse was out of the barn so to speak, she had to agree. Besides, to say she wasn't thinking about their one night together would be a lie. She was thinking about it. Way more than she should. Would he still find her desirable now that she was pregnant?

"I'm going to bed," she said, loath to bother him when he was working. "It's been an eventful day and I'm beat."

She'd probably fall asleep as soon as her head hit the pillow. That was normal these days.

Jared gave her a crooked grin. "It has been and you were terrific about everything. I need to get some paperwork done and then I'll come to bed."

Just like an old married couple. Her flannel pajamas and robe didn't inspire a burning lust from the looks of things, so she'd take herself to bed before she did something embarrassing. Like kiss him goodnight.

"Well, goodnight."

"'Night, Misty. Sweet dreams."

He didn't look up from his paperwork so she padded back to the bedroom and slid between the covers. In the blink of an eye everything in her life had changed. She'd gone from being all alone to now having a family albeit, a rather dysfunctional one. Her "sister" hated her, one brother was sweet, and the other was an alcoholic. And a womanizer. The father was very old-fashioned and tragically losing his memory to boot. Jared was obviously the middle son who kept the peace and tried not to make waves. And how did she fit in? If she did at all. This was going to take some getting used to.

✧ ✧ ✧ ✧

Jared shoved the paperwork back into the file folder and tossed it on the coffee table. He wasn't in the right mindset to get anything done and he'd known it before he even tried. But he thought Misty might be more comfortable going to bed without him on her first night here. She'd looked exhausted and he needed to remember that she was in her first trimester. The book had said she'd be tired all the time and it was his job to make sure she didn't overdo.

And that included sex.

Damn if she hadn't looked adorable in her red plaid flannel pajamas and her face scrubbed clean of any makeup. He'd had to fight the urge to lift her up in his arms, carry her straight to bed, and show her how much she aroused him. But she needed her sleep, not an all-night marathon lovemaking session with some horndog of a guy.

It was times like this he really missed his mother. She would have known what to do or say to get Misty to marry him. Even if she didn't, she would have made a pan of brownies for her middle son and talk to him about anything and everything as if she had nothing else in the world to do. As if he was the most important thing in the universe to her.

He glanced at the clock and realized a couple of hours had passed since she'd gone to bed. She should be deeply asleep by now and hopefully he wouldn't wake her when he climbed in bed. Pulling off his shirt as he made his way to the bedroom, he tossed it in the hamper along with the rest of his clothes. Misty was a motionless lump under the covers so he quietly shut the bathroom door behind him and brushed his teeth.

She didn't have many personal possessions but her few toiletries now sat next to his on the bathroom vanity and in the shower. He felt a rush of satisfaction as he regarded her pink toothbrush sitting next to his in the holder. He would be able to watch over her and the baby now that she had moved in.

Sliding between the cool sheets, he tried not to move too much in case it woke Misty. She must have heard something because she murmured a few unintelligible words and turned over, cuddling against him. Her body was soft and warm and he had to grit his teeth not to reach out and run his hands down her gorgeous curves. Instead he carefully laid his arm over her, not hugging her but still giving them both physical contact. Her response was to glue herself to him even closer, throwing her leg over him and resting her head on his shoulder, her breasts snug against his ribs.

Fuck, he wasn't made of stone. She was beautiful and he hadn't slept with anyone since their night together. He'd had offers but no one had interested him enough after her sweet innocence and fiery passion.

He stroked a hand down her long silky hair. "Misty?" he queried softly. "Are you awake?"

Her fingers rubbed his bare chest and his cock stood up and paid attention. His skin tingled where she touched him.

"Jared?" Her voice was sleepy and he couldn't tell if her eyes were open or not in the darkness of the room. "What time is it?"

"Midnight. I didn't mean to wake you up."

Her hand pushed back her hair and she shook her head, scooting several inches away. He missed the warmth and softness of her immediately. "No big deal. I don't have anywhere to be early tomorrow morning. I can sleep in if I need to. Did you work all this time?"

He could hardly call staring sightlessly at paperwork while he secretly envisioned her naked work, but she didn't need to know that.

"Yes, and I tried to slip into bed as quietly as possible but you must have heard me."

In a drowsy state, she'd cuddled up to him but later had pulled away. What did that mean?

"I'm not a great sleeper. I wake up every couple of hours and sometimes I can't go back to sleep."

"What do you do then?"

"I work or watch television or read. Sometimes Rayne can't sleep as well so we watch movies or something. There's always something to do. If I'm really not tired I'll clean the apartment."

Jared chuckled and very slowly, so she could pull away if she wanted to, wrapped his arm around her shoulders, tugging her close. "The cleaning service was just here a few days ago so I think we're good there. But I guess I need to set up a place where you can work that has good light."

He hadn't seen anything she'd painted but was anxious to. He had a feeling she was extremely talented. He knew it wasn't easy for an artist to make a living with their art and she was doing it. Experimentally he began rubbing circles between her shoulder blades and the tight muscles loosened under his fingers.

"That feels good." He stopped for a moment and then moved the massage to her lower back which drew a moan from her lips. "And that feels really good. My back is always bothering me. Part and parcel of being a painter."

"I'll rub your back anytime," Jared offered and he meant it. His cock was already hard and aching but he ignored it, wanting only to make her feel good. The woman carrying his child needed to be spoiled and cosseted, not ravaged like an animal.

"No strings attached?" Her question came out as a whisper even as her own fingers began to stroke his bicep. She was playing with fire and an innocent like her had no idea.

"Of course." The words sounded strangled as her fingers drifted lower to his abdomen. His cock throbbed and jerked for attention and he had to grit his teeth to keep his libido under control. "You should close your eyes and go back to sleep."

Misty yawned. "I doubt I'll sleep for awhile."

Swallowing hard, Jared reached for the bedside lamp. "We could watch some television."

Her palm rested flat on his belly, searing the skin. "Is that what you want to do?"

He was a jerk and a horny asshole. But he wasn't a liar. "Not really. I'd rather make love to you."

A pause. "I think I'd like that too."

"Are you sure?" This time he did switch on the lamp so he could see her expression. "I know you're tired and the book said you might not be in the mood until the second trimester."

Misty rubbed her eyes at the light and smiled. "I got a few hours and I feel better. As for that book, it may not be entirely correct. I–I've been thinking about it since that night."

He had too. Over and over again until he tossed and turned most of the night.

"I just don't want you to think I moved you here just so I could have sex on tap or something. That wasn't my intention."

Laughter bubbled from her lips. "Sex on tap? What an interesting expression. I think I might like that if it was you."

"You're bold tonight." He leaned down to nuzzle the soft skin above her collar. "I like it."

"I wouldn't be if I couldn't tell that you're…interested." Her knee nudged his hard cock. "That night was so amazing and I want to see if it can be that way again."

He'd make it even better. Now that she wasn't so tentative and unsure it would be more than wonderful.

"I'll go nice and slow like last time," he promised, plucking the buttons on her pajama top. "You just tell me if I do something you don't like."

Her finger was tracing patterns on his bare chest. "That's the thing. It was great last time and you were so patient. But you don't need to be like that this time. I mean…you can be more like how you normally are."

The flannel top drifted away and he slid his hands into the elastic waistband of her bottoms to glide them down her legs. "How do you think I am normally?"

She pressed her now bare body to his, her skin heating his own. "Um, more passionate and maybe—I don't know—rougher?"

This conversation was certainly taking an interesting turn. Jared had been with plenty of women and many of them wanted it fast and hard, not to mention the ones who wanted to be submissive during sex. Was Misty one of them?

"You want me to take you rough? Are you sure about that?" He was careful to keep any judgment or emotion out of his voice. He'd love to ravish Misty but he wanted her to want it as well.

"I just don't want you to be so careful this time." Her fingers skated down his back and then up to his shoulders.

"All you have to do is say no if you change your mind," he said right before he captured her lips in a kiss. If Misty wanted passionate, she was going to get it. In spades.

✧ ✧ ✧ ✧

This was what Misty had dreamed about.

His lips had captured her own, staking a claim as only a man like Jared could. He took pleasure in her body, his hands roaming up and down her curves as if he owned them. She surrendered to his mastery, letting her mind go blank and trusting in his promise of pleasure.

His lips traveled down to her nipples and he sucked one into his mouth, letting her feel the slight edge of his teeth. The combination of pleasure and pain was almost too much and she felt herself climbing higher, and yet they'd barely begun.

He repeated his pleasurable torture on the other peak turning it pebble-hard. She squirmed and wriggled under his hard body but he held her down easily, not allowing her to get away from his relentless onslaught. He cupped both of her breasts and scraped his teeth along one nipple and then the other until she was a shuddering mess underneath him, her pussy already wet and waiting.

Digging her fingers into his muscular shoulders, she arched her back in supplication, offering herself up on a silver platter. But only for this one man. He seemed to understand her unspoken message and began to kiss a wet trail down her belly before he pushed her legs wide apart.

This time she didn't cover herself, although she still felt her face and chest grow hot at his intent inspection. She braced herself for the first touch of his tongue but it didn't cool the trail of heat he left in his wake. Up and down, side to side, he traced the folds of her pussy and then tongue fucked her until she was on fire and begging for mercy. His mouth closed over her clit, the suction sending her over in a whirlwind of sound and light. The room spun and she had to grab hold of Jared's solid frame as she flew through a sea of stars before coming back to earth gently.

He was kissing the sensitive skin of her inner thigh and she sighed with pleasure as he continued all the way down her leg to the instep of her foot. He dropped a light kiss on her toes and looked up at her with a big grin.

"Are you ready for me, baby?"

She shook her head and instead beckoned him closer. "I want to make love to you too."

He crawled up her body his thighs on either side of her chest and her palms on his hard thighs. "You don't have to do this, you know."

"I know," she replied her fingers already gliding up and down his thick cock. "I want to."

She didn't have much experience but she wanted him to feel the way she did. Ravished.

Piling a few pillows behind her head, she was able to easily reach him with her tongue. Running it from base to tip and then back again, she traced each vein before engulfing the head with her mouth. Jared hissed and his head fell back and she watched the expressions flit across his features as her head bobbed and her tongue flickered. His jaw had tightened and his teeth were gritted and bared. He was so damn sexy her arousal amped up simply looking at him.

He pulled away slowly and with a groan. "I can't take much more of that. For someone who said they don't have a lot of experience, you're a quick learner."

She giggled and swiped at him again with her tongue. "It's good that you appreciate enthusiasm as much as skill."

She'd thought it might feel awkward or strange to be in bed with Jared but it felt natural and right. He was the father of her child and the man that had introduced her to real pleasure.

And he was fun. She hadn't expected to laugh in the bedroom but his sense of humor stretched even to sex.

He slid down so he was pressing her into the mattress, a delicious weight. "I'm pretty enthusiastic. In fact I'm fixin' to show you how much right now."

Misty barely had time to catch her breath. Jared lifted her hips and pushed forward relentlessly, the walls of her pussy wet and hot, easily giving way. He wrapped her legs around his waist as he pulled out and then thrust forward, sending electricity through her body and making her clit swell with arousal. Over and over he fucked her hard and fast, just as she'd fantasized it could be.

Their breaths were ragged and labored and her fingernails had scored the flesh in his back as she teetered on the precipice of release. She was so close, her climax shimmering just out of her reach.

"More," she gasped. "Harder. I need–"

His mouth came down on hers before she could finish but he did indeed fuck her harder, their bodies grinding together with each stroke of his cock. When she exploded her scream was lost but the sensations twisted her into knots before releasing her to float somewhere above the bed. Jared came at the same time, every muscle in his body tense. He whispered something dirty in her ear as the pleasure began to drain from her body leaving supreme satisfaction in its place.

They cuddled together for a long time, his hand idly stroking her hair and back. She'd never felt such peace and contentment. She'd been so terrified of letting herself go but she had and it hadn't increased her hunger for men.

It had only increased her hunger for Jared. And that scared her more than anything.

Chapter Fourteen

"You're spoiling me," Misty scolded as she lounged in bed one morning a few weeks later while Jared brought her tea and toast. He'd insisted doing it every morning and it had certainly helped the nausea. In fact he'd shown clearly that he was devoted to making sure both she and the baby were happy and healthy.

"You say that every morning." Jared set the cup of tea and small plate of toast down on the bedside table. "I want you to eat all of it because I don't want you to have any tummy problems today. I've got the day off and I thought we could spend it together."

Jared had been so busy he hadn't had much time off since she'd moved in. One of his deputies had been out sick and he'd had to work long hours to make sure all the shifts were covered. Luckily the fake calls had ceased and things were back to what passed for normal. Although she knew he was frustrated about the Boyd Hicks case. The SUV appeared to be set on fire because of a cigarette thrown into a pool of gas underneath the vehicle. The thrower of that cigarette had somehow managed to stay out of range of the cameras except for a shot of the man from the back. He had been too non-descript and Jared hadn't been able to identify his suspect. She hoped things were calmed down for good, if only for Jared's blood pressure.

She nibbled on the toast and took a sip of tea. Her stomach gurgled but in a few minutes it would settle down for the day.

"What did you have in mind? A movie? Lunch?"

She was almost used to going out in public with him. The town didn't hide the fact that they pointed and stared but he was right. This was their problem, not hers. He'd apologized for how his sister had acted that first night but she'd waved it away. It wasn't his fault his sister was a bitch. Besides, she was only saying what everyone else was thinking.

And he'd defended her. To his own flesh and blood. She'd never forget that and how much it meant.

"Sure, lunch." His tone was deliberately casual and her attention perked up immediately. She was getting to know this take charge man more and more and there was one sure thing she'd learned. He liked to get his way and wasn't above being a little sneaky about it. If that didn't work he'd use his bull in a china shop strategy. "I was thinking we might do some shopping too."

Even with him that sounded like hell. Misty hated to shop. She wrinkled her nose in distaste.

"I think I'd rather see a car chase shoot 'em up kind of movie."

"Really? Which one?"

Misty shrugged and finished the last bite of her toast. "I have no idea but there's always one around. Wouldn't you rather do that? Or maybe you want to hunt or fish? Or wrestle a bear?"

"I wrestled a bear yesterday," he teased with a grin. "Almost threw my back out so we'll need to do something less active today. Like shopping."

Misty groaned and rolled her eyes. "I don't wanna go and I can't believe that you do. Don't men hate shopping?"

That brought a scowl to Jared's face. "I don't love it but it has to be done every now and then. And the fact is, young lady, you need clothes." She started to protest but he raised his hand. "Don't bother denying it. I'm sure you could go on wearing your too large clothes for the better part of your pregnancy, but honestly they need to be thrown out or burned. We couldn't even give them to charity. You're gorgeous and I want to show you off. We also need to get you a new phone while we're out."

She'd known her wardrobe left something to be desired but she didn't go out much so it hadn't mattered. But he had a point. Those clothes represented the repressed, scared woman she'd been before meeting him. It might be nice to have a few things that she actually looked nice in. Something to tempt Jared. Not that he needed much encouragement in that department. He was happy to make love to her every single night at least once if she was in the mood.

He'd also had a lawyer look at her Seattle lease and found a loophole. Her money had been returned to her so now she had a few dollars she could spend. A day at the mall with Jared might be fun. Or at least more tolerable than on her own.

"Let me call Rayne. We talked about meeting for lunch today."

"Have her meet us at the mall," he offered. "She's your best friend and I barely know her."

Jared had been working so much he hadn't had time to get to know Rayne, but this might be a good opportunity for them to spend some time with each other. Misty hoped they would get along although Rayne's tattoos and piercings might put Jared off.

"She'll try and get you to fix her up with one of your handsome single friends," Misty laughed. "She hasn't had a boyfriend in a few months."

"I'm not sure I have any handsome single friends unless you count Royce and Ty."

"Ty's spoken for and Royce isn't here. Maybe you can think of someone else."

Jared grinned wickedly. "There's Dare Turner. He's the grouchiest man I've ever met. I mean nothing makes that man smile."

"That doesn't sound very nice. Why is he so unhappy?"

It seemed sad that someone spent day after day that way.

"Who knows? Maybe his underwear is two sizes too small. Now…are we going shopping or not? And no is not an acceptable answer."

Jared was wearing a charming smile on his face and he smelled absolutely wonderful. He seemed to know how to convince her to do things she didn't want to do. In the last two weeks, she'd eaten Brussels sprouts, taken up walking on a treadmill, and drinking milk – albeit chocolate.

"Then I guess we're going shopping. But don't expect me to buy a bunch of stuff. I'm going to be growing for the next several months so I think it's best to be conservative."

He dropped a kiss on her nose and then stood, picking up the plate and cup. "Meet you downstairs in half an hour?"

She nodded and he left, giving her some privacy to get ready. Despite making love to him almost every night, she was a little shy when it came to showering and getting dressed. It seemed intimate and the way she was starting to feel that might not be a good idea.

Jared Monroe was a wonderful man who treated her with care and respect. How was she supposed to hold out against someone like that? If she wasn't careful, she'd embarrass herself and fall for him.

✧ ✧ ✧ ✧

"It's not expensive, Misty," Jared argued, keeping his voice down. "You need it and I want to get it for you."

Misty's lips were set in a mutinous line. She'd been like this all damn day, giving him a hard time whenever he wanted to buy her something. He'd lost more battles than he'd won but he had still managed to persuade her into three pairs of jeans, four sweaters, four blouses, new boots, and some very fetching satin and lace lingerie that he was planning to take off of her at the first opportunity.

Now they were at the phone store in the mall and she was insisting she didn't need a new one.

"My phone works just fine," she insisted. "I don't need anything new."

"Your phone barely holds a charge for an entire day. It's not safe. What if the weather gets bad and you're stranded somewhere? This phone has GPS and I'll be able to find you."

Misty sighed and regarded the smart phone dubiously. "It also has a million features I have no idea how to use. I don't even know how to make a phone call. All I have to do with my nice flip phone is open it up."

The salesman had drifted a discreet distance away when they'd started to disagree about her need for a new phone but Jared knew the man was listening in. "It's easy. You just press a few buttons."

Jared demonstrated but she didn't look any more sold on the phone. She was regarding it a little like a poisonous snake. "You can put all sorts of apps on it too if you want. And you and Rayne will be able to text each other. Didn't you say she wanted to do that?"

He'd said something right.

"She did say that." Misty reached for the phone again and inspected it closely. "I guess I could get used to it. But I want to pay for it myself, Jared. You've paid for everything today and it's not right."

"You're my woman and that's my baby. Nothing is more right than taking care of you." Jared had never had to argue with a female to get her to take something he'd purchased for her. They'd been more than happy to receive rather than give. Misty was the opposite. She was only comfortable when she was giving or caretaking for someone else. It was a nice and welcome change. He should have asked her out years ago except that she was only twenty-five to his thirty-nine.

"That's one fancy phone." An amused feminine voice made him turn around and watch Misty launch herself at the young woman. Dark-haired with several earrings in one ear and a small stud in her nose, the attractive woman had several tattoos. Misty had already warned him. This was Rayne.

They shook hands and he liked the woman right away. She was warm and friendly and she clearly adored Misty. The feeling was obviously mutual. Misty was smiling and relaxed and Jared couldn't help but feel a little jealous. She never looked quite that way with him. But then relaxed wasn't how he felt around her either.

How he felt when she was near was becoming rather complicated. He liked her. He respected her. And damn if he didn't want to get her naked as often as possible. She was an incredibly talented artist and a sweet, loyal woman who was fun to be with. She was going to make one terrific mother.

And a wonderful wife. Only if he could convince her of course, but lately he hadn't even tried. She was so set about wanting a husband who loved her. The entire subject made him uncomfortable so he'd dropped it for the time being.

Rayne helped him convince Misty to let him buy the phone for her and they headed to lunch. Sitting in the restaurant, Rayne helped Misty learn to text while they all chatted about the latest news in town. She had a quirky sense of humor that meshed well with Misty's quieter personality.

They were working on their entrees when Jared's phone rang. "Excuse me for a minute?"

The ladies nodded and he checked the screen. Deputy Knox. "Hey, Knox. What's up?"

"It's Boyd Hicks, boss."

In the last few weeks Boyd Hicks had become a non-issue. The fake callouts had ceased which was good for everyone. The only news had been when Jared had checked on the little girl, Tilly. It turned out Lindsey's premonition was right. Boyd Hicks had requested visitation with his daughter but it was caught up in family court as to whether it would really happen. In the meantime Lindsey's request for custody was looking like it was going to be granted at her upcoming hearing. That was good news for the mother.

"What's he done?" Jared asked, bracing himself for the answer. Boyd had always been up to no good.

"That's just it. He hasn't done anything. He's dead." Knox paused as if waiting for Jared's reaction but then continued. "His body was found in the pasture on the Hawkins place. Chris is already there."

Knox recited the exact location and Jared jotted it down on the paper napkin. Rayne and Misty had stopped talking and were watching him closely, aware that something was going on.

The shock of hearing Hicks was dead was starting to wear off. In fact it hadn't been that much of a surprise. Guys like Boyd Hicks lived dangerously and on the edge of regular society. Their lives were in precarious positions every day. Trust the wrong person. Double cross someone. Lose their life.

Jared didn't like murder in his town and it was best to stamp it out before it spread like wildfire. It didn't matter if the victim was a good guy or a bad guy. He needed to find out who killed Boyd Hicks and why.

Chapter Fifteen

By the time Jared arrived at the remote location, the coroner Dr. Ron James was already leaning over the body of Boyd Hicks. Chris was there as well, taking the statement of the two ranch hands who had found the body. A few days of above freezing temperature had melted a patch of the snow in the pasture and that's where they'd found the body. Whoever had killed Hicks had probably assumed – or hoped – that his body wouldn't be found for months. If ever.

"Hey, Ron. What do we got?" Jared asked, kneeling down next to the coroner. The body wasn't a pretty sight but it was fairly well preserved thanks to the time of year.

"Looks like a couple of bullets to the chest," the older man observed. "Although it's hard to tell. I'll need to get him on the table to be sure. There's no blood pool so he was killed somewhere else and dumped here."

"How long has he been dead?"

"That's a good question. The snow and cold has preserved a great deal of the tissue but I'll hazard a guess to say several days. Maybe more. I'll know more once I open him up." The coroner reached behind him and pulled out a clear plastic bag. "You'll want this. I found it under the body."

A cigarette. If luck was with Jared it belonged to the murderer. That was the good news. The bad news was that everyone in Boyd's life appeared to smoke so it didn't narrow the list of suspects.

"Thanks, Ron. Hopefully this will lead us to the killer. Anything else you can tell me?"

"No defensive wounds. They either took him by surprise or he didn't think they were a threat. I'm assuming from what I see that he was shot while facing his killer but I'll need to confirm that. Your deputy has the victim's personal effects."

"Thanks, Ron. I'll leave you to finish."

The man nodded as Jared stood and walked over to Chris and the two ranch hands. Both of them looked a little sick but then this was a grisly discovery neither one of them had been expecting. Jared had seen the men in town and neither one of them was a hellraiser. If they had been he would know much more about them.

"Gentleman." Jared nodded politely as he stepped into the conversation. "Thank you for calling the authorities about this."

The shorter one clutched his hat in his hand more tightly. "No problem, Sheriff. Tom and I were just coming out here to the far pasture to check things out. From a distance we thought it was a dead cow. Didn't realize what it was until we were right up on it."

"Did either one of you touch the body?"

"No, sir." The one named Tom shook his head vigorously. "We could tell he was good and dead."

That he was. After being shot in the chest a couple of times Boyd Hicks probably didn't linger in this world long. Jared put his hand on Chris's shoulder. "Let me read their statements when you're done."

"Will do," Chris agreed. "We're almost finished."

The coroner was zipping up the body bag as Deputy Knox arrived at the scene. "What can I do?"

Jared pointed to an area of the pasture where the snow was packed down hard and hadn't melted due to the shade of a tree. "There's tire tracks over there. Take some pictures and get an impression so we can try and match it to a vehicle. Len Hawkins doesn't use trucks all the way up here and they don't look right for ATV tires. I'm hoping we can match those tracks to the killer's vehicle. And when you get back to the office, call the warden at the prison. I want to know if he was ever in any violent altercations with other prisoners. Maybe somebody had a vendetta against him. In fact, just request his whole file."

"I'm on it. What about Dale Hicks?" Knox asked.

"I'm definitely going to be talking to him again considering he admitted that he and his brother were on the outs. It's going to be hard to nail down time of death for an alibi check though."

His deputies tasked, Jared began the laborious process of combing the area for any other clues. Hopefully the cigarette butt and tracks would be the key but anything else they could find would help. He should call Misty and let her know not to wait dinner for him. It looked like it was going to be a long day.

✧ ✧ ✧ ✧

Rayne had graciously offered to drive Misty home from the mall when Jared had been called out. He'd been wearing a grim expression when he'd left, telling her he might be late. From the conversation she knew that someone had been murdered and the body had been found in a pasture. It was frightening to think there was a killer walking around Fielding and no one knew who it was.

She hung up her new clothes and stowed the bags and boxes in the garage. She shouldn't have given Jared such a hard time about buying her things but his spending money on her went against the grain. She'd always taken care of herself. However she couldn't deny the thrill she'd received when she'd look in the mirror as she was trying them on. She'd looked…nice.

Settling down on the couch with her sketchbook, she lost herself in her drawings until she heard a thump on the front porch. She hopped up and scrambled to the door, hoping it was Jared. Already the sun was beginning to set in the west and soon it would be pitch black outside.

Pushing the front door open, she stuck her head outside and saw what had made the sound. Gerald Monroe was sitting in one of the rocking chairs not saying anything, just staring out into the quiet early evening.

"Mr. Monroe," Misty began tentatively. "Aren't you cold out here?"

He turned to her and for a moment she thought he didn't recognize her. But then his expression cleared and he shook his head. "It's warm today."

"But getting colder. The sun will be down soon and you'll freeze out here. Why don't you come inside and let me fix you some hot chocolate. We have marshmallows."

The same instinct that had made her pull over that night when Jared was slumped in front of the B&B was urging her on now. Gerald Monroe looked lost and sad. Something inside of her wanted to make it better. Of course she hadn't been able to make it better for her own mother. Every time Misty had sobered up Annette her mother would promise to never drink again, but within a few days she'd be doing it again. Nothing Misty had done made any difference.

The older man hesitated and then stood to follow her into the house. He settled into a kitchen chair while she retrieved a sauce pan from the cabinet and some milk from the refrigerator.

"I don't remember your name," he finally said as she stirred the liquid that was beginning to steam. "I forget things now that I didn't used to. I like to go for walks but sometimes I get turned around. That's why I was sitting on your front porch."

"My name is Misty," she answered, her heart twisting in her chest for this proud man to have to admit that. "Misty Foster. My mother was Annette Foster. I live here with Jared."

"I remember that. You're having a baby but you won't marry him." Gerald smiled. "That must have been a shock for him. He's never had too much trouble with the womenfolk before. I bet he thought he'd be able to pick and choose."

"I think I did surprise him," Misty agreed, adding the cocoa and sugar. "What was Jared like when he was younger?"

"Bossy," the old man laughed. "Even then he liked to tell people what to do. Don't let him steamroll you into doing everything his way. Otherwise known as the right way. According to him."

Misty giggled and poured the hot chocolate, added marshmallows, and carried the two mugs over to the table. She set one in front of Gerald and set the other across from him where she sat down.

"He does like things a certain way, doesn't he? He has all his shoes lined up in the closet from lightest to darkest. His clothes too."

The old man pulled a face. "That's my fault. I was in the military and I taught all my kids to do the same. I didn't like chaos in the house which is almost constant when you have four children."

"I guess you and Jared are a lot alike," she said, watching Gerald's expression closely. She was aware that Royce was his favorite. At least Jared and Ty thought so.

The older man scowled. "He treats me like I'm sick. Hell, they all do. I'm not sick. I just have trouble remembering things." He wrapped his hands around the mug. "You know what the funny thing is? I can't remember what I had for dinner last night. I couldn't remember your name. But I can remember the summer of 1976 like it was yesterday. Isn't that strange?"

"Was that a good year?" Misty sipped the hot liquid, letting it warm up her stomach. "Why don't you tell me about it?"

Gerald Monroe smiled slowly, a light shining in his eyes. The same blue eyes as Jared. "Royce was three, Jared was one, and Rita was pregnant with Ty. It was the summer of the Bicentennial and I swear to the good Lord that everything was red, white, and blue. The town was having a big celebration with a parade, picnic, and fireworks. The town council had decorated the main square and some people were wearing Abe Lincoln hats or George Washington wigs. It was quite a sight to see."

Misty had a thought. One she hoped would help Gerald remember for a long time. "Wait here a second. I have an idea."

She ran to the couch and grabbed her sketchpad and colored pencils before running back. "If you describe it to me I can draw it. Then you'll have a picture in case the memory starts to fade."

Gerald grinned and pulled his chair closer to hers. "I like that idea. I have so many memories I'd like to put down on paper."

Misty smiled back and placed her hand on his arm. "Then we better get busy. By the way, why don't you stay for dinner? I'm making spaghetti."

"That's my favorite, Misty. I think I will stay. Now where was I? That's right. The Bicentennial. Well, pretty much everyone was in the town square. And it was hot. We were having a heat wave that week. And of course you can't have a picnic without potato salad, right? Bless Rita's heart, she'd slaved all day on the third to make about ten pounds of potato salad and there it sat out in the heat. You know where this story is going, don't you?"

She giggled, her pencils busily whisking across the paper. She'd found a way to connect with Jared's father – a way to perhaps be part of the family. Someday she'd tell her son or daughter all about their grandparents and about the picnic in Fielding on the Bicentennial.

✧ ✧ ✧ ✧

Jared was tired and hungry when he opened his front door after spending hours at the Boyd Hicks crime scene. Plus he and Knox had driven up to talk to Dale but the man wasn't home.

The cigarette and the tracks were in the hands of the state forensics lab so he needed to be patient for the results. And patience wasn't exactly one of his virtues.

"Hey, you're home." Misty and his father were sitting at the dinner table. Jared instinctively stiffened but they both looked relaxed and happy. In fact he didn't remember the last time his dad had looked that calm. But then Misty had a way of making a man forget his problems.

"I am. Something smells good." Jared closed the door behind him and shed his coat and hat. "Dad, it's good to see you. Is everything okay?"

"See?" Gerald waved his fork in the air. "He's always worrying, acting like I've got one foot in the grave. Tell him everything is fine."

"Everything is fine," Misty repeated dutifully, patting the older man's lined hand. "Your dad took a walk and came to visit me. He's been telling me great stories and I've been drawing pictures for him."

Jared noticed the pile of papers on the kitchen counter. He picked up the top one and his face split into a grin. How had his father remembered this? Jared had forgotten until now.

"This was such a great Christmas. We all got new bikes from Santa and of course the snow was piled up outside. We all bundled up in our pajamas and winter coats and rode them outside until Mom shooed us back into the house."

Jared couldn't stop smiling as he studied the drawing. Every detail was just right down to the color of bikes each child had received. Jared's had been blue with a red stripe and he'd ridden it all through junior high and high school. Damn, he'd loved that bike. He didn't know what had happened to it. Somehow it had disappeared while he was in college. He swallowed a lump that had somehow taken up residence in his throat.

His father still remembered that day. But for how long?

"Your mother made chocolate chip pancakes every Christmas morning," his father said with a smile. "I can still taste them."

"So can I," Jared choked out, tears pricking the back of his eyes. Thoughts of his mother always managed to do that to him. "She made them on my birthday too."

Misty stood and pulled another plate from the cabinet above the sink. "Sit down and I'll fill your plate."

"One more minute." Jared was mesmerized as he leafed through the drawings. His past come to life. A few he didn't remember, perhaps he was too young, but most brought back a rush of memories he didn't want to push away. Would they think he was crazy if he simply stared at them for the rest of the night? He missed his mother so much sometimes it physically hurt but Misty had brought her to life on these pages. His father must have described Rita Monroe in detail so true to life were these drawings.

Finally he sat down as Misty and his father were finishing dinner. Her phone rang and she jumped up to answer.

"It's Rayne on my new phone. Will you handsome gentlemen excuse me for a moment?"

They nodded and she drifted into the bedroom leaving Jared alone with his father. His dad had cleaned his plate and was enjoying a cup of coffee.

"I got lost," Gerald Monroe said gruffly. "Misty didn't say that but that's what happened."

Jared's hand tightened on his fork. "Did you take your medication today?"

"Yes, and it still happened. Misty didn't make a big deal out of it and I don't want you to either. I was just being honest, that's all."

"Fine, but I wish you wouldn't go walking by yourself anymore," Jared said carefully, not sure what icebergs where hidden in the water he was navigating. "I'm glad Misty was here. Maybe she can walk with you if I'm not around."

"She's a fine woman. You've done well for yourself." His father folded the napkin in his lap and set it on the table. "Why won't she marry you?"

"You didn't ask her?"

"I'm asking you," Gerald retorted, amusement in his features.

"She wants a husband who loves her." Jared couldn't picture the man good enough for Misty though. She needed someone really special in her life.

"And you don't?"

How did he say this? "I care about Misty. A lot."

Gerald snorted. "Care? What a namby pamby word. It means nothing and says nothing. But if that's all you can say then you don't love her. Too bad. She's one to keep. She'd be good for you too. She's not like those other women I've seen you date. Misty feels things. Deep down. If she ever decided to love someone they'd be one lucky son of a bitch because she'd love them forever."

Yes, whomever Misty loved would be a very lucky man.

"Dad, you barely know her, although I'm not arguing that she's wonderful. She is."

Jared was wondering why he was arguing at all. Except he didn't like the idea that his father thought he knew something about Misty that Jared didn't.

"I might forget things but I still got eyes. I can see. She's got a good heart. Whose idea do you think it was to draw those pictures for me? She has empathy. She gives a damn. She'll be a good mother."

That was something Jared knew. "She's worried she won't, I think. Her mother wasn't exactly parent of the year."

Gerald shrugged. "Neither was I and you turned out alright."

This was the closest thing to a compliment Jared had ever received from his father. "Well, thank you."

"You and Ty work hard. I know Royce needs some tough love." Gerald sighed, his face aging before Jared's eyes. "And Becky needs a good man in her life."

"Royce and Becky need to grow up," Jared scoffed. "Hopefully they'll do just that."

"I've never had to worry about you though," his father said softly. "That's what your mother used to say. 'We don't have to worry about Jared. We know he'll do the right thing.'"

For the second time that night, Jared found it hard to swallow. "I miss Mom."

Gerald nodded, his expression sad. "I do too, son. More than you can possibly know. Someday when you fall in love you might understand what it feels like to have her taken from you too soon. But I know she's waiting for me. We'll be together again."

"Not too soon, Dad. You've got things to do here." Jared's voice came out thick but his father didn't seem to notice. He was gazing off somewhere in the distance. Or perhaps to the past.

"No, not too soon. But someday. I'm not afraid of death. But I still have things to teach my children and grandchildren. I'm not done yet. That's what I'm really afraid of…running out of time."

Jared had to blink back the tears that had sprung to his eyes. "I'm afraid of that too."

"That's why I like telling the old stories. If I can hold onto them maybe I can hold onto me for a little longer."

"Tell me the one about when you were in high school and you and your friend stole the other team's mascot. I love that story."

Gerald chuckled. "That was Roscoe. Best friend a man could ever have. Died a week after graduation. Tractor tipped over on him and he was crushed underneath. I still miss him."

"You never told me that part. I just assumed he moved away from Fielding."

His father turned to him, his expression solemn. "When you have children you tell them the happy stories. It's only when they're all grown up that you can tell them the unhappy parts. The real life parts."

"Am I grown up enough?" Jared asked, his throat tight and his eyes burning.

Gerald nodded. "Let me try and remember the things I didn't tell you. Let's start with Roscoe."

Jared settled back in his chair as his father began the story he'd told so many times before, only this time it would have a new ending. A more honest ending.

For the first time in a long time Jared really listened as his father spoke. He didn't get impatient or interrupt. He didn't glance at his phone or think about all the things he needed to do. He just listened.

Chapter Sixteen

Misty and Jared were cuddled in bed watching television. He'd taken his father home about an hour ago and had barely said a word since he'd returned. He wasn't a man given to brooding but his thoughts seemed very far away. She hated to interrupt him but she was worried he was upset with her.

"Jared?" She pillowed her head on his chest, breathing in his clean, masculine scent. "Is everything okay?"

"Everything's fine," he answered, clicking the remote from one channel to another. "Why do you ask?"

She was walking a fine line here. She wasn't his wife and he didn't owe her any explanations. She was however the mother of his child and his life affected hers.

"You've been acting kind of not like yourself tonight. Are you mad at me for inviting your dad to dinner or for drawing those pictures? I just wanted him to have something to look at that reminded him of the past."

Jared sat straight up, dislodging her from her comfortable spot. "Shit no. I thought it was really sweet. Especially as Dad didn't exactly roll out the red carpet that first night at dinner."

"He had a lot to deal with that night between you, Royce, and Ty. I won't even mention your sister." She propped herself up with a couple of pillows. "I found your dad sitting on our porch. He looked…lost."

Jared's lips twisted and he rubbed the back of his neck. "He was lost. Literally. I talked to him about it when I walked him home and I think he won't try to take a walk without one of us from now on." He gave her a sheepish smile. "I kind of volunteered you for that if I'm not around."

"I'm happy to do it. He's a nice man, which I have to admit I didn't expect from the way you've described him. He doesn't seem like the drill sergeant you've told me about."

Jared lounged back and crossed his long legs. "Tonight was the first time in a long time that he's opened up in any way to me. It probably won't last but I was glad it happened."

Misty stroked Jared's arm, trying to soothe his troubled mind. "When was the last time?"

"When Mom died. For a few days after the funeral he was different. Kind of like he was tonight. Then he went back to being Gerald Monroe. I love him no matter which one he is but I have to admit tonight was nice. He said I turned out okay."

"You definitely turned out fine. Did you have any doubts about that?" Misty wondered. Jared was a man among men in her eyes. She'd never known any better in her life.

Jared looked at her and for a moment she saw the uncertain little boy he must have been trying to please a demanding father. "I think I do alright. But I wasn't sure he knew. That he even really noticed me."

It was no wonder they'd been pulled toward each other that wintry night. They'd both tried to win their parents' love and approval. Misty had done it by caring for her often drunk mother who would be out all night with some strange man. Jared had competed with his brothers and sister for his larger-than-life father's attention.

"Looks like he has. I think he's noticed a whole bunch of things about his children but he's just not one to say too much. Kind of like you."

She pointed her finger at Jared's bare chest and smiled.

"Like me, huh? I don't talk enough for you? What do you want me to say?" A grin spread across Jared's face and he scooped her up in his arms, keeping her prisoner while he nibbled at her shoulder. "How about I tell you that your spaghetti sauce is really good? Is that what you want to hear?"

Misty giggled as his tongue tickled a sensitive spot but her heart squeezed in her chest at his words. Those weren't what she wanted to hear and that was the sad thing. She wasn't begging for her mother's approval anymore.

She wanted Jared's.

And that was the last thing she would ever ask him for. He wouldn't want that and she would never put him on the spot.

"I have a great idea." Jared was still smiling and his blue eyes were lit with mischief. "How about we go to the cabin when I get this case buttoned up? Just you and me. We'll make love, go for a hike, maybe eat some s'mores. What do you say?"

"I didn't even know you had a cabin. Please tell me it has indoor plumbing. I'm not much for roughing it."

"It's a cabin, not a tent. Running water and electricity. I haven't been there for ages."

And she knew why. He had more responsibilities now – her and the baby. But she did want to be alone with him away from the prying eyes of the town.

There she'd admitted it. She liked Jared, she liked living with him, and she liked making love with him.

"Then let's go," she agreed. "When do we leave?"

"As soon as I solve this case," he declared. "I do have some important things to take care of in the next few days but mostly I'll be waiting on the state crime lab."

Her puzzled expression must have clued him in that she had no idea what he was talking about.

"The call I got earlier. It was about a murder," he explained.

"That's what I thought. Do you know who did it?"

"No, but I have a strong suspicion. But Boyd Hicks wasn't a well-liked man, so honestly there could be several people who wanted him dead."

"Charming," she observed. "It sounds like it might be a tough case to solve."

"We'll get him." Jared's tone held complete confidence. "There was some evidence at the scene. Hopefully it will link back to the murderer. Then we add in motive and we take the case to the prosecutor."

"Easy peasy," she teased. "At least you make it sound that way."

"Some cases are and some aren't. I know which way I want this one to go."

"Maybe you'll get lucky."

His lips skimmed down into the valley between her breasts. She sucked in a breath at the trail of heat his lips created. "I'd like to if you're in the mood."

When Misty was with Jared she was always in the mood. Wrapping her arms around his neck, she whispered in his ear. He reared back in surprise but his expression was one of delight.

"Are you sure?"

She nodded happily. "Rayne told me about it and I'd like to try it. Can we?"

"Honey, I love your try anything spirit. Let's get these clothes off."

His fingers plucked at the buttons of her pajamas and she sighed in pleasure with every touch. She wasn't her mother but Misty intended to enjoy tonight with Jared very much indeed.

✧ ✧ ✧ ✧

Jared slammed down the phone and growled with frustration, glad that it was only him and Knox in the station house at the moment. Luckily it was a quiet day. No ringing phones, no petty issues dragging him away from the Boyd Hicks case. Just the smell of burnt coffee and stale donuts. He needed to walk over to the diner and put some real food into his stomach.

Not being the most patient of people, dealing with the state crime lab never put him in a good mood. They were always backed up and everyone thought their evidence was more important than anyone else's.

"I take it the news wasn't good?" Deputy Knox was standing over Jared's desk with an amused smile.

Jared exhaled slowly to calm himself down. "The DNA off the cigarette won't be ready for at least a week. Maybe more. Have you made any progress on those tire tracks? The lab is telling me weeks on that too."

Knox was a damn good deputy who had been on the forensics side of the fence earlier in his career. Jared had been lucky to hire him and that's why he'd made sure to give Knox plenty of responsibility and recognition.

"You were right. They're not an ATV. They belong to an oversized type of truck like an F-250 or larger."

"The kind of truck you might use to transport a dead body," Jared confirmed. "It makes sense."

Unfortunately that didn't narrow it down much. Every damn cowboy from here to Billings drove a truck like that.

"I sure wouldn't try moving a body in my girlfriend's Prius," Knox laughed. "But I'm also guessing that the truck might have a top on the truck bed or at least a tarp. They wouldn't want anyone seeing a dead man back there."

The phone rang again and Jared rubbed his temples before answering it. "Monroe."

"Hey, Jared. It's Griffin."

Griffin Sawyer was the sheriff of Hope Lake and a damn good one but he usually didn't call the office during the day.

"What can I do for you? Is Jazz okay?"

Griffin chuckled on the other end of the phone. "Jazz is amazing and wonderful. No, this call is about what I can do for you. I found that Dale Hicks you were looking for."

Jared had let all the men know about Boyd Hicks's murder and Dale Hicks as a person of interest.

"Have you talked to him? Where is he? I need to talk to him."

Finally something about this case was going right. Jared picked up a pen to write down the address.

"He's staying at a friend's campsite near here. Deputy Levi stopped them about some litter early this morning. He had no reason to detain them so he had to let them go. But he called me and I told him to sit on them until you get there. He's watching their campsite from a ways away so they don't get spooked."

Jared scratched down the location, his blood pumping in his veins. "Listen, I appreciate you keeping your eyes out for him. This will really help our investigation."

"No problem. I know you'd do the same. Good luck. I hope you get your man soon." Griffin signed off and Jared snagged his car keys from his desk drawer.

"Knox, you're with me. We're headed for Hope Lake."

Dale and his friend could be armed and dangerous. Jared didn't want to walk into a situation like that alone.

During the drive Jared and Knox discussed the strategy of how to deal with Dale. Doubtful the man would be cooperative.

Jared pulled alongside an official Hope Lake SUV and rolled down his window. The deputy in the truck did the same.

"Sheriff Monroe?" he asked.

"That's me," Jared confirmed, reaching out of the window to shake the deputy's hand. "You must be Deputy Levi."

"I am," the man nodded. "The man you're looking for is staying in a makeshift campsite just up the road less than a quarter of a mile. This is a dead end so no one has been in or out since I called Sheriff Griffin. Do you want me to hang around for back up?"

Jared liked the odds of three officers better than two. "Hang back and stay by your radio in case this gets out of hand. Hicks is unpredictable."

Jared and Knox followed Levi's vehicle until they could see the tent from the road. Pulling off to the side, Jared parked his truck and slowly exited, his gaze darting from left to right and then back again. Levi had done as Jared asked, staying in his SUV but he had a shotgun perched on his dashboard just in case.

Jared and Knox hiked up the small slope to the campsite, their guns drawn and ready. Dale came out of a scrub of trees carrying a large bucket. When he saw Jared and Knox he tossed the bucket at them and took off running in the other direction.

"Dammit, not again," Jared growled. But this time luck was on his side. The man tripped on a tree branch and landed face down, his arms and legs sprawled in all directions. Knox snapped cuffs on Dale and dragged him over to a chair by the campfire.

"Where's your friend?" Jared asked. "We know you're not here alone."

Dale spat on the ground but jerked his head toward the trees. "He's hiding in there. We ain't done anything wrong."

"Then tell your friend to come out. With his hands where I can see them."

"Royal!" Dale yelled. "Get out here!"

An older man with salt and pepper hair came out of the trees with his hands in the air. Knox escorted him to the other chair after patting him down for weapons. The deputy stayed close to the friend so that Jared could concentrate on Dale.

"Your brother Boyd is dead, Dale."

The man looked up at Jared, his eyes narrowed. "I heard. Is that what you came to tell me? Then you can leave because I already knew it."

"News travels fast," Jared observed. "You were certainly someone who wanted to see your brother dead."

Dale didn't deny it. "Didn't kill him. Now let me go about my business."

"You don't seem too broke up about Boyd's untimely passing. Maybe you and Boyd argued. Yeah, that's what I'm thinking. You argued and things got out of hand. Maybe he even tried to kill you first. That's self-defense."

Clyde scowled and shook his head. "I ain't seen Boyd for weeks so we couldn't have argued. And I couldn't have shot him because my gun disappeared. Besides, there's plenty of people that wouldn't mind seeing Boyd six feet under."

"Your gun disappeared?" Jared snorted. "Now there's an excuse I haven't heard in almost an hour. Your gun just up and vanished. Like so many firearms do."

"Well, it did. It was in my house and now it's gone. Maybe Angie took it."

"You'll throw anyone under the bus won't you? A real gentleman. Who else could have taken your gun?"

"Lots of people. Angie likes to have people over."

"So anyone could have used your gun and killed Boyd? Except none of them have motive like you do."

"I told you I haven't seen him. I've been in Cheyenne. I just got back here the day before yesterday. I couldn't have killed Boyd."

"Cheyenne, huh? And I suppose you were all alone and no one can confirm your whereabouts?" Now Dale was just grasping at straws.

"Wrong, Sheriff," Dale taunted. "I was in the county lockup there. I did fourteen days for not paying a traffic ticket. I was supposed to do thirty but they let me out for good behavior. I was a model prisoner."

"I can check that, you know," Jared warned. The man wasn't a genius but he had to know that his alibi could be easily confirmed or disproven.

Dale crossed his legs and smiled. "You should do that. I'll wait."

"You'll wait at the station. With me."

With a deep sense of satisfaction, Jared and Knox placed Dale into the back of the SUV.

"I didn't do it, Sheriff. I swear on a Bible."

"I'll call Cheyenne, don't you worry. Wonder what they're going to tell me?" Jared kept his eyes on the road. He wasn't going to be pulled into Dale's drama.

"That I was in jail," he growled. "I didn't kill Boyd."

"Then you've got nothing to worry about," Jared answered mildly.

As soon as Jared arrived back in Fielding, he'd call Cheyenne, Wyoming and put Dale's alibi to rest once and for all.

Chapter Seventeen

"So when are you going to marry him?" Rayne asked Misty at lunch. They were munching on pizza and catching up. "How many times has he asked you anyway?"

"I don't know. Maybe three or four." Although he hadn't lately. In fact, he'd been decidedly silent on the subject for over a week. For all Misty knew he'd changed his mind. "It doesn't matter because I'm not going to marry him. That's not the kind of marriage I want."

"Yeah, I wouldn't either." Rayne rolled her eyes. "Who wants a gorgeous husband who treats you like a princess? That would suck big donkey balls."

Jared was handsome and sexy. And he was good to her. Great, really. But...was it wrong to want someone to love her? She could easily fall in love with Jared of course. If she let herself. But could he love her too?

"Looks aren't enough," Misty argued. "Marriage is for a lifetime. Forever. If you don't love someone I would imagine it feels even longer."

"He cares about you. Anyone can see it."

Jared did care about her. He liked making love to her as well but that wasn't enough to build a family. Not the lasting kind.

Rayne tilted her head and smiled. "I think you're falling in love with him. And can I say I don't blame you? He's a good guy, Mist. It's okay to fall for guys like him. Your ex-boyfriend? Not so much."

"He doesn't love me." Misty avoided the question. "How could he? I'm the girl from the wrong side of the tracks, remember? He's practically royalty here in Fielding. The only reason I'm in his home is because I'm having his baby."

Rayne tapped her chin. "Let's see…how are babies made these days? Ah yes, by sex. He didn't care that you were the girl from the wrong side of the tracks when he was getting horizontal with you, and I doubt he cares now. He's not the type."

"I don't want to sit here." A loud voice interrupted their conversation. "Not next to her. Or her trampy friend."

Misty wanted to sink into the booth and never be seen again. Two older women – she didn't know their names – were standing next to Misty's table with looks of distaste on their faces. The only thing she knew about the women was they were members of the Ladies Auxiliary and had always made a point to cross the street whenever Misty was walking down the same sidewalk.

The host who was trying to seat them looked lost and unsure. The pizza place was packed as it always was at lunchtime and few other tables were to be had. Certainly none that had been cleaned by the busboy.

Rayne slapped the table, her expression militant. "For such fine ladies of Fielding, you have some nasty mouths on you. Who died and made you queens?"

Why didn't Rayne just ignore them like Misty's mother always said to do? She admired Rayne's bravado but it would only make things worse. She simply didn't understand.

The taller of the two women sniffed in disdain. "I know trash when I see it. Look at you," she scolded. "Tattoos and piercings. I know what your kind is like. It's shameful, that's what it is."

Misty's hand tightened on her glass and her heart beat wildly in her chest. This was why she'd wanted to leave Fielding. She'd never understood the hate this town had for her mother and for herself but she doubted she'd ever get used to being the whipping girl for every citizen.

The other woman tut-tutted, holding her handbag as a shield as if Rayne or Misty were planning to mug them or pull a knife. "And you, Misty Foster, sitting here with decent folk as if you had a right. Everyone knows you've trapped the poor sheriff with some story about a baby. If you are having a child – and I doubt it – the father isn't a good man like Jared Monroe. You should go to the church right now and repent all of your sins and lies."

"And what should I do, Mrs. Petitt?" Jared's voice, deep, compelling, and yes, a little angry sounded behind her. "Should I also repent my sins?"

Jared stepped into view, a thunderous look on his face. His eyes were almost gray and his lips were a flat line of displeasure. Mrs. Petitt's hand fluttered to her chest, her lined cheeks turning pink.

"Sheriff, how good to see you. How is your father?"

"My father is fine but I'm concerned about you," Jared answered evenly. "You seem to be under the mistaken impression that Misty has somehow trapped me with a baby. So I'm going to say this once and for all. Since you're the biggest gossip in town I'm sure it won't take long for everyone to hear it."

Mrs. Pettit flushed a deep red and her mouth gaped open like a fish trying to breathe out of water. Her companion wasn't any better; her hand covered her mouth and a look of chagrin and horror now covered her features.

Jared leaned down so he was eye to eye with Mrs. Pettit. "In no way have I been trapped. If anyone is trapped it's Misty. She was an innocent girl and I, an older man, took advantage of that innocence. And trust me when I say the baby she carries is mine. All mine. Are we clear?" The woman nodded faintly but Jared wasn't done. "When she told me how this town treats her I couldn't believe my ears. But I had to believe it since I heard it myself today. Perhaps you should go repent your sins, Mrs. Pettit, and we both know you have your share now, don't we?"

There was an edge to his voice as he posed his question. Both women had gone from bright red to pale in a matter of seconds. Whatever Jared knew about their secrets his words had hit home. Hard.

The women scuttled out of the restaurant that had gone eerily quiet when Jared had shown up. He looked around as if daring anyone else to say another word before sliding into the booth next to Misty.

"I guess they lost their appetites," Rayne said loudly. "Too bad."

The rest of the patrons began to go back to their meals. The show was over. Misty, however, was mortified. She pressed her hands to her hot cheeks and closed her eyes, trying to block everyone out. If she'd moved to Seattle this wouldn't have happened.

Jared put his arm around her shoulders but she wouldn't look at him. This was exactly what she'd been afraid of. Had warned him about. But he hadn't listened to her.

"It's over, honey."

That pissed her off because she knew better. She lifted her head and their gazes locked. Hers angry and his gentle.

"It's not, Jared. It will never be over. I could save a school bus full of children from a burning building and they wouldn't care. I should have left when I'd planned to."

"You're going to let a couple of women run you out of your hometown?" Jared asked, his fingers massaging her shoulder. "You're stronger than that, Misty. To put up with that shit your whole life you've got to have a spine made of steel. You should have just told her to go to hell."

Misty tugged nervously at her braid. "Mom always said to ignore them. What you did just now? Believe me it will only make things worse. I've tried to fight back and it doesn't work."

"It's not going to get worse because I won't allow it. Everyone now knows that you're under my protection. And as for fighting before, you were a child—now you're a grown woman," Jared reminded her. "I see what your mother was saying but when someone comes at you like that…"

Rayne pursed her lips and made a face. "Those two old battleaxes can go fuck themselves. Judging me for tattoos and piercings. Thinking they know me or you, for that matter. They don't know shit and I won't hesitate to tell them that. I have no idea how my sister can stand to live in this town."

"Now don't you go putting ideas of leaving into Misty's head," Jared warned. "I'll just come after you, honey."

"And drag me back?" Misty crumpled up the paper napkin in her hand. "I said I would stay for awhile and I meant it. I'm not a liar."

"No, you're a good person who has allowed a few people in town to make you think that everyone feels the same way they do." Jared pointed to the diners in the restaurant. "Do you think these people care what you or Rayne do? I mean…honestly? They're busy worrying about their own lives. They don't have time to worry about yours. Sure, they might like to hear some juicy gossip about how I knocked you up but that's only to take their mind off their problems."

His vernacular lightened the mood which she was sure he intended. "Knocked me up? I'm not sure I like the sound of that."

"I liked it when we did it."

Misty shook her head and elbowed Jared. He was trying to make her forget what had happened and she had to admit she wasn't feeling as badly as she had ten minutes ago. He had unquestionably stood up for her and for that she was grateful. Having him – and Rayne – here did make it somewhat easier.

But that didn't mean she wanted a repeat performance. She'd just as soon never see Mrs. Pettit and her friend ever again.

"Not in front of everybody."

Her friend laughed and took a generous bite of her pizza. "The way you two look at each other there was no doubt you both enjoyed it." Rayne pushed the pizza closer to Jared. "You might as well join us for lunch. We'll never eat all of this."

Jared helped himself; his appetite she'd learned was always hearty. "Don't mind if I do. It's been a busy morning."

"You always have a busy morning. You haven't had a full day off in awhile." Misty placed her napkin beside her plate. She'd lost her appetite. "I need to get going. I have a doctor's appointment in half an hour."

Jared grinned. "I know. They called the house to confirm and the call was routed to my phone. That's why I'm here. I'm going with you."

"You don't have to," Misty replied automatically, too used to doing everything on her own. "I'll be fine."

"I'm sure you will but I'm still going. I have questions for the doctor," Jared replied confidently. "Are you asking me not to go?"

"Of course not. I just didn't think you'd want to go to a doctor's office with a bunch of pregnant women."

"I'm sure they'll be partners there. I'm a part of this, Misty. Don't shut me out."

Rayne was watching the back and forth with great interest. Misty needed to end this conversation immediately. "Then we should get going. The receptionist said I would have new patient paperwork to fill out when I got there." She pulled her wallet from her purse but Jared's hand stayed her movements.

"I've got this."

Rayne smiled and lifted her glass of iced tea. "Thank you, Jared. You're such a gentleman. A real keeper."

Misty didn't miss the meaningful look from her friend. After Jared's display of chivalry today, Rayne was never going to shut up about marrying him. She was firmly in the pro-Jared camp, obviously dazzled by his looks and charm.

Jared paid the bill and took Misty's arm as they exited the restaurant. She was determined not to let what had happened dampen her excitement about seeing the doctor for the first time. No matter what, she had her baby.

✧ ✧ ✧ ✧

Dr. Farber was a smiling middle-aged woman with kind brown eyes. Her nurse had taken Misty's blood pressure, weighed her, and then finally had her pee in a cup. Misty had kept Jared up by her head during the doctor's exam but the entire time he'd peppered the poor woman with questions. She must have been used to it though because she never lost patience, even when Misty was ready to slap her hand over his mouth.

"Now we're all done with that part of the visit. Would you like to see your baby?" the doctor asked with a knowing smile.

Who was going to say no?

"Very much." Misty nodded her head along with Jared. The doctor wheeled a large machine over next to the examination table and began typing on the keyboard.

"Let's take a look at your baby."

The doctor inserted the wand inside of Misty and while at first it was uncomfortable she quickly forgot all about it as she stared at the screen. There was a small light pulsing and Misty couldn't seem to tear her eyes from it.

"That's your baby's heartbeat." The doctor pointed to the light. "Nice and strong. He or she is still pretty small but everything looks as it's supposed to."

Her heart in her throat and practically shaking with excitement, Misty turned to Jared but his expression stopped her. He too was staring at the screen but his expression had gone white as if in shock and his hand was now pressed to her abdomen.

"Jared?" she prompted. "Are you okay?"

His hand slid from her belly and his fingers entwined tightly with her own. "It's just so…real."

Dr. Farber beamed at the two of them. "For a woman who is experiencing morning sickness and fatigue, the baby is real almost from the first minute. But for men, it often doesn't become real until now when you can actually see him or her. So yes, Sheriff, your baby is real. Real and healthy. In about seven months you'll be parents. Congratulations. Now I'll leave you to dress. We'll see you in four weeks, Misty."

The doctor handed Misty the pictures and then bustled out of the door. Misty started to lever up but Jared leaned forward and laid his head on her stomach, a sheen to his beautiful blue eyes.

"Thank you, Misty. Thank you for telling me and thank you for not leaving Fielding."

She ran her fingers through his silky dark hair in awe that this strong man was as affected as she was by a blurry black and white picture. Did all parents feel this joyous at the first glimpses of their child? Did they feel scared and overwhelmed but so happy that it didn't matter?

And did the mothers feel this incredibly close to the father of their baby? Misty cupped Jared's jaw gently, his whiskers scraping her palm despite the fact that he'd shaved that morning.

"I'm glad I stayed too. This is something too good not to share." Her throat felt tight and it was hard to speak. Overflowing with emotions she couldn't name or control, tears rolled down her face.

"Hey, easy there, honey." Jared brushed her wet cheeks. "This is a happy day."

She pushed at his shoulder, but he'd pulled her into his arms despite the fact that she was naked from the waist down and covered with a paper sheet. "I am happy. I've never been this happy. That's why I'm crying."

Jared looked at her like she'd lost her mind and maybe she had. The pregnancy hormones were working overtime. She wanted to kiss him and tell him how much he meant to her.

Was that love?

Extricating herself from his arms, she quickly pulled on her panties and jeans before stepping into her boots. She needed to pull herself together and fast. Being this emotional made her too vulnerable.

Dabbing at her eyes with a tissue, she took a deep breath and smiled. "All ready to go. No more tears."

"Honey, you can cry on my shoulder anytime."

He meant it but she didn't want to take him up on it. Grabbing her purse and the pictures, she shrugged into her coat.

"We should show these to your father."

Jared grinned and nodded. "That's a great idea. I'll give the house a call. Ty will want to see them too."

He looked every inch the proud papa as they marched out of the doctor's office and into the cold. Jared Monroe was going to be a terrific father.

She could say with honesty – at least at this very moment – she was glad she'd stayed in Fielding. She wouldn't have missed this with him today for anything in the world.

She'd remember it and hold it in her heart forever.

Chapter Eighteen

"You had to let him go, boss," Deputy Knox said to Jared. He was back at the station house after Misty's doctor's appointment and the day had rapidly gone to hell.

"How can this be?" Jared asked, holding up the email he'd printed out and had been carrying around for the last thirty minutes. "Is he some kind of Houdini?"

Jared had received word that Dale Hicks had indeed been in the county lock up near Cheyenne serving time on unpaid tickets. Although Boyd's time of death couldn't be pinpointed exactly, it was highly unlikely Dale was anywhere in the vicinity to commit the murder. So Jared had reluctantly let the man go with a warning not to leave the area.

"That man is no Houdini," Knox declared as they watched Dale climbed into a red hatchback with his girlfriend at the wheel. "But he's not as stupid as he looks. He's got street smarts and that will take you pretty far in the criminal world."

"Can it help you commit a murder when you're out of state?" Jared asked wryly.

"No, but it's not like he doesn't know other criminals. People who might do the job for him while he was so conveniently in Wyoming."

"I thought about that too but we've got no evidence in that direction."

"What about Lindsey Jackson or her husband?" Knox asked, sifting through the file. "Where do they come in? Are they just victims of Hicks? And there's Bonnie too."

"All smokers with motive, although Bonnie says she doesn't have one, but knowing Boyd Hicks like I do I find that hard to believe." Jared shook his head. "We've got nothing on any of them. Now all our hopes are on the DNA from the cigarette and the tire tracks. And I've been thinking about the truck. Maybe someone saw the truck up there that day. It's a popular hiking spot."

"Not as much this time of year." Knox grimaced. "But we could run something in the paper asking if anyone saw a truck up there around that time. It's worth a shot. We don't have much else to go on."

"Let's do that. It's back to basics. Who would want Boyd Hicks dead? Absolutely everyone and anyone that might have a motive. Has that file from the state pen shown up yet?"

"Not yet. The wheels of bureaucracy move slow."

"And in the meantime our killer could be getting away right now. Or even planning another murder. Jesus, I can't fucking stand red tape." Jared grabbed a pen and made some notes. "Let's start leaning on our snitches a little bit. See if they know of anything that Boyd had going on since he got out. The smallest thing could be the lead we need. I'll call Terri at the newspaper."

Knox pointed to the clock on the wall. "Aren't you supposed to be somewhere? Something about dinner with the family and showing off your baby pictures."

"Aww hell, if I'm late Dad will never let me hear the end of it."

Gerald Monroe liked his home run with military precision.

"Then go. I'll call the newspaper and we can get a start on this stuff first thing in the morning." Knox was already picking up the telephone.

"Then you go home too," Jared ordered. "I mean it."

"I won't argue." Knox grinned and winked. "I've got a date tonight."

Knox was a charming, good looking guy and very well liked by the female population of Fielding and several of the nearby towns. He wasn't a playboy per se but he had a small devoted following of ladies that made sure he wasn't alone unless he wanted to be.

"I won't even bother to say have fun because I know you will," Jared smirked. "I'll just say thank you and see you tomorrow."

A new day to start working the Hicks case. All over again. But this time he'd get it right.

✧ ✧ ✧ ✧

Misty rinsed and stacked the dinner dishes in the sink of the family house. Gerald had protested and said the housekeeper could do them in the morning. Misty couldn't stand the idea of dishes sitting out on the table all night. After some spirited discussion they'd had found a compromise. Misty wouldn't wash them but she would clear the table and get the dishes ready for the housekeeper.

The photos from the ultrasound earlier in the day had been a huge hit at dinner. Ty and Gerald had been suitably impressed with the tiny peanut-shaped object in the picture. Becky had skipped dinner which Misty shouldn't have been happy about but she had to admit she was. It certainly made for a more peaceful dining experience.

Ty also had good news. Royce would be coming home next week. Jared had even talked to his older brother a few days ago and he seemed like a new man. It wouldn't be easy but hopefully Royce could stay sober and clean when he got out of the clinic.

She dried her hands on a dishtowel and placed the last of the leftovers into the refrigerator. Crossing from the kitchen into the living room, the men were nowhere in sight. Standing still for a moment, she heard voices coming from the back porch. Gerald had said something about smoking a cigar. Wrinkling her nose at the thought of the smell, she'd hoped Jared wouldn't join him.

A wool throw lay on the back of the couch and she tossed it around her shoulders before heading to the back door. She heard her name just as her hand touched the doorknob.

"Have you locked things down with Misty yet?" Gerald Monroe asked. His deep voice easily penetrated the glass and wood of the French door.

"Not yet. But I'm making progress," Jared said, a confident air in his tone.

Had her growing feelings been so transparent? It was embarrassing to think he knew she was falling for him when she'd tried so hard to keep it to herself.

"I hope so. The last thing this family needs is a messy custody battle. You can't allow her to take the baby out of Montana, son. You'll have no leverage at all if she falls in love and marries someone else."

Despite the warmth of the throw wrapped around her, Misty suddenly felt cold, a chill running through her veins at Gerald's words. She'd thought they'd made a connection the other night but perhaps it was all about the baby for him.

Jared said something she couldn't make out and then he said, "Don't worry, Dad. I've got this under control."

Stepping back, her hand dropped from the doorknob as pain sliced through her chest, almost bringing her to her knees. She was being played. All this time she was thinking they were growing closer, but this was really all about *control.*

Screw Jared. Screw the entire Monroe family.

She'd been fine without a family before and she'd be fine in the future. She didn't need them.

But it hurt. This was why she'd never let herself be vulnerable before.

Straightening her spine, she pasted on a smile and opened the door. The pungent stink of cigars slapped her in the face and before she could say anything witty or profound she was coughing and hacking from the thick smoke hanging in the air.

"Jesus, Misty, you shouldn't be back here with all this smoke." That was Ty's voice. She couldn't see very well because her eyes were watering and her dinner had crawled its way up to her throat. Misty didn't like cigar smoke at the best of times but apparently the baby liked it even less.

Strong arms lifted her from her feet and carried her back into the house. It was Jared she was sure. She'd know him anywhere; even through the stench of cigar smoke she could detect his woody citrus scent. He laid her on the couch while someone else pushed a glass in her hand.

"Drink," he commanded. "It's just ginger ale for your tummy."

She sipped at the cool liquid as he dabbed at her watery eyes with a handkerchief. "I'm okay. I guess the baby doesn't like cigars."

"I heard you gagging," Jared confirmed. "I don't know what we were thinking going out there to smoke. Even if you hadn't stepped outside I would have reeked of the stuff. I'll get undressed in the garage when we get home."

"You okay, honey?" Ty asked, rubbing his forehead. "We're sorry we made you sick."

"Very sorry." Gerald strode into the room with a sheepish expression. "It was my idea. I'd forgotten cigars made Rita sick as a dog too."

How could she stay mad at three handsome men who looked so chagrined? Wait, she could stay mad at them for trying to control her and the baby. She handed the glass back to Jared and took a deep breath, determined not to show how upsetting their conversation had been.

"Can we go home now? I'm very tired."

"Of course. I'll get your coat." Jared was gone before she could protest that she could do it herself. Ty and Gerald were looking at her as if she might explode or puke or both. Luckily it meant she didn't have to say anything even as Jared returned and bundled her up in her coat and gloves.

She hugged Ty and Gerald and then followed Jared to his truck, thinking of what she would say when they got home. His smooth moves and charm might work on other women but she was done being bamboozled.

Misty was mad and she wasn't going to be silent about it.

✧ ✧ ✧ ✧

Misty had been quiet during their five minute drive back to the house. She'd stared out the window ignoring Jared, and then as soon as he stopped the truck she'd jumped out and stomped up the porch steps. She must be really pissed off about the cigar smoke making her sick and she was right to be. He should have known better.

But he knew how to get on her good side.

After shedding his coat, he slid his arms around her and dropped a kiss on top of her head. "Why don't I run you a nice hot bath? While you're in there having a nice soak I'll make some hot chocolate. Extra marshmallows."

She was stiff in his arms when she normally melted against him. "Misty honey, I'm sorry about the cigar smoke. Dad was right, we should have known better."

Misty was looking at him like he'd lost his mind. Shaking off his embrace, she stepped back and crossed her arms over her chest. "Why are you apologizing, Jared? After all, you have me *under control*, right? Isn't that what you told your father? Misty is *under control*."

Jesus, Mary, and Joseph, she looked mad as hell. Her cheeks were red, her lips pursed, and she was tapping her toe as she waited for his response. So tiny, she looked like a pissed off golden-haired fairy. But now was not the moment to say that out loud.

Rubbing the back of his neck, Jared tried to think of how to explain. She'd obviously overheard part of his conversation with his dad and completely misunderstood what he was trying to say.

"Misty, let's sit down and talk about this. Like adults."

Her violet eyes narrowed to slits. "Are you trying to say I'm acting like a child?"

Son of a bitch.

"No, that's not what I'm saying at all. I'd just like us to sit down and talk."

"I don't want to sit down," she retorted, beginning to pace back and forth across the living room. "I want to tell you how angry I am with you. You're trying to control me and I won't have it, Jared. I won't have someone pulling my strings."

Her voice had gone up an octave and he didn't have a clue as to how to calm her down. He only knew she didn't understand.

"I am not trying to control you," he argued, holding on to his temper. Her stubborn posture was keeping her from really listening to him. "You have to know that, Misty."

"Then why did you tell your father that I'm under control if you're not trying to do just that?"

"That's not what I said." *Not exactly, anyway.*

"All I know is that since I've met you, I've given up on my dream to move to Seattle and I've let you railroad me into living here. Now I have new clothes and a new phone. Next thing I know we'll be married and I'll be running around to have dinner on the table by six and making sure Jared Junior's shoes are all in a row in his closet. Everything has been Jared Monroe's way. When do I get my turn?"

He could feel the back of his neck grow hot. She was angry and he understood that, but she was deliberately making things sound worse than they were.

"You needed a place to live and you needed new clothes and a phone. Yes, you could have purchased them yourself but it made me happy to buy them for you," he said through gritted teeth.

"And as long as you're happy that's the important thing," Misty replied, nodding her head.

"Yes. Shit. I mean, no. Of course I want you to be happy. That's why I've done all these things. So you'd be happy and taken care of. Are you trying to tell me that you're not happy after all I've done?"

She'd turned her back on him and he could see her shoulders tremble with emotion. When she looked at him again there were tears shining in her eyes.

"Jared," she said softly. "You did those things for you. Not for me. I'm not saying what you did wasn't nice or good or that I'm not appreciative. I am. I'm saying that ultimately you did it because that's what you wanted. You want me to live here. You want me to have different clothes. You want us to get married. Why? Because it makes you happy. You want to change me into someone you could be with. Someone your father, and siblings, and yes, even the town could approve of. I didn't need any of this to be happy. I already was. I was happy just being with you and having this baby."

He didn't know what to say.

So he didn't say anything. He turned and stomped out of the house and into the night, anger churning in his gut and driving him away. If he didn't leave he'd say something he didn't want to or didn't mean. He'd be cruel and nasty. He could defend himself in a hundred different ways and show her how wrong she was but he was too mad to even form the words.

Nothing she said was true. It couldn't be. Because if it was it meant he was a real asshole.

Chapter Nineteen

Jared had been gone for hours. It was times like this Misty wished she drank coffee. Right now she was curled up in a chair in front of the fireplace and sipping some of the apple cider she'd begun to crave a few days ago and wondering if she screwed everything up.

Was she completely wrong?

Was the feeling that she had been doing all the compromising incorrect and selfish? She didn't want to think she was the ungrateful type. She never had been before – that she knew of. But the niggling feeling in the back of her mind that kept saying over and over that while Jared's actions were sweet and giving…he was getting pretty much everything he wanted.

She couldn't shake the feeling that she was being subtly manipulated and by someone who excelled at it. Was he so good he didn't even know he was doing it? That would explain his stunned expression when he'd practically run out of the house.

Or maybe pregnancy hormones were making her crazy and paranoid.

She wanted to be a real partner to Jared. If she was going to marry him, and right now the answer would be a resounding no, they had to come to the relationship as equals. She wouldn't allow herself to be marginalized. That's how she'd been feeling lately and she didn't want a lifetime of it. She'd spent most of her formative years that way and she wasn't anxious to keep doing it.

Caring about Jared didn't mean not seeing his faults. It meant accepting them but he had to accept hers as well. He couldn't mold her into being someone else.

He had to love her for who she was right now. Not the person she might be someday.

And that was the crux of all of this. She wanted Jared to love her. *Her.*

Tonight when he'd boasted to his father that he had her under control it had hurt deeply. She was falling in love with this bossy, maddening man with a gentle way about him. She'd wanted him to feel the same and it looked like his feelings were far from her own. It was all about winning. About being on top.

Boy, Gerald Monroe had really done a number on his middle son. Jared was so competitive he was even competing with her. He wanted to win so badly he was willing to squash her own dreams and desires. If he wanted to make this work between the two of them he was going to have to give. Just a little.

Jared need to show her that he recognized that there were two people living in this house. Two sets of needs. Two sets of wants.

But she had to own her part of this. It wasn't all on Jared.

She'd allowed this to happen. Heck, in her own way she'd encouraged it. She was so used to her needs and wants not mattering – to her own mother, no less – she'd given in right and left to Jared's subtle demands.

No more. If this was going to work, there needed to be more compromise and less folding like a cheap tent when the pressure was on. Now the only issue was how to explain it to Jared.

✧ ✧ ✧ ✧

Jared had walked in the cold dark for a long time trying to work off the anger Misty's words had inspired. With every step he'd told himself that she didn't understand. She was being selfish and petty. Even ungrateful. By the time he found himself on Ty's front porch, he was completely sure he was in the right and Misty in the wrong.

Ty opened the door with his usual grin. "What brings you here, big brother? Shouldn't you be home taking care of Misty?" Ty's smile fell instantly. "She's okay, isn't she? Is she sick?"

"She's fine and I tried to take care of her. Not that she appreciates that." Jared brushed past Ty into the house and knelt in front of the fireplace. He was frozen in spots that no man should ever have to thaw out. "So I decided to take a walk and clear my head."

Ty crossed his arms over his chest, a smile playing on his lips. "At night? Without a coat? That doesn't sound like a bright idea, Jared. Why don't you tell me what really happened and why you're here? While you do that I'll make some coffee. You look half frozen."

Ty went into the kitchen that overlooked the living room while Jared held his hands out to the warmth of the flames and tried to put the evening into perspective.

"Misty thinks I'm trying to control her."

Ty flipped a switch on the coffee maker and then leaned against the counter. "Are you? Knowing you as I do, it wouldn't stretch my imagination to believe it."

Jared scowled at his brother. Ty was supposed to take his side, dammit. "I am not. She's not thinking straight. I'm trying to make our lives better. Make her life better and she's damn ungrateful."

"Humor me. How are you making her life better? And be specific."

Unused to being questioned, Jared shifted uncomfortably. "For one thing, she's out of that poky little apartment. She has a real home now."

Ty nodded. "What else?"

"I bought her some new clothes and a new phone. Her things couldn't even have been sold at a garage sale. And they looked terrible on her."

"Keep going."

"I bring her breakfast in bed so she won't puke every morning. I think that's pretty wonderful."

Ty sighed and shook his head. "And she never says thank you? That's terrible."

"Well, actually she says thank you every day."

With a beautiful, sleepy smile on her face.

"So she's not a complete bitch. That's good news." Ty rested his chin on his hands. "Anything else?"

"I take care of her." Jared shrugged, not sure what his brother wanted to hear. "I make sure she eats her vegetables and drinks her milk. Gets some exercise and takes her vitamins. Stuff like that."

Ty straightened up and whistled. "And she doesn't appreciate that? Who the fuck does she think she is? Doesn't she know that you know how she should live her life? That you know better?"

Jared opened his mouth to vehemently agree but then realized Ty was being a total sarcastic shit.

"I guess I know whose side you're on," Jared said dryly. "So much for blood is thicker than water."

"This has nothing to do with love and everything to do with who we are," Ty replied mildly, pulling two mugs down from the cabinet and filling them with the dark, steamy brew. "Let's face it, brother. Gerald Monroe is a great man but he lacked some basic parenting skills. He pitted us against one another and everyone else like gladiators in the ring for his amusement. And look how we turned out. We're bossy, stubborn, and bulldoze anyone who doesn't do things our way – all in the name of being the best. Showing Daddy that we won. It's not pretty and it pisses people off. They can only take so much of our shit before they rebel."

Jared stood and took one of the mugs from Ty, trying to digest what his brother had said. He knew he liked to get his own way and could be pushy…he had high standards…but was he as bad as Ty said?

"You make us all sound like monsters. Like terrible people."

"In a way we are monsters. Dad created us and let us loose onto the unsuspecting village. Shit, looking at you is like looking in a damn mirror. You have exactly the same expression of disbelief that I had when Kyle told my ass off several months ago. He'd had enough of my crap and he called me on it."

"Maybe he was wrong," Jared argued almost desperately. He didn't want to be the bad guy in this scenario.

Ty sat down at the table and took a sip of his coffee. "He wasn't, although it took me about a week to come to that conclusion. Misty's not wrong either. Did you hear yourself tonight talking to Dad? He was pressing you about marriage and you told him you had everything – including a female, which is a laugh – under control. Did Dad ever have Mom under control?" Ty held up his hand. "Don't bother to answer because we both know the truth. He did not. She ran circles around his ass and the only control he had in his own home was his kids. Hell, even we rebelled now and again. Except you. You toed the line."

"You sound like Royce." Jared didn't like the picture Ty was drawing. "And I have rebelled. I became sheriff even though Dad didn't want me to."

Ty chuckled and propped his feet on the round wooden table. "Once. A broken clock is right twice a day. All you were trying to do tonight was make Dad happy. You didn't think about Misty's happiness once, did you? This was about what you and Dad wanted. Shit, do you even *want* to get married to Misty?"

"It's the right thing to do," Jared said, stalling for time. Did he want to marry Misty?

Ty snorted coffee out of his nose. "Okay, so you offered and she turned your ass down. Is it the right thing to do to keep bugging the shit out of her about it? Is it the right thing to do to try and wear her down? Sneak under the radar? Is that the right thing to do?"

Jared slapped his mug down on the table, irritated more with Ty than with Misty. At least she had an excuse. She was pregnant and not feeling like herself. "Clearly I came to the wrong place. I'll borrow a coat and head out."

"Yep, if you came here for a pity party then I'm the wrong guy. If you came here for some advice to fix things with Misty then maybe I can help you."

"What would be your advice, o wise one?" Jared asked sarcastically. "I can't wait to hear this."

Ty dropped his feet to the floor and leaned forward, an earnest expression on his face. "Stop being an asshole."

"That's it?" Jared laughed and reached for his brother's coat. This had been a waste of time. "Stop being an asshole. Not very helpful, Ty."

Ty stood and got face to face with Jared, invading his personal space. "I'm going to give you some news that's going to come as a shock. It's not all fucking about you. Believe me, when Kyle landed that blow it just about knocked me on my ass. But he was right. I was acting like only what I wanted counted. And I wasn't above some pretty underhanded shit to get my way. Then I'd act like he should be grateful. Does this sound familiar? It should. So far Misty has given up a new life in Seattle, moved in with you, been forced to eat food she doesn't like and do exercise that wasn't her choice. Now you want her to dress for you and be fucking happy about it. Oh, and don't forget she needs to fall in with our dad's plans about what's acceptable. Does that just about sum Misty's life up for the last few weeks or have I left anything out?"

Jared stared into his brother's eyes, a blue mirror of his own, before falling down into a chair defeated. He'd messed everything up. As each day she'd lived with him played in front of him like a movie, the horror of what he'd done grew. No wonder she'd been pissed off tonight.

"How did you fix it?" Jared asked his brother. "I think I might be falling in love with her."

Ty retrieved the coffee pot and refilled their mugs. "Now you're talking some sense. We can figure this out if you're ready to be open-minded."

Jared was ready to get his ass kicked by a tiny little blonde with violet eyes. If that wasn't love he didn't know what it was.

Chapter Twenty

Misty didn't know how long she'd been asleep when she heard the bedroom door open. She groggily pushed herself up on her elbows before reaching for the bedside lamp. Snapping it on, she blinked several times to adjust to the sudden light.

Jared was standing a few feet away from the bed, his shoulders slumped in dejection. "I guess I messed up. I'm sorry."

She sat up and pulled her knees into her chest. "I'm sorry too. I did some thinking and it's my fault just as much as yours. Maybe more."

Jared shook his head and came to sit on the edge of the bed. "No, it was me. I had a long talk with Ty tonight and he helped me see a few things. About me. About Dad. About how fucked up as a family we are in general. I'm sorry that you got caught in all my baggage. It's not fair to you."

Misty shrugged, relieved that he was willing to even discuss the whole issue. "Life's rarely fair and I don't expect it to be. I just want us to be a team. Partners. I want us to be in this parenting thing together, making decisions that are best for all three of us."

Jared's hand reached out and grasped her own, warm and strong. "I'm sorry you didn't get to move to Seattle."

Smiling, she raised his hand to her lips. "It's okay. Really. It would have been wrong for me to take the baby that far from you. I know that and I'm okay with the decision I made."

"I'm still sorry. And I'm sorry that I'm such a shit to live with and make everything difficult. I think you look fine in anything you wear and I won't push you to walk on the treadmill or eat broccoli if you don't want to."

Misty slapped her hand over her mouth in shock. "Wow, what did Ty say to you? It's like another Jared here in front of me."

"Just a few home truths," Jared sighed. "He and I talked about how Dad made us compete and how it's pretty much messed us up. I see now that I was pushy and manipulative to get my way because in my messed up mind I equated it with winning and being the best. I know that it was wrong."

"There's nothing wrong with wanting your way. It's how you go about getting it. We need to talk about things and compromise. Sometimes I'll get my way and sometimes you will. I think that walking on the treadmill is a good idea so I'm going to keep doing that. But I'm not eating Brussels sprouts again. Ick. They were not good."

Jared smiled and slid closer. "I promise there will never be another Brussels sprout in this house. Good enough?"

"I don't care if you eat them." She leaned down and rested her cheek on their entwined hands. "I know that part of this is my issue. I'm used to taking care of my mom and putting my needs on the back burner. I'm even used to the good people of Fielding treating me crappy. I can't continue to let this happen. I won't let my son or daughter see me being disrespected. I don't want them to end up like me."

He placed a finger under her chin and lifted her face so she was looking into his eyes. "I sure as hell don't want them to end up like me either. I think I need to have a long talk with my dad and let him know that I won't be competing for his love and approval any more. If he can't deal with us not getting married – or any other life decision we make – then that's his problem."

"That ought to be an interesting conversation. I guess it's too late to have that with my mother."

"She might be listening, you never know. I think the important thing is we both want to change. We want to be better. But I know that I'm going to fall into old habits. I'm counting on you to call me on it."

Misty nodded. "Me too. If I start acting like a doormat you need to let me know. I'll tell Rayne too. She loves to point out that behavior."

"I knew I liked that girl." Jared grinned and began to pluck open the buttons on his shirt. "I've got to be up for work in five hours. Maybe we should both get some sleep. I never realized a fight between a couple could be so exhausting."

Misty peeked up at him from under her lashes. "This was our first fight. Does that mean we should kiss and make up or something?"

His shirt fell away revealing his broad chest and flat stomach. "We probably should. I've heard that make up sex is pretty awesome."

He wore a wicked grin as he stood to kick off his boots and jeans. Misty had to control the urge to lean forward and run her tongue over his delicious abs.

"I've heard that too, but of course I've never experienced it. Have you?"

Standing before her completely naked, his hard cock reaching almost up to his belly button, he was sex on a stick. Everything she'd ever dreamed about or wanted.

"I haven't, so I guess that I'm kind of a virgin. Be gentle with me, Misty," he smirked.

She shook her head and pulled her pajama top off. "I'm afraid I can't promise that. Get over here, cowboy, and show me how sorry you are."

Jared put one knee on the edge of the bed and leaned over her. She could feel the heat emanating from his skin and she reached out to run her hand up his chest. Jared grinned and wrapped his fingers around her wrist.

"Yes, ma'am," he drawled, moving her hand down his body, his smile promising all sorts of dirty delights. How had she ever thought she could live without this?

✧ ✧ ✧ ✧

The fatigue that had been weighing Jared down fell away as he tugged the last of Misty's pajamas from her beautiful body. Every curve fit his palm perfectly as if she had been made just for him. He ran his hands from her breasts to her hips and back up again, luxuriating in the silky softness of her skin.

But one thing had changed. Her waist, always tiny, appeared to have thickened ever so slightly. A sign that the baby was real and growing. Healthy and strong. This woman was the mother of his child and the thought still brought him to his knees. Maybe it always would.

His fingers lingered at the indentation of her waist, teasing the sensitive flesh. "Your body is changing. It's so fucking beautiful, Misty, to watch this. I don't even have the words."

"Just don't treat me like I'm made of crystal," she whispered, her soft breath caressing his cheek as he leaned down closer to capture those soft pink lips. He took his time, not hurrying the kiss, but letting his tongue explore the warm cavern of her mouth. Still learning all that aroused her, he tickled her tongue with his own until she was squirming underneath him.

His own arousal had gone from zero to sixty in mere seconds. His cock was already painfully hard and his balls throbbed with each beat of his heart, which was pounding out of his chest.

"You promised not to be gentle with me either," Jared whispered against the fragrant skin just behind her ear. She answered by digging her nails into his back, the pain mixing with the pleasure and heightening the latter.

She dropped kisses onto his shoulders, his chest, and down his abdomen, scooting her body under his until her mouth hovered over the head of his cock. She ran her tongue around the head and then blew softly. The sensations rocketed through him and headed directly back to his dick, making it swell even larger and ache with need.

"Witch," he hissed with a chuckle. "You're a fast learner, my sweet."

She didn't bother to answer, simply taking his cock in her mouth and swishing her tongue back and forth until he couldn't take it anymore. His body trembled as he reluctantly pulled away, his heart galloping in his chest.

Her soft hands still cupped his balls, stroking and kneading. Groaning at the effort to stem the tide he sat back on his heels, instantly missing her hot mouth and teasing tongue. Strong emotion tightened in his chest as he gazed down at Misty. She wasn't just beautiful, she was...his. And without a doubt he was hers as well. She held his heart in her small hands.

He hadn't planned it, and if he were honest, he wasn't even sure he'd wanted it. But she'd come into his life unexpectedly and brought love, acceptance, humility, and hope. She'd created a family with him.

✧ ✧ ✧ ✧

The way Jared was looking at Misty had swarms of butterflies doing aerial loops in her stomach. His eyes were all soft and his expression almost worshipful. He was looking at her as if she was the most beautiful thing he'd ever seen.

Could she be that lucky?

She never had been before but everything in her life had changed since the night she'd given a sheriff who'd had one too many a ride home. He made everything better even when he was being difficult and stubborn. His strength made her stronger, and hopefully the love she felt growing in her heart each and every day would inspire the same feelings. It wasn't simply that she carried his child. It was more than that. It was the way he made her feel.

Like she was special.

Lifting her foot, he pressed his lips to the toes and then the instep, drawing a moan as frissons of electricity ran straight up her leg to her clit and honey spilled from her pussy. He continued kissing a wet path from her calves to her inner thigh and she wound her fingers into his silky dark hair, needing his tongue in her slit so desperately.

When his tongue finally touched her clit she cried out his name even as he lapped at the button, torturing it until she was on the edge of orgasm. Her legs shook and her fingers clawed at the sheets as he expertly kept her on the precipice, not letting her go over.

Closing her eyes, she let the pleasure flow through her like water as he kissed his way inch by inch up her torso, stopping to nibble on sensitive, delicate spots now and again. By the time he captured her lips again his cock pressed against her entrance. With a moan of need she lifted her hips so his cock slid in further. He pulled back and then surged forward, filling her completely and taking her breath away.

Each stroke rubbed her G-spot and she wrapped her legs around him as his thrusts sped up. He rode her hard and fast, just the way she liked it, each stroke building her arousal. His breath was hot against her neck as he whispered naughty things he wanted to do.

"Honey, I can't–" Jared's voice broke and he groaned with the effort of holding back. Misty anchored her hands on his wide shoulders and pressed a kiss to his chest, the tang of salt on her tongue.

"Yes, Jared," she exhorted. "Now."

He reached between them and touched her swollen clit, sending her into heaven. The room tilted and the stars rocketed around the ceiling, spun in circles, and then dissolved into a golden haze. Jared reached his own pinnacle, his body growing taut. His cock swelled inside of her and the heat of his seed flooded her pussy.

When it was over he held her close, running his fingers through her long hair and tickling her nose with the strands until she giggled. She'd never felt closer to anyone than she did to this man at this moment.

She was in love with Jared Monroe.

Chapter Twenty-One

"Boss?" Deputy Knox asked, cradling the phone between his neck and his shoulder as Jared strode into the station house. "I need to speak to you right away. It's the Hicks case."

Jared headed straight for the coffee machine. He and Misty had stayed up half the night making love and he was ass dragging today. In the last three weeks not only had the sex become off the charts amazing, but their relationship had grown closer. He was working hard to take her thoughts and opinions into account and they'd managed to compromise several times, including on the nursery decor. They'd decided on a zoo animal theme fit for boy or girl. Secretly Jared was leaning toward wanting a girl who looked like Misty.

"I'm listening," Jared replied as Knox hung up the phone. "What do you have for me? We could use some good news."

"We got the traffic camera footage from the road heading into the Hawkins place." Knox was wearing his usual grin but his enthusiasm was infectious. Jared found himself smiling with excitement at the thought they might get a break in the case. Finally.

"Damn, it took long enough," Jared groused. "Have you looked at it yet?"

"Just got it." Knox shook his head. "It's going to take time to look through it. They sent us two weeks' worth of footage since we don't know time of death. It's like looking for a needle in a haystack."

"Except that road is rarely traveled," Jared observed. "I would imagine we can fast forward through hours of nothing to get to a part where a truck shows up. We already know we're not looking for a regular car."

"Then I guess I better refill my coffee cup and get to work." Knox grabbed his mug from his desk and made a beeline for the coffeepot. Jared settled at his own desk and opened one of the files. He might as well give Knox a hand. He was all about not asking his deputies to do shit work he wasn't willing to do himself.

"I'll let you know if I see anything suspicious," Jared said to Knox. "I'll start with the first week of video."

The morning dragged on as Jared went through each day of twenty-four hour footage. Whenever any vehicle appeared he'd slow the file down to take a closer look. His eyes were tired and his stomach was growling when a large truck came into view. He stopped the tape and then rewound, starting again at normal speed. The road was dark and deserted and Jared couldn't see the driver, but the truck was oversized just as the tire tracks indicated.

"Knox," Jared yelled. "I want you to see this. I think we've got something."

His deputy abandoned his own laptop and came around to Jared's desk, peering down at the screen. "What am I looking for?" Knox asked as Jared restarted the tape. "Never mind, I see it. Damn, it's too dark to see who's driving it or the license plate."

Jared chuckled at his deputy's naiveté. "I can zero in on the back of the truck and hopefully see the plate or at least a partial. Give me a minute."

Tapping at the keys, Jared isolated the part of the picture he wanted enlarged. The software zoomed in and Jared could clearly see that the truck was a dark color with some sort of pin striping on the tailgate. The last part of the plate was shadowed but he could make out HJ345.

"All we have to do is run this partial with the search criteria of only trucks and that should narrow our list down significantly. If we're lucky there will only be a couple of vehicles that match."

Jared input the partial plate and waited as the system began its search. Knox perched on the edge of Jared's desk. "What are you thinking, boss? Is it Dale? Or someone completely different? Someone we don't even know yet?"

That very question had been bugging Jared for days, since they'd been forced to let Dale go. When Jared had interrogated Dale a second time he'd felt there was something going on there. Something not quite right. Jared's gut was telling him Clyde wasn't completely innocent but what he'd actually done was a mystery yet to be solved.

Jared's laptop beeped as the search came to a halt. Three names met the criteria. One looked damn familiar.

David Jackson. Lindsey Jackson's husband.

Looks like they needed to have a chat with him. Now.

✧ ✧ ✧ ✧

Jared took a few quick photos of David Jackson's truck sitting in his driveway before they knocked on the door. Lindsey had a smile on her face when she answered but it quickly disappeared when she saw who it was and this time Jared had Knox with him. Although Knox wouldn't be going into the house to question David Jackson. He had a job to do outside. Meanwhile Chris was also nearby, just a radio call away if they needed him.

"Sheriff Monroe, what can I do for you this evening?"

Her tone was short and unwelcoming but he'd heard worse. Jared tipped his hat, determined to be polite. What Lindsey's role in all this was he didn't know. Victim or willing accomplice?

"Ma'am, I'd like to speak with your husband if I may."

Lindsey's eyes went wide. "Why on earth would you want to talk to David?"

Before Jared could answer a deep voice sounded from somewhere inside the house. "Lindsey, let them in. I'll talk to them."

"Fine, come in then." She stepped back but looked unhappy about it. The door swung shut behind him and David Jackson stood in the middle of the living room. "Have a seat. What do you want to talk to me about?"

Jared sat down on the sofa while David sat in a chair across from them. Lindsey sat on the arm of his chair, her hand on his shoulder, the knuckles white.

"Sorry we stopped in without calling but I'd like to ask you a few questions. Have you loaned your truck to anyone recently, Mr. Jackson?"

The man frowned and shook his head. "No. No one drives that truck except me."

Lindsey smiled and patted his arm. "It was his birthday present to himself. He doesn't even let me drive it, not that I would want to. It's too big for me. I prefer my Accord."

Jared had seen the light blue four-door Honda in the driveway.

"Does anyone else have keys to your truck?" Jared watched David's expression carefully. The man's shoulders were stiff and his complexion had turned pale.

"No. What is this about, Sheriff? I told you no one drives my truck but me."

Jared pulled a photo from his pocket and set it on the coffee table between them. It had been made from the footage and showed the partial plate clearly. "This photo was made from footage taken on the road to the Hawkins pasture. It's the only road in or out so the killer would have had to drive on it."

David picked up the photo and quickly scanned it before setting it back on the table. "I'm not sure why you're asking me about this. Is this picture supposed to mean something to me?"

Jared had to hand it to David Jackson. He was holding himself together pretty well but Jared could see the tells – a sweaty forehead, a darting gaze. The man was nervous. It could be because the cops were questioning him. It could also be because he'd done something illegal…and was now being questioned by the cops.

"That appears to be your license plate, Mr. Jackson. Are you saying that it's not?"

David picked up the photo again, this time his hands shaking slightly. "I don't think it is. I mean, you can't really tell in this picture. So no, I don't think it's mine. Sorry I couldn't help you."

"So you've never driven on High Cross Road, Mr. Jackson?"

David Jackson sat back in his chair and reached for Lindsey's hand. "No, I can't say I have. It's not really near any place I would go. Are we finished here?"

"Not quite. I need to talk to my deputy for a moment." Jared rose from the couch and walked to the door where Knox was waiting. Letting him into the house, Jared knew instantly what

Knox had found by the look on his face. Knox held out two pieces of paper with tire tracks on them.

"Thanks, Knox." Jared walked back and sat down again. "Mr. Jackson, what would you say if I told you that your tires match the tire tracks at the spot where we found Boyd Hicks?"

The once pale face turned bright red. "There are lots of trucks with those tires, Sheriff."

"That's true, except all those other trucks didn't drive on the road to that location." Jared leaned forward and looked the man in the eye. "Don't make this difficult, Mr. Jackson. I'm getting a warrant for your truck right now. We'll impound it and go over it with a fine tooth comb. I'm thinking we'll find evidence that Boyd Hicks was in the back of your truck and you transported him to the Hawkins pasture from wherever you killed him. Am I right?"

David Jackson opened and closed his mouth several times and then his shoulders began to shake. Lindsey fell to her knees next to him. "David, what's wrong?"

He buried his face in his hands and the sound of sobs filled the room. "I did it to protect my wife. I wasn't going to let that low-life hurt her or Tilly again."

The words were choked but Jared could make out the confession. Exultation at finding the killer mixed with dismay that it was David Jackson. Lindsey wore a stricken expression at her husband's statement of guilt. She kept shaking her head and trying to pull his hands from his eyes but he was whispering over and over, "I did it for you. I did it for you."

"Mr. Jackson, are you confessing to the murder of Boyd Hicks?"

David Jackson still didn't look up but he nodded his head, sobs still wracking his body. "I did it to protect Lindsey and Tilly."

"Mr. Jackson, did you act alone? Was anyone else involved in the commission of this crime? Did your wife know about this?"

Jackson shook his head again. "No. I didn't want her to know. I killed Hicks so he would never come near her again."

"She didn't know? She wasn't there?" Jared asked sharply, watching the reactions of both man and wife. Lindsey Jackson appeared to be in shock but Jared needed to be sure.

He wasn't unsympathetic to the couple's plight. If Boyd Hicks had been threatening and harassing them Jackson may have felt he had no choice. But he should have gone to the police and not taken things into his own hands. Unless it was truly a case of self-defense where Boyd was ready to kill Lindsey. And that wasn't out of the question.

"I tell you she had no idea. I went to see Hicks to confront him. That's when I killed him."

Satisfied at least for the time being, Jared reluctantly nodded to Knox who helped the man to his feet before snapping cuffs on his wrists. Lindsey cried and tugged frantically at her husband's arm.

"Tell the sheriff this is all a mistake, Dave. Tell him you're just kidding."

"I love you, Lindsey. There isn't anything I wouldn't do for you."

Sobs wracked the woman's body and she pulled at her husband's shirt. "Don't do this, Dave. Don't do it."

"I love you, baby. I love you."

Lindsey turned to Jared, her hands together as if in prayer. "Sheriff, Dave doesn't mean it. He couldn't do something like this. Don't take him. Please don't take him away!"

With each sentence her voice had become increasingly desperate and ragged. Her ashen skin was streaked with mascara as her tears continued to fall. Jared felt a twist of sympathy for what this woman had endured first with Boyd and now with David Jackson.

"Ma'am, I have to take your husband in. But I suggest you call a good lawyer, especially if he was simply protecting you from harm."

Lindsey was shaking but she nodded her head. "Can I kiss him before you take him away?"

Jared nodded to Knox again and the deputy stepped away from Jackson. Lindsey pressed her palms to her husband's chest and looked up at him with a pleading expression.

"I'll get a good attorney. Don't make any statements until he gets there, okay? Don't say a word."

It was actually good advice. Lindsey kissed her husband before Knox led him out of the house and into the truck. They'd take him to the station, get him booked, and then wait for his attorney to show. Jared had many questions for the man including how, when, and where the whole thing happened.

"He'll be arraigned in the morning, Mrs. Jackson. At that time the judge will set bail," Jared explained as the stricken woman watched her husband being led away in cuffs.

"He only did this because he loves me," she whispered, falling to her knees and wrapping her arms around her torso as if in comfort. "No one has loved me until now. Dear God, he loves me."

Digging in his wallet, Jared pulled out a card from a social services group that worked in the area. They helped the families of the incarcerated with a multitude of programs, not the least of which was counseling.

"Mrs. Jackson, this group may be able to help you. They can recommend a lawyer or help you fill out forms for aid. They also offer counseling to prisoner's families." Jared held out the card and she reached up to take it with shaking fingers. "We need to take your husband to the station now. Is there anyone I can call to come stay with you?"

The crying had stopped and her eyes were glazed over as if she was in some sort of trance. "There's no one."

Jared pointed to the card he'd given her. "Then you should call them. They'll send someone here to be with you."

She looked down at the card and then at Jared. "I will."

"Good. I'm sorry about this," Jared said awkwardly. He wasn't sorry about arresting a killer but he was sorry that this woman had experienced way too much trauma in her life. She needed someone – preferably a professional – to help her through the days and weeks to come. It was going to get worse before it got better.

Chapter Twenty-Two

"So the case is closed?" Misty asked as she and Jared sat down in a booth at the diner. She'd been working all day, so by the time he arrived at home they'd decided to eat out.

"Well, the prosecuting attorney will evaluate the evidence and decide if it's enough to indict. I'm still waiting on DNA from the crime lab and information from Hicks's prison stay, although that's a moot point now since Jackson confessed."

Jared handed Misty a menu and began perusing his own.

"So sad that things got to the point that David Jackson felt he had no choice but to do what he did. Has he made a statement yet?"

The waitress interrupted and Jared ordered a coffee for him and a hot chocolate for Misty. Their server moved to the next table quickly, the diner filled with patrons.

"He did when his attorney arrived. He says Hicks was harassing Lindsey about seeing Tilly and threatening Lindsey's life if she wasn't supportive of his petition for visitation. Things came to a head when he went to see Boyd at his house and tell him to leave Lindsey alone. Things got hairy and Boyd pulled a gun on Jackson but Jackson shot first, firing two bullets into Hicks's chest. Then he got scared and dumped the body in the Hawkins's pasture. He admitted that he'd worked there several years ago as a ranch hand and knew the layout well."

The harried waitress slapped down their drinks and pulled out an order pad. "Are you ready to order?"

"I'll have the pot roast with potatoes and carrots." Misty closed the menu and set it on the edge of the table. The waitress scrawled on her pad and looked at Jared.

"I'll have the pot roast as well," he decided. Since the night of their argument he'd stopped nagging her about vegetables and milk, which in turn made her want to be sure she ate her veggies and drank her milk. Chocolate milk. Hot or cold.

The waitress shoved her pencil in her pocket. "Pot roast for the sheriff and for Man Trap Misty. Coming right up."

The words were muttered under her breath but Misty easily heard them. She assumed she was meant to. Sucking in a shocked breath, her first instinct was to ignore the woman. Hadn't Annette Foster always said to turn the other cheek? But look where that had gotten her. A town that treated her like dirt and a man who for awhile only thought about his needs.

She'd stood up to Jared but it was time to stand up for herself. Especially if she was going to live in this town and raise her child.

"Pardon me?" Misty asked sharply before Jared could ride in on his white horse and come to her defense. "Did you mention my name? Is there a problem?"

Apparently the last thing the woman expected was to be called out about her rude behavior. She turned a bright red and her mouth fell open in surprise, no words coming out.

"Well?" Misty prompted. "Is there a problem with my order?"

"Um–" The waitress began but the manager interrupted. A kindly older man, Tim Siddell, had owned the diner for as long as Misty could remember.

"What's going on here?" he asked, looking back and forth between Jared, Misty, and the waitress. Jared started to stand but Misty grabbed his hand and shook her head. She needed to handle this herself.

"Hello, Mr. Siddell. I was just asking your waitress if there was a problem with my order."

"Is there, Ada?" he asked, his tone hard and uncompromising.

"No, sir." Ada shook her head vigorously. "I was just taking their order back to the kitchen."

"Then get to it," he replied with a chilly tone. "We're busy tonight and people are waiting."

The waitress dashed away and Mr. Siddell sighed as he watched her disappear into the kitchen. "Now that Ada is gone, what did she really do?"

Misty wasn't one to try and get people in trouble, especially as she'd made her point. She wasn't going to be anyone's doormat any longer. Period. Full stop.

Jared, however, had no such inhibitions. "Ada used an unflattering name for Misty. If it happens again we won't be coming back, Tim."

Misty patted Jared's hand soothingly. He was more upset than she was. "If it happens again I'll react exactly the same way, which is to call them on it. No need to make threats or promise a boycott. It's that simple."

Mr. Siddell's face split into a grin and he leaned down close to Misty. "Good for you. I always thought people were crappy to you for no reason. You tell them off once and for all." He straightened and looked grimly at Ada, who had returned and was now taking an order at a nearby table. "And I'll deal with Ada. I'll make it clear to her and anyone else who works for me that we respect our patrons. All of them. Thank you for your patience and tolerance, Miss Foster."

The manager strode away and Misty felt a little sorry for Ada. From the look on Tim Siddell's face she was about to get her rear end chewed.

"I agree with Tim," Jared said softly. "Good for you. I have to admit this side of you is kind of sexy."

Misty giggled and sipped her hot chocolate. "You think everything is sexy. Is that all you can think of?"

"When you're around? Pretty much. It's all your fault and I'm just a poor victim of your feminine wiles."

"I'm changing the subject. What were we talking about before Ada interrupted?"

"Murder," Jared responded promptly. "But I've told you pretty much everything. The only other issue is that now Jackson is in jail the state will probably postpone Lindsey Jackson's custody hearing for her daughter until after David Jackson's trial."

"That could be years," Misty exclaimed, her hand instinctively covering her stomach protectively. Heaven help anyone that wanted to try and take her child away from her. "So sad for Lindsey Jackson. She lost her daughter and now she's lost her husband."

"It's tragic," Jared agreed. "I hope she avails herself of some of the social services I discussed with her. She appears to be all alone in the world."

"I know what it's like to be alone and she'll be okay. I'm sure she's a strong woman after all she's been through," Misty observed.

"Speaking of strong women." Jared smiled and brought her fingertips to his lips. "Now that the Hicks case is pretty much buttoned up how about you and me taking the weekend and going to the cabin? Just you and me and a roaring fire. Clothing optional."

"Will there be chocolate too?" she asked with a giggle. Truly it sounded like heaven with or without the chocolate. With everything going on they didn't get enough alone time together. And when the baby arrived it would surely be in short supply.

"Chocolate, strawberries. You name it. Your wish is my command, pretty Misty. So what do you say?"

"I say yes. I can't wait to be alone with you. I may keep you naked all weekend," she teased, loving the naughty twinkle in his blue eyes.

Jared raised his coffee cup. "Here's to naked weekends and warm fires."

How lucky could a girl get?

✧ ✧ ✧ ✧

Jared wiped his boots on the welcome mat of the family home a few days later. The temperature had risen and it was a nice warm day.

"Hey, Dad. Are you here?"

"In the kitchen, son. I'm making myself a sandwich," Gerald called from the other room. Jared pulled off his jacket and dropped it on the back of a chair before joining his father.

"Want one?" Gerald held up a loaf of bread. "We've got some tasty shaved ham if you're hungry."

Jared was hungry but Misty had sent him a text that she was making roast chicken for dinner. "Misty's fixing dinner but I could go for a handful of those potato chips to tide me over."

Gerald chuckled and pushed the bag closer to Jared who settled on a bar stool at the kitchen island.

"What brings you here? Is Misty doing okay?"

Funny how now that Misty was pregnant everyone asked about her and no one gave a shit about him. He didn't mind; it was kind of funny really. It reminded him about what Ty had said.

It isn't all about you.

"Misty's fine. She's working on this amazing painting of the view from the front porch at sunrise. I'd never really looked at it before until I saw what she'd painted. It was like seeing it through new eyes." Jared popped a few chips into his mouth. "I came to tell you that Misty and I are going to the cabin this weekend. Ty says Royce has decided to stay a little extra at the rehab center so we won't miss him coming home."

Jared had spoken to Royce the week before and for the first in a long time, his brother had sounded sober and clean. Happy and looking forward to the future. Jared was damn proud of Royce and what he'd been through. Hopefully now he could be a real part of this family while their father could still remember things and participate.

"He came by at lunch and let me know that. Royce sounds good. Let's hope he can stay that way." Gerald added Swiss cheese on top of the ham and some mustard before slicing the sandwich in half. "Are you sure you don't want some of this?"

"I'm sure." Jared chuckled at the look of delight on his father's face. Lately he'd calmed down and was hardly ever angry. He also seemed to be enjoying the little things in life more than ever. Whether it was the medication or something else Jared didn't know, but it made the entire family more peaceful.

"Well, I hope you and Misty have fun at the cabin. It's good to get away for a few days. Are you planning to ask her to marry you while you're there?"

The perfect opening for the conversation they needed to have. Now Jared needed to scrape up his courage to talk to his father and possibly upset him.

So much for happy and calm in the Monroe household. It was good while it lasted.

"Dad, about that. The whole question of marriage is between me and Misty. It's nobody else's business."

No point in beating around the bush. Jared threw down the gauntlet.

His father set the sandwich down on the plate and frowned. "This is about an innocent child being brought into the world without married parents, son. This is also about a child being born into the Monroe family without our name. That is my business."

"No, it's not," Jared replied. "It's no one's business, actually. This is a private matter. As for what name this child will have Misty and I have already discussed it, and the last name will be Monroe whether she and I marry or not."

"This is about the Monroe family reputation. How will it look if you and Misty aren't married?"

That made Jared laugh. His father was grasping at straws. "The Monroe family reputation? Are you kidding? Our reputation doesn't hinge on whether a tiny little blonde marries me, Dad. Our reputation is about how we treat people. If we're honest and give a shit about our fellow man. That's what people care about. If they judge us for whether my child is born in wedlock or out, well, then they aren't the kind of people that I care to be around."

"What about me?" Gerald Monroe placed his hands on the kitchen island and leaned forward so his face was inches from Jared's. "Don't you care how I feel about this?"

Jared smiled and shook his head. He was truly free and he had Misty to thank for it.

"No, I don't." He held up his hand before his father had a chance to launch into a long lecture for his middle son. "I love you, Dad, but I'm done competing for your approval. You either love me the way I am or you don't. I'll be sad if you don't but I'll have my self-respect from being my own man. Would I like to marry Misty? You bet I would. I love her and I'm figuring out that she's the one for the rest of my life. But I am not going to manipulate her into saying yes so you're happy. You're going to have to decide to be happy or unhappy on your own because it's crazy to have it be dependent on whether you can get your children to give into your whims. Royce won't do it. Ty won't do it. Hell, Becky only did it for the money. I'm out of the Gerald Monroe pleasing business as well."

He could see he'd shocked his father. The man's brows pulled down and a muscle ticked in his jaw. "I've never made you compete for my approval, Jared Andrew. I've simply wanted you to do what's right."

Hearing his father was like listening to himself. It's what he'd always said to everyone. He just wanted the people around him to do what was right. But now he knew better.

Right by whom? There was more than one way to work, eat, play, and live a life.

"Actually you have," Jared said quietly, not wanting to upset his father any further. This wasn't about arguing or who was wrong or right. He wouldn't be pulled into a discussion like that. "You've done it our whole lives and we were doing it to the people we cared about. It's what we saw and knew. But I'm breaking the chain. I'm going to make a life with Misty and that means that her opinions count just as much as mine."

"You would put her before your family?" Gerald asked gruffly.

"She's carrying my baby. She is my family," he said simply. "She's my life."

There was a long silence and then his father picked up the sandwich again. "Well, that's fine. If that's what you've decided. I wasn't pushing you, you know. I was just giving my opinion."

Someone alert the local newspaper.

Gerald Monroe had given in to his middle son. He'd backed down and let something go. But they'd both won because Jared had set the tone for the future. Mutual respect. Just like Misty had at the diner a few days before.

In their own way they'd each had the same issue. It might be one of the reasons they felt drawn to each other.

They were stronger and better together than apart. He'd never been able to say that about any woman before but he could say it about Misty. Sweet, strong, beautiful Misty. Thank heavens she'd picked him up that cold night and given him a ride home.

Chapter Twenty-Three

Jared's cabin was adorable. Perched next to a small lake, the tiny log home sported only one bedroom, one bathroom, and a great room area with a roaring fireplace. It wasn't fancy but it would certainly do for the romantic weekend they both had planned.

While Misty explored the cabin Jared brought in their bags. "How about we go for a little walk by the lake?"

The temperature was in the sixties, sunny and mild, although it would be much cooler in the evening. It would be a pleasure to walk hand-in-hand with Jared or even just sit on the porch and rock. They rarely had time for just the two of them and she was really looking forward to this weekend.

"That sounds like a wonderful idea. But we should unpack the food first and put it away so that nothing gets spoiled."

Jared laughed and shook his head. "Always so practical. Let's get to it so we can get out and enjoy this day, or what's left of it."

Quickly she and Jared made short work of unpacking the groceries. "Leave a package of chicken in the refrigerator," Jared said. "I'll cook it on the grill for dinner tonight."

"I love barbecue chicken and I love the idea of you cooking it," Misty sighed. "I really am on vacation."

"You'll be in charge of everything else so don't relax too much," Jared warned with a chuckle. "But I am planning to make some of my famous barbecue sauce, so prepare to be amazed."

That explained the bottle of molasses in one of the bags plus all of the spices. Even though they'd stopped for lunch on the way, Misty's appetite was ready for what sounded like a wonderful meal.

"Ready?" he asked as he stowed the last of the food in the pantry and grabbed a blanket from the back of the sofa.

"What's that for?" Misty pointed to the blue and red quilt he'd tucked under his arm.

"In case we want to sit and enjoy the sunshine. I thought it would be nicer if you didn't have to sit on the ground."

They had been cooped up in the car for most of the morning and Misty was glad to be out in the clean, fresh air. She placed her hand into Jared's and let him lead her down the front porch steps and around the back of the house to the large lake. The sky was a soft blue with only a few fluffy clouds here and there. The sun glistened off the water and a warm breeze caressed her face. So much has happened in these last few weeks it felt good to just relax with the man she loved.

And she did love Jared Monroe. She could admit it now, at least to herself. Every day that thought became clearer in her mind and every day the emotion grew deeper in her heart and soul. Of course she hadn't told him yet. There simply hadn't been an opening, the right moment, to tell him all that she was feeling. She still wasn't sure that he felt the same, although when they were together like this she felt that he loved her.

But that nasty fear held her back. What if he only loved the baby? What if he only loved sleeping with her, making love to her? The thought of telling him her feelings and having them thrown back in her face, or the very least simply not returned was frightening.

But today she wasn't going to think about all the things that could go wrong.

"We could go for a walk or there's a rowboat we could take around the lake. It's up to you, honey."

"Do I have to row?" Misty teased. "I am the pregnant one here."

"Your slave will do all the work," Jared laughed. "But I may need a backrub later after all my efforts."

"I think I know exactly what you need. In fact it will be my pleasure to give it to you." Misty slid her arms around Jared's waist and pressed her cheek to his wide chest. She was learning to flirt for the first time in her life. And she definitely wanted to flirt with Jared today and let him know that she wanted this weekend to be the perfect romantic getaway.

Jared dropped a kiss on the top of her head and then nibbled his way down to her ear, gently biting the lobe. A shiver ran up her spine and her body flushed with heat. Misty wasn't sure she was going to be able to wait until tonight to make love to this most perfect man.

"Maybe we should take that boat ride later," she suggested. "I have a feeling we'll both be thinking about the same thing the entire time we're out on the water."

"Misty, are you suggesting that we forget about this beautiful sunny day and go inside and make love?"

She knew Jared wasn't upset. In fact, he had a gigantic grin on his face and his hand was tracing circles on her back. As usual their bodies were perfectly in tune.

"That's exactly what I'm suggesting," she replied boldly, running her hands up his arms and onto his shoulders. "What do you think? The lake will be here all weekend."

"I think we can have both." Jared waggled his eyebrows and walked down to the banks of the lake before taking the blanket from under his arm and shaking it out. He spread the blanket on the ground and held out his hand. "Your bed awaits, my princess."

Shyness made her look around as if they might be watched. "I'm not sure about this."

Jared settled on the quilt and beckoned to her. "I promise we are the only people for miles. The Monroe family owns all this property around here. Now what do you say? I'd love to make love to you at here in the sunshine."

"Isn't it a little chilly?" she asked but she was already moving forward to join him on the blanket. The ground was soft and springy and her arousal was beginning to hum at the mere idea of lovemaking…al fresco.

"I'll keep you warm," he assured her with a wicked smile.

"What about bugs?"

"They'll have to find somewhere else to have sex. This blanket is just for us." Jared grinned and tugged her into his arms so they were lying side by side. "Unless you were talking about the birds and the bees."

Her fingers went to the buttons on his shirt, plucking them open one by one. "My mother never had the birds and bees talk with me and I didn't have any friends that I could ask questions. I had to learn it by reading her *Cosmopolitan* magazines that she kept around the house."

Jared threw back his head and laughed. "My brothers and I used to sneak into my dad's office and read his *Penthouse*. We were probably in our mid-twenties before we realized the chances of having sex with a hot pizza delivery girl were slim and none."

The shirt slid off his tanned chest and she went to work on his belt buckle. "Common sense didn't tell you that? Never once has it occurred to me to have sex with anyone that delivered anything."

"A guy's gotta have hope. We were three horny teenage boys. With an emphasis on horny."

His jeans slid down his legs and he kicked them off along with his boots before reaching under her cotton sweater. His hard cock slapped against his belly and she reached out and ran her fingernails lightly up the sides, the skin like velvet over pure iron. He groaned in response and captured her lips for a long, drugging kiss. He tasted of the coffee he'd drank in the truck as they'd driven here, and although it wasn't a flavor she normally favored she couldn't get enough of it from Jared's lips. When he lifted his head he nibbled his way down her neck and shoulder.

"I don't think much has changed," Misty giggled as his fingers tickled her ribs. He tugged the sweater over her head and casually tossed it away. His fingers went to work on her jeans and before she knew it they were lying naked in the sun, his body partially covering hers. He had promised to keep her warm.

"When you're around I can't help it," he breathed against the skin of her throat. He kissed a trail down to one breast, fuller and more sensitive now than they were that first time together and gently laved at the nipple. Electricity rocketed to her pussy and clit and she shivered under his masterful touch. He ran his tongue down into the valley between her breasts before lapping at the other nipple until it was hard and erect.

Closing her eyes, she let her other senses come wonderfully alive. The fresh smell of the grass. The squawking of birds as they flew overhead. The feel of the sun and breeze on her bare skin. Making love outdoors made her feel decadent and free. Perhaps next time they could make love under a full moon and a sky full of stars.

"Jared," she whispered as arousal tightened in her belly. "Need you now."

"Soon." He licked her nipple and then blew on the wet tip, sending arrows of pleasure to her curled toes. Kissing and nibbling his way down her belly, he pushed her legs apart and traced patterns on her inner thigh with his tongue. The flesh was sticky with her honey and she moved restlessly as he teased her with his mouth, never quite giving her what she needed to go over.

His large hand pressed against her stomach, warm and reassuring as his lips nuzzled her belly button. He did this more and more these days, hoping to feel the baby move. It was still too soon but she couldn't wait for that day either.

His tongue was drawing lazy circles on her lower abdomen right above her clit. His mere touch fired off a round of sparks that made her entire body shudder and quake. She couldn't take his teasing any longer. She needed him now, fucking her deep and hard.

Reaching down she wrapped her fingers around his impressive cock. Stroking up and down she dragged a groan from his lips, his breath ragged and labored.

"You are a torturous witch," he chuckled under his breath. "Just for that I'm going to lie back here and relax while you do all the work."

Taking her with him, Jared rolled over onto his back. Distinctly uncomfortable, she braced her hands on his hips as she straddled his thighs. Always during their lovemaking he had taken the lead and been in charge. Now he was reclining back, a smile on his face as he waited for her to do…something.

"I don't know what to do," she admitted, hiding her face behind her long hair.

"Honey, I'm going to love everything you do. Just do what comes natural. It'll be okay."

Still unsure, she ran her palms up and down his torso, delighting in the feel of his skin, so different from her own. Hovering over him she lowered herself down onto his cock slowly, inch by inch, until she was seated in to the hilt. She hissed at the pleasure that bloomed inside as she experimentally swiveled her hips. Once. Twice. Three times.

"Holy hell," Jared muttered, a sheen of sweat on his forehead. His fists twisted the fabric of the quilt as she moved and swayed. Finding a sweet spot she bounced up and down, riding him fast and hard. Pleasure flowed through her, joyous in its intensity.

The coil of arousal in her belly tightened and then finally exploded as their bodies moved in synchronicity. Slamming herself down on him one more time, she screamed his name as she tumbled over the cliff. Her nails dug into his biceps as she gave her body over to her orgasm. Colored lights sparkled behind her lids even as Jared reached his own pinnacle.

When it was over, she lay on top of him exhausted and wrung out. The warm sun on her back and the smell of newly awakened grass mingled with the heavy musk of their lovemaking. Jared played with her hair, running his fingers through the long strands while the birds chirped.

"I hope you never cut your hair," he said after a long while. He'd wrapped them in the blanket so she wouldn't feel the chill, cuddling her close to his warm body. "It's so goddamn beautiful and it feels like silk."

"I don't remember the last time I got my hair cut. I like it long except for washing it. That's kind of a hassle so I only do it every other day."

"I promise to help," he vowed, his lips near her ear. "I know it's none of my business what you do to your own hair."

"Lots of women cut it after they have a baby," Misty conceded. "We'll see what happens."

Immediately his hand covered the slight swell of her belly. It wouldn't be long and she'd need new clothes again. Maternity clothes this time.

"I should probably get you inside," he said, pulling away reluctantly. "You and Junior need your rest and maybe a snack."

Misty giggled as he unwrapped them from the blanket and began to find their clothes piece by piece. "What are you going to do if Junior is a girl?"

Jared grinned and tossed her panties and bra toward her. "Spoil her. Just like I intend to spoil her mama."

It sounded like a first class plan.

Chapter Twenty-Four

The next morning Misty was making the bed while Jared fixed breakfast. They'd had a wonderful first day and night of their mini-vacation and she was feeling the need to tell Jared how she felt – that she loved him. Surely he couldn't look at her and make love to her the way he did if he didn't love her? She didn't know much about love and sex but every time she was with Jared it felt so right and perfect. He had to feel it too.

Tucking in the sheet, her hand came across something stuck under the mattress and she tugged it free. She frowned as she stared at what looked like a leather belt attached to the headboard at one end and a loop that fastened with velcro at the other. Crawling to the middle of the bed, she dug under the mattress and found another one just like it.

She stared at it for a long time and then almost smacked herself in the head with her hand when it finally dawned on her. These were for bondage. She'd read about it but of course had never experienced it herself. A cursory inspection of the bed revealed two more leather tethers, one at each corner of the foot of the bed. She also tried looking in the closet and dresser drawers, finding nothing. But strangely the bedside table drawer was locked tight. What did Jared have hidden in there? Men didn't lock up their underwear and socks.

Sitting on the bed, she inspected the leather straps closely. Jared had never mentioned wanting to tie her up or do anything all that kinky. Of course she'd been so inexperienced when they first went to bed together that it probably wasn't the moment to drag out the sex toys. She wasn't against the idea, but Jared was absolutely the only man in the universe she'd even contemplate this with. She wouldn't trust anyone else to tie her to a bed. Ever.

The idea did have its appeal. Helpless with Jared. All his attention focused on her. No decisions to make. Nothing to worry about.

Yep. The more she thought about it the better it sounded.

Her fingers ran over the butter soft leather. Wanting to experiment with Jared didn't make her a whore. It didn't make her easy or anything like her mother. It made her a woman in love that wanted to explore her sexuality with a man she trusted. That was all. There was nothing to be ashamed about. Millions of women probably did things like this all the time.

"Misty," Jared called from the kitchen. "Did you fall back asleep? Breakfast is ready."

"Coming," she yelled back, furiously tucking the leather straps back under the mattress and smoothing down the comforter. She'd never asked a man if he wanted to tie her up before so she wasn't quite sure how to bring this up to Jared.

The direct approach was usually the best but she still blushed at everything. Hopefully that habit would eventually cease, but as of now she was constantly hiding behind her hair and staring at her toes.

"Everything smells delicious." She reached for a plate but Jared shook his head and pulled out her chair. Sitting down, she spread her napkin in her lap while he set a full plate of food in front of her. The last few days had been wonderful with nary a moment of nausea morning, noon, or night. Her energy had also returned along with a healthy sexual appetite. Jared didn't seem to mind though and appeared to be thrilled that she was so enthusiastic about their physical relationship.

"Thank you. I made scrambled eggs, bacon, hashbrowns, and toast." Jared handed her a fork. "The hashbrowns have cheese in them."

Misty bit into a piece of bacon and hummed her appreciation. Everything was better with bacon. Jared didn't even give her a hard time about it as long as she didn't eat it every morning. In fact he was piling it a mile-high on his own plate.

"This is fantastic. You're quite a chef." Misty sipped her orange juice. "What do you want to do today?"

"Whatever you'd like to do. We could go for an easy hike after breakfast and then maybe have a quiet afternoon. The temperature is supposed to drop later in the day so we could build a fire and watch a movie. I don't have any chick flicks but I probably have a few that you might like."

"A hike sounds good. I've got my energy back." Misty quickly polished off the bacon and eggs and started in on the hashbrowns. "We've got that pot roast I can make for dinner."

"It sounds perfect." Jared yawned and stretched his arms over his head. "Damn, I needed this vacation. With everything going on with the Hicks case, Dad, and Royce it feels good to just relax and watch the world go by for a change."

"Don't forget dealing with a pregnant woman," Misty teased. "Moody, sick, and tired isn't a fun combination."

"I'd take you any day over Dad. He's never been a day at the beach and of course now he's even more difficult." Jared paused and wiped his mouth with the napkin. "I did have a talk with him, by the way. I told him whether or not you and I get married is none of his business and he needs to lay off."

Misty was sure that the conversation hadn't been easy for Jared but she was proud of him that he'd had it. His habit was to do whatever it took to make his father happy and gain his approval. Now he was doing the exact opposite.

Just as she was beginning to think that being married to Jared might be pretty wonderful.

"How did he take it?" she asked, finishing her last bite of toast. She'd cleaned her plate and once again marveled at her new pregnant appetite. Before the baby she'd grab a muffin or a toaster pastry before getting to work.

"He was shocked but then he backed off when he realized I was damn serious. I told him that you and the baby come first."

Jared said it with such conviction she had no doubt he was serious and if it came down to it, he would choose her and the baby before his father. The thought was more than overwhelming. It was the stars and the moon. He was committed to her whether they had a piece of paper between them or not. So why not add the piece of paper and make it truly official?

All he had to do was ask her again.

"That had to be difficult for him to hear. Was he upset?" She liked Gerald Monroe. He was only trying to do what he thought was right even if it was none of his business.

"Actually he gave in kind of easy." Jared saw the look on her face and laughed. "Yeah, I was shocked too which leads me to believe that was only the battle. He's saving up ammunition for the war. He always was a long game player if you know what I mean."

"He won't give up?"

"My father doesn't know the meaning of the word surrender. He's full speed ahead at all times."

Jared stood and began to clear the table while Misty ran suds in the sink for the dishes. "Even now?"

He sighed and stacked the plates on the counter next to the sink. "I don't know. His emotions have become erratic and unpredictable this last year. He might drop it forever or be loaded for bear the next time I see him. There's no way to know. But I'll make sure I'm prepared if he does bring it up again. This is between you and me."

She laid her hand on his arm and gave him her best encouraging smile. The situation with Jared's father was likely to only get worse and never improve. The medication had stabilized his condition but it wouldn't work forever. "I'll be here with you every step of the way."

Jared pulled her into his arms and she shrieked as her sudsy hands made contact with his t-shirt. He simply laughed and pulled her closer, not caring about being wet and soggy in the least.

"You and the baby are the best things in my life. I want you to know that."

"I feel the same. I'm really happy," Misty confessed, words of love on the tip of her tongue. But a rash of fear ran through her and she lost her nerve. There was still time this weekend to tell him of her love. Besides, if she were honest, she hoped he'd say it first. This morning he'd come so close. Closer than she'd ever imagined.

✧ ✧ ✧ ✧

Misty and Jared were lying in front of the fireplace later that day watching television. Misty had slid the roast into the oven and Jared had put on a movie. He was correct when he said he didn't have any chick flicks but he did have a great sense of humor and they settled in to watch *Beetlejuice* as the temperature outside dropped.

"More hot chocolate?" Jared asked, pausing the film and pointing to her mug. She nodded and he padded into the kitchen in bare feet to warm up more milk. "Are you sure you're okay watching this movie? It's one of my favorites."

"Mine too." Misty played with the fringe on the blanket they were lying on. Screwing up her courage, she sat up and took a deep breath. She'd been waiting for the right moment all day. "So I've been meaning to ask you…I found some leather straps attached to the bed when I was making it this morning. Is there anything you'd like to tell me about that?"

Jared froze, the spoon in his hand ceasing the circles it had been making in the cocoa mixture. "I'm not sure what you're talking about."

Misty stood up and walked over to where he was standing in front of the stove. "You need to turn the burner down if you're not going to stir that."

Muttering an expletive, Jared lowered the heat on the pan. "This will be done in a minute."

"So you're plan is to convince me I didn't see what I actually saw?" Misty queried. "Does that usually work for you?"

Jared sighed and let his head fall back so he was staring at the ceiling. "No. Shit, I don't want you to think I'm some sort of pervert or monster."

Misty took the spoon from his hand and stirred the cocoa before lifting it from the heat and pouring it into the two mugs on the counter. "I don't think either of those things but I do think you're avoiding my question. Obviously I'm not the first female you've brought up here."

"No. Does that make me a jerk? Do you hate me?"

He looked genuinely concerned that she was pissed off.

"Jared, what you did before you met me is something I really can't be angry about, now is it? I know you've dated more than your fair share of women and I assume you slept with most, if not all of them," she explained patiently. "From all appearances, you may have had kinky sex with some or many of those women. I'm going to assume not all of them were into bondage but I could be wrong. So long story short? No, I'm not mad. Are you ashamed of your sexual peccadilloes?"

She lifted both mugs and walked back in front of the fireplace, settling on the blanket. At first it didn't look like Jared was going to follow her but he finally did, sitting across from her. "I am not ashamed. I just don't want to scare you."

"I'm not a child that needs your protection from the outside world. I may have been sexually inexperienced but that does not mean that I'm naïve about what goes on between a man and a woman. I'm also very open-minded and I'm not scared." She blew gently on the steaming cocoa. "You know what's funny? I thought that I'd be the one all embarrassed and blushing, not able to talk about this. But you're the one that wants to squash the topic. If you don't want to talk about it that's fine. I'll drop the entire subject and never bring it up again."

"It's not that." Jared shook his head. "I think you've figured out that I like to be in charge. In control. Well, that extends to the bedroom. I like to be dominant in bed and through the years I've met women who prefer to be submissive when it comes to sex."

"So you tied them up?" she asked. "What else did you do? And does it have anything to do with the locked nightstand drawer?"

A streak of red appeared on each of Jared's cheekbones. "You have been a busy bee. Yes, there are some…what do they call them? Marital aids in that drawer. I locked them up because

I occasionally lend the cabin to a friend and they don't need to know anything about my personal life."

Misty took a drink of her hot chocolate to give herself more time to formulate her question. "But you were willing to marry me and not do any of this ever again? That sounds like quite a sacrifice."

Shrugging, Jared stretched out his long legs. "I never saw it that way."

"Were you ever going to suggest we use some of these *marital aids*?"

"Honestly? As innocent as you were when we first went to bed together, I figured the last thing you'd want to do is have kinky sex with me. So no, I was not planning to suggest we use them. Maybe someday way in the future I might have."

"When the sex got boring," Misty finished for him. He hadn't said it but it was right there hanging in the air between them.

Jared scowled and set his cup on the side table. "No. I was thinking about when you were more – I don't know – more open to experimentation. Shit, I'm not sure I like being interrogated like this."

He probably didn't like it at all but she wasn't done.

"Jared, I was inexperienced, not innocent. Two different things. If this is something you need that makes you happy sexually, it kind of bugs me that you were planning to keep it a secret."

"I don't need it," he argued, hopping to his feet. "I just like it."

"It? Can you be more specific? I really want to know what you're willing to give up for me. What is it that you enjoy so much? Tell me."

He smacked the back of an easy chair, his brows pulled down in frustration. He was pissed off at her for not dropping the whole thing but this was important. He was planning to shut off an important part of himself. It was a recipe for disaster if she let him. He'd grow to resent her eventually.

"You want to know what I like in the sack, Misty?" Jared's mouth was tight and a muscle ticked in his jaw. "I love tying a woman down and making her helpless for anything I want to do. I like denying her an orgasm until she begs. I like to spank naughty girls with my hand or a paddle until they beg me to fuck them. I like using nipple clamps and vibrators to drive a woman out of her mind with pleasure." He threw up his hands. "Are you happy now? Does any of this make you feel any better? It can only scare the shit out of you. Make you afraid of me. I never wanted that."

Misty slowly exhaled with relief. "I am happy. It wasn't near as kinky as I feared. From what I've heard from Rayne about sex you're actually pretty mainstream. I thought you might want a threesome or to tickle me with feathers." She frowned and shook her finger at him. "I do not like being tickled on my feet. Got that?"

Mouth hanging open, he swallowed hard, his Adam's apple bobbing in his throat. "I don't have any feathers. And I don't want anyone else. I only want you. Are you saying you're okay with this?"

Now it was her turn to blush. "I'm opening to experimenting with you. I trust you. I don't think you'd ever hurt me." She tilted her head. "You don't want to hurt me, do you?"

"Fuck no." Jared shook his head, a smile starting to bloom across his face. "Well, I'll be. You might want to try a few things?"

It was as she feared. He really did want this part of his life but he'd planned to try and bury it deep so she'd never know.

"Yes, but you have to promise me something."

"Anything. You name it."

"Never, ever try and keep a secret like this from me. This is obviously an important part of you. If we have any hope of a future together we have to be open and honest with one another."

"Can I be honest now?" he asked with a grin. His palm rubbed the fly of his jeans where the outline of his hard cock could be clearly seen. "Now that we've talked about sex, I'm really in the mood to do it. Can we go to bed?"

The movie and her hot chocolate were going to have to wait. She stood and walked toward the bedroom, giving him a shy smile over her shoulder.

Misty Foster was about to experiment. She was going to break out of her good girl mold once and for all. It was time to put the past firmly behind her and look to the future with the man of her dreams.

Chapter Twenty-Five

Misty slid naked under the covers as Jared shed the last of his clothes. Shaking with excitement, she tried not to show any trepidation in case he misinterpreted it as fear. The fact was she was nervous but not afraid. Jared was so protective of her on a day in and day out basis he'd never do anything that would harm her. Or the baby.

Jared joined her on the bed, taking his time to kiss and caress her body. His rough hands stroked and touched her breasts until the nipples were hard and tight. Moving restlessly, she lifted her hips in suggestion but he simply chuckled and shook his head.

"From this moment on I'm in charge. That means I decide what we do and when we do it. If you want an orgasm you have to earn it."

He'd given them freely up until now. "What do I have to do?"

"Obey," he replied promptly. "Do as you're told. Good girls get rewarded with pleasure. Naughty girls have to wait."

Misty smiled teasingly. "Then I definitely want to be a good girl."

Jared piled up some pillows against the headboard and then relaxed back on them, his hands folded behind his head and a smug smile on his face. "The first thing you need to do is get to work."

She didn't understand. "Work? Do you want me to wait on you or something? Bring you a drink?"

He pushed back the covers so his naked body could be seen. Damn, he was gorgeous, all muscle and tan skin. How did he manage to be that tan this time of year? It had to be natural. "I want you to get to work. On me. Make love to me. You can use your hands, lips, whatever." He waited but she didn't move. "Anytime now would be good."

It wasn't that she didn't want to. It was more that she didn't know what to do or where to start. Taking a page from his playbook, she straddled his body and tentatively pressed her lips to his. At first he let her do all the work, barely moving underneath her. Eventually he took control of the kiss leaving her breathless when it was done.

He still hadn't moved his hands from behind his head and he was clearly waiting for her to move on. She trailed baby kisses down his throat, over his collarbone, and down his chest. She paused, hovering over his flat male nipples, and wondered if his were as sensitive as her own.

There was only one way to find out. She swiped her tongue around the brown disc and felt him shudder, his breathing becoming more ragged. A surge of feminine power ran through her and she ran her tongue along his ridged abdomen before giving his cock a long lick from base to tip.

Shiny pre-cum smeared on his belly and she lapped at it experimentally. It tasted salty and a little sweet and she traced the slit on the head of his cock with her tongue to get every drop.

Jared's fingers tangled in her hair. "Aww fuck, honey. That feels so good."

Engulfing his cock in her mouth, she bobbed her head up and down, keeping her lips tight. She swept her tongue side to side and his hips lifted off of the mattress.

At some point he'd wrapped her long hair around his arm and his hand was anchored to the back of her head, pressing his cock deeper into her mouth. She sputtered and coughed a little when it touched the back of her throat and he paused, letting her get used to the feeling. Relaxing her jaw, she was able to take him farther, his dick heavy on her tongue.

"That's it, honey. You can take me. Yes," he hissed as her tongue fluttered over the sensitive spot on the underside of the head. His hand softly caressed her cheek and he tugged at her hair to get her attention. "Do you need to stop? We can if you want."

Misty knew what he was asking. If she didn't want to swallow she could pull off now. His balls were pulled tight to his body and his cock was pulsing in her mouth. Jared was close to coming and he was giving her a chance to gracefully exit this particular activity.

What was the old saying? In for a penny, in for a pound? Or was it something else? Either way, she'd started this and she was damn well going to finish it. Tonight was a night for trying new things so she might as well go big or go home.

Shaking her head, she redoubled her efforts. A string of curses fell from his lips, his back arched, and he dug his heels into the mattress. Hot seed jetted to the back of her throat and she had to swallow quickly to keep up. When he was done his muscles relaxed, and she laid her head on his belly and let him stroke her hair and back.

"You didn't have to do that," he said some minutes later as she crawled up his body to tuck her head into the crook between his shoulder and neck.

"I know. But I wanted to try it."

With a finger under her chin, he tilted her head so she was looking into his blue eyes. "And what was the result of your experiment? Never again or definite maybe?"

"Hmmmm…definite maybe. It wasn't unpleasant." Misty wasn't sure how to explain it. She didn't want him to think she hated it because that wasn't the case.

"It wasn't exactly birthday cake and ice cream?" he guessed. "Let me put it in different terms. You'd do it to please me but it does nothing for you?"

Laughter bubbled from her lips. Her man was so eloquent. And on the money too. "That sums it up. If you enjoy it I want to make you happy but yeah, I don't think I'd seek it out if you didn't."

"I can be fine with you never doing it again," he declared with a grin. "Now there are other things I'd like more. Much more."

He rolled her from her side to her back and grinned wickedly down at her. "Time to play, Misty. All you have to do is say no at any time and everything stops. Got it?"

She nodded, a knot growing in her throat. She'd said she wanted to try things and the night had only just begun. Jared lifted her arm above her head while he fished under the mattress for the leather ties. She had to swallow hard when the fur-lined cuff was wrapped around her wrist and buckled in place. He lifted her other arm and repeated the process before sitting back on his heels.

"Pull at them," he commanded, his gaze hot as he swept it down her naked form. She jerked at the tethers hard but they didn't budge. He put his hand out and shook his head. "Easy, honey. Even though these are lined you could bruise if you pull too hard."

Jared moved her hands so her fingers could wrap around the soft leather of the strap. "Put your hands here and if you need to you can pull. Nothing is going to budge that headboard. It's made from solid oak beams."

Her breath hitched in her chest as the fact that she was effectively helpless dawned on her. He could do just about anything he wanted to and she couldn't stop him. Instead of making her afraid, the idea ratcheted up her arousal into the stratosphere. Honey dripped down her thighs and her nipples tightened painfully under his scrutiny. This was more than she ever could have imagined and her fantasies were currently running wild.

What would he do next?

✧ ✧ ✧ ✧

Misty was laid out before him like the most delicious buffet of bare flesh he'd ever seen. A sexy decadent angel, her long golden hair was spilled around her like a halo. Despite the fact that he'd gotten off only minutes before, Jared had to rein in his arousal to keep from falling on her like a starving dog on a steak.

Jared's hands cupped her breasts, his thumbs brushing back and forth over the already hard nipples. She twisted underneath him, her lush lips parted as her breath came in pants.

"I can do whatever I please and there's nothing you can do about it," Jared intoned. It wasn't the truth of course. One word or even a frown and he'd have her out of those bonds in seconds. He hoped pointing out her predicament would amp up her arousal even further.

He ran a finger through her drenched folds and chuckled as his finger slid inside her pussy easily.

"I think you like being in bondage, honey." A finger brushed her clit and a moan was torn from her lips. "I think you like it a lot."

Jared should have known she was like no one else. Instead of denying it or acting coy, she nodded her agreement. "Yes. I like it. Are you going to do my legs? Or maybe spank me?"

She'd be the death of him and it was all his own fault. She'd been innocent – no, wait – inexperienced when he met her, all blushes and giggles. Now she was practically Mata Hari seducing him with a smile or a turn of her shoulder. But he sure as shit wouldn't complain. He had everything he'd ever wanted all wrapped up in this bundle of golden haired trouble. He'd never let her go.

"You will not get a spanking." He reached around and patted her bottom. "Not while you're pregnant. I'm sure it would be fine but I'm not taking any chances with you. As for your legs, not this time. I want you to wrap them around me while I'm fucking you. Can you do that for me?"

Misty nodded toward the nightstand. "And the drawer?"

There were several things in that drawer she would enjoy but one item took Jared's fancy. Misty's nipples were sensitive and she enjoyed having them played with.

"Maybe," he answered casually, not wanting to give away the surprise. "I have a couple of ideas but you have to be a good girl, remember?"

She scowled. "I am being a good girl."

"Good girls don't ask so many questions. Nor do they try and control things, which is what you're doing. Relax and trust me to take care of you. I promise you'll enjoy it so much more."

Her expression immediately softened. "I do trust you, Jared. More than anyone else in the world."

An arrow of pain shot through his heart at her softly spoken words. She had no idea how much they meant to him. He loved her. Adored her. Worshipped her. There was nothing he wouldn't do for her.

She was everything. And more than he deserved. So arrogant and full of himself, he hadn't been able to see how perfect she was that first night when she'd driven him home. It had taken him time to see they were made for each other. She didn't take any crap from him and kept his feet firmly on the ground.

Not able to speak at the moment, he instead turned back to his goal – making Misty scream with pleasure.

Reaching around to the back of the nightstand, he plucked the small key from its hidden hook and unlocked the drawer. Misty craned her neck to see but tied down as she was she didn't have a good angle. She would have to wait and see what he had in store for her.

Rummaging in the drawer, he pulled out a pair of tweezer-type nipple clamps with weighted beads hanging from the ends. They would tug nicely on the hard tips of her breasts every time she moved, heightening her pleasure.

Jared held up the clamps in front of Misty. "These are nipple clamps. I'm going to put them on you and leave them there for a little while. If you don't like them I'll take them off immediately." He grinned wickedly. "But I think you're going to love them, honestly."

Holding them closer for her examination, she nodded again. "You promise?"

"I promise," he vowed. "Just give yourself a minute to get used to it."

Bending his head, he drew first one nipple and then the other into his mouth, worrying them with his tongue and teeth until they were hard and tight. He placed the clamp on either side of the bud and tightened the clamp until he heard the swift intake of her breath.

Ratcheting the tension down slightly, he applied the other clamp and sat back with satisfaction. Her cheeks and chest were a rosy hue and her breathing was ragged. Her expression was one of indecision as if she wasn't sure she liked it or maybe she wasn't sure she was supposed to like it. He reached out and brushed the heavy beads so the clamps tugged at the nipple.

Misty moaned and twisted, her teeth sinking into her lower lip. "Jared," she whispered.

Reaching for the opposite breast, he held his hand only a few inches from the beads. He didn't touch them. He just held his fingers ready. Waiting.

"Please," Misty gasped. "Please, Jared."

So beautiful when she begged, he could refuse her nothing. He swept the beads to the side and she groaned even as her hips lifted. This wouldn't be the last time they used these clamps. He might buy a pair with purple beads to match her eyes.

✧ ✧ ✧ ✧

Misty was lost in a maelstrom of sensation. Some small part of her was saying she shouldn't enjoy the ache of the clamps on her sensitive nipples but she'd shouted that voice down. It felt too good to be wrong. Everything she did with Jared was good and perfect.

His callused fingers ran over every inch of her flesh, sending flashes of heat through her veins and lightning skimming across her skin. He parted her thighs, his thick digit pressing inside of her – first one and then two.

Hooking his fingers, he rubbed a sweet spot inside of her that made the room spin and her body quiver with arousal.

Trembling on the precipice, she cried out in abandonment when he pulled away.

"I want to be inside you when you come, Misty. I want to feel you fall apart all around me. I want to feel the way your sweet pussy hugs my cock when we fuck."

Three months ago those words would have embarrassed the hell out of her. Now they turned her on, sending her arousal soaring even higher and making her shiver in anticipation.

"Make love to me," she urged, tugging at the leather straps that kept her from touching his smooth golden skin. "Don't make me wait."

He didn't.

His large muscular body covering hers, he lifted her legs so they were wrapped around his waist. Tilting her hips to just the right angle, he plunged deep inside of her – in to the hilt in one stroke. He filled her totally and completely, pleasure bubbling through her like champagne.

Jared fucked her deep and hard – each stroke building the heat inside her that was threatening to detonate. With each thrust her breasts jiggled and the beads tugged, sending jolts of pleasure straight to her clit.

"Now, honey," Jared rasped into her ear as he thrust one last time. His fingers plucked one of the clamps off of her nipple and then the other. The bite of pain as the blood rushed back in sent her over the edge, her orgasm exploding inside of her like dynamite – hot and powerful. Jared's touch seared her skin as she shattered apart into a million tiny shards, glinting and dancing in front of her eyes.

Jared groaned his own release, his body tight and his jaw flexing. His eyes closed for a long moment and then her name fell from his lips as he sucked air into his lungs.

Fluttering down to earth, she luxuriated in his attention as he pressed open mouth kisses on her neck and shoulders. Finally he uncuffed her wrists and she wrapped her arms around him, her palms tracing the dips and planes of his muscles.

"So…I guess I like kinky," she said after they'd both laid there for a long time watching the shadows on the wall and the moon through the curtains. Misty didn't think she'd ever be shy or embarrassed again after tonight. If being open-minded meant the sex was that amazing she needed to do it more often.

Jared chuckled and turned so she could tuck her head onto his shoulder. "I guess you do. There are lots of things we can explore together. All you have to do is say the word. Whatever you want."

"What if I want that spanking? I think I might like it." She was ready to admit that pain heightened pleasure for her and a spanking sounded…naughty and decadent all at the same time.

"Not while you're pregnant. You'll have to pick something else. Not that I'm not dying to spank that cute little bottom because believe me, I am. I just won't be doing it for awhile. Tomorrow morning I'll let you go through the nightstand drawer. Maybe you'll find something you want to try in there."

"I want to try everything." She traced a line with her fingertip from his shoulder down to his hand.

"Easy, honey. I'm pushing forty. Let's take it one night at a time, okay?"

They had all the time in the world.

Chapter Twenty-Six

Jared dropped their bags in the bedroom. It was the last load from unpacking the truck. The weekend in the cabin had been everything he'd wanted it to be. He felt closer to Misty than ever before.

But.

He'd totally wimped out and not told her how he felt. Deep in his heart he believed she felt the same way he did. Of course she hadn't said anything about love either but wasn't he supposed to man up and be the first to say it?

What was the worst thing that could happen?

Images of Misty refusing him raced through his mind and he shook his head to chase them away. This was no time be a pussy, as his friend Logan would say all the time. If she didn't love him after what they'd shared this weekend then she never would.

Filled with purpose and determination, he stomped into the kitchen where she was unpacking the cooler.

"Misty," he began. "Things are different between us now than they were in the beginning. I think we're closer. Hell, I know we are. More intimate. We know each other better and we seem to fit together. And I don't mean sexually. I mean our lives. Do you know what I mean?"

Jesus, he was rambling. He needed to fucking pull himself together here. She shut the refrigerator door and took her time answering, confusion written across her delicate features.

"I'm not sure I do, actually."

She'd thrown the ball back into his court. "I mean we're a good couple, don't you think? We make each other happy. At least I know I am."

Her lips curved into a smile and her shoulders seemed to relax. "I am too. Very happy. In fact I don't think I've ever been this happy."

"So we're good together," he persisted. "We mesh. Blend. That sort of thing."

"Yes, I think we do," she replied, her hands gripping the counter. "But I'm not sure where you're going with this."

Jared wanted to cut through all this bullshit. He either believed in the two of them or he didn't. He loved Misty and by God, she was going to love him. If not today, then someday. He'd do whatever needed to be done to make that happen in his lifetime.

Throwing caution and good sense to the wind for the second time since meeting her, Jared dropped to one knee and grabbed her hands in his.

"Dammit, Misty. I love you. I doubt I've done a very good job of hiding it so I assume you know. I love you and I want us to spend our lives together. And it's not just because of the baby, although that's a bonus as far as I'm concerned. I'd be happy with just you. You said you wanted the man you married to love you. Well, I do. More than I can even express in words. So will you put me out of my misery and marry me, woman? I don't think I can rest until you do."

Tears were running down Misty's cheeks and Jared didn't know if that was good or bad. It was only when she cried out his name and fell to her knees, wrapping her arms around him and whispering "Yes" over and over that he realized she was doing that happy crying thing that women were known to do.

He pulled her closer and captured her lips in a kiss that he hoped said everything he didn't have the words for.

How she'd changed his life and made him a better man.

How he couldn't wait to be a husband and father.

How he'd love her for the rest of his life and beyond.

"I love you too." The words came out choked with emotion but he could see the happiness shining in her violet eyes. "I love you so much and I wasn't sure if you loved me too. I couldn't be sure. I thought you might though."

"I damn well do. You're going to marry me, right? I won't let you out of the house until you say yes."

Misty giggled and pressed a kiss to his jaw. "I've already said yes but I'll say it again. Yes. Yes, I'll marry you."

"I want you to have the wedding of your dreams. White dress. Big fancy cake. The whole nine yards. I want to put on a wedding this town will talk about for years."

"I don't need it." Misty was shaking her head but Jared was adamant.

"We're not going to run off like we're ashamed, honey. We're going to stand up tall and proud and proclaim our love and commitment. And I sure as hell want everyone in Fielding to know that I'm in love with Misty Foster and plan to spend the rest of my life with her." Jared tilted her chin up so she was looking him in the eye. "You do need this. You need to exorcise any remaining ghosts."

"You're being bossy again." Misty didn't look like she minded though. In fact, she was looking at him like he was sliced bread or fried chicken.

"I am," he agreed because—well, he was. "But you know when to put me in my place. You're the first woman who has ever been able to, you know. It's one of the reasons I love you."

She was chewing on her lip in thought. "I'll think about the wedding. We don't have to make the decision today."

"We need to tell Dad and the family. Maybe we can schedule lunch with everyone tomorrow and tell them the good news."

"Can Rayne come too?" Misty asked eagerly. "I don't want her to hear from someone else."

"Of course. She's going to be family. Maybe we can fix her up with Royce," he teased.

"I'm not sure we're in any position to match-make," Misty warned with a laugh. "Besides, Rayne is very picky about men. I think she might be single forever."

"We'll inspire her with our happiness." Jared stood and swept Misty up into his arms. "I think there's a bed calling our names."

"You're insatiable but I like that about you." Misty ran her fingers through his hair and gave him a brilliant smile. His heart ached in his chest at the thought that he'd be seeing that smile every day for the rest of his life. Damn, he was one lucky son of a bitch.

"Your engagement ring is in the bureau in the bedroom too," he revealed. He couldn't wait to see her face when he slid the platinum and diamond ring on her dainty finger.

"I don't need a ring. I only need you."

"Lucky for you you're getting both."

Jared was getting everything he'd ever hoped for. It was turning out better than he'd ever dreamed.

✧ ✧ ✧ ✧

"Ty and Royce are going to meet us at the diner," Jared said to Misty and his father after she parked her economy car along the main road in Fielding. He made a mental note that they needed to replace that vehicle as soon as possible. With everything going on he'd overlooked how old and unreliable it was. He didn't want her driving around in a car that wasn't completely safe.

Gerald Monroe slapped Jared on the back and grinned. "Damn, it's a gorgeous day. I think the warm weather is here to stay."

It was beautiful, warm and sunny. After a long, cold winter everyone was anxious to shed their coats and gloves and enjoy the good weather. Gerald did most of all, as he'd been stuck in the house the last week with a head cold.

"I think it might be, Dad, although we're supposed to get another cool snap by the weekend."

"I don't mind cool," Gerald chuckled, rubbing his arms. "It's the cold that gets into my bones. Getting old is hell."

Misty linked her arm through his. "Don't even go there. You're still a handsome man. I know where Jared gets his looks."

Misty had Gerald Monroe wrapped around her little finger. He beamed at the compliment and patted her hand. "My Rita would have loved you. You have her same spirit."

Jared cleared his throat of the lump that had formed at the mention of his mother. It was times like today that he missed her most. And yes, she would have adored Misty.

"Are you two done with the mutual admiration society? We need to grab a table at the diner. It's always busy this time of day."

Gerald winked at Misty. "I think he's jealous."

"I think you're right," Misty said as they followed Jared down the block and into the restaurant.

It was busy this time of day but Ty was already sitting at a table he'd commandeered, sipping an iced tea and chatting with the diners next to him. That was Ty all over. He was friends with pretty much every human being, dog, cat, and maybe even cow in the entire county.

"Where's Royce?" Jared asked as they sat down, Misty next to Jared and his father on her other side while Ty sat across the table.

"He's not going to be able to make it." Ty signaled the waitress. "He had to meet with that counselor and the only time she was free was now. The rehab place recommended he see someone for the first year after getting sober."

Jared felt a stab of disappointment that Royce wouldn't be joining them but also pride that his brother had finally grown up and taken control of his life. Since being back Royce was like a new man. Or maybe like his old self. Either way it was damn good to see.

"Rayne's not here yet?" Misty frowned, looking around. "I hope she's not stuck at the shop."

There was no way Misty would want to make their announcement about being engaged without Rayne there. As it was Misty had shoved her left hand in her pocket so no one would see the sparkly new ring on her finger.

Misty checked her phone, her frown growing deeper. "She's not answering my texts either. I'm going to run down there and see if she's stuck with a customer. I won't be long."

Jared stood at the same time as Misty. "I'll go with you."

Misty rolled her eyes in that manner that told him he was being bossy and controlling again. "I think I can manage to walk two blocks there and back without something bad happening to me. You stay here with your family. I'll text you if Rayne is stuck with a client."

They were going to be her family too as soon as he could convince her to schedule the wedding, but she was right. The tattoo shop was only a couple of blocks away and she'd be fine. He was worrying too much again. Misty was the picture of health these days. It was true what they said about a pregnancy glow.

Jared dropped back into the chair. "Fine. We'll order drinks. What do you and Rayne want?"

Misty gave him their order before exiting the diner, her pale gold hair shining in the midday sun. She was wearing her new clothes today, her belly just a slight curve under the loose crimson blouse but Jared knew it was there. He'd run his hand over it this morning as they'd lounged in bed an extra ten minutes after the alarm had gone off.

"Damn, you got it bad," Ty drawled. "Never thought I'd see the day the great Jared Monroe would be felled by ordinary love."

His and Misty's love was anything but ordinary.

"I wouldn't call myself great but you can if you want to," Jared laughed. "And if you're asking if Misty and I are happy the answer is yes. Were you rooting against us?"

Ty held up his hands in surrender. "Not at all, but things weren't looking too good last time I saw you both together."

"Things have changed," Jared said softly. No one but he and Misty truly understood how much each of them had changed since the day they'd met. She had embraced her sensual nature and was no longer ashamed of her desires. He'd been more cognizant of trying to push her – and everyone else – to bend to his will. He'd caught himself several times and when he hadn't? She had let him know, no longer silent on the issue.

Things between them had never been better.

Chapter Twenty-Seven

Misty breezed into Rayne's tattoo shop and found an empty front room. Shaking her head, she went through the curtain that separated the back office area. Rayne must have lost track of time working on some paperwork. She always had tons of it stacked up on the rickety old desk shoved in the corner of the back room.

"C'mon, girl. You're late." Misty laughed as she spied Rayne sitting at the desk chair. "Are you ready to go?"

Rayne looked at her watch and groaned. "Shit. I lost all track of time. Dammit, you should have called."

Misty giggled and pointed to Rayne's phone sitting on the desk. "I did. Is your phone dead again? You always forget to plug it in."

Rayne checked her phone and then tossed it back down in disgust. "Deader than a doornail. And yes, I forgot to plug it in. Again. I've been so busy lately I'd forget my head if it wasn't attached."

"Business is good. That's nothing to complain about."

"I'm not complaining, just observing." Rayne reached for her purse hung on a hook. "It will be nice to get outside. I opened the front and back doors but it's not the same."

Midday sunshine streamed through the open back door giving the drab gray workroom a more cheery appeal.

"Let me lock the front of the store and post the *Closed* sign and we can go out the back." Rayne left her purse on the desk and headed to the front through the curtain.

Misty walked around the room admiring the photos on the wall of designs Rayne had created. She was incredibly talented with a special flair for capturing the essence of each client.

A thud from the front room caught Misty's attention. It sounded as if Rayne had dropped something heavy.

"Rayne," Misty called, heading toward the curtained opening and her friend. "Do you need some help?"

After only a few steps, the curtain lifted and a woman with a gun walked into the back room. Misty's heart skipped a beat and her breath caught in her throat. Somebody was robbing Rayne's tattoo shop. And where was Rayne?

"Have a seat, Miss Foster," the unknown woman invited, her dark hair in disarray and her cheeks red. "You and your friend won't be going anywhere."

"How do you know who I am? And where is Rayne?"

"Rayne is fine. As for me? I'll be happy to tell you." The woman waved her gun toward a chair. "But first...have a seat and stay there. No heroics or I'll have to pull the trigger and that would ruin everything."

On shaking legs Misty dropped down into the chair, her gaze darting around the room looking for something – anything – she could use as a weapon or perhaps another exit she'd never noticed. Of course there wasn't one and there were several objects that she might throw, but nothing that was going to neutralize a woman with a gun. The back door, however, was still wide open and if Misty could distract the woman perhaps she could make a run for it.

A protective hand instinctually pressed against her abdomen and the stranger noticed the action. "Worried about your baby? I know what that feels like. I'm a mother too. I have a daughter. At least I did."

"You're a mother? Then why are you doing this? If you need money there has to be a better way than robbing someone."

Perhaps reasoning with the woman might work. Misty didn't have any other options. She needed to talk this woman out of robbing the shop and she needed to make sure Rayne was okay. Misty strained to hear a sound from the front of the shop but it was silent.

"I'm not robbing anyone." The woman sat down in a chair opposite Misty and pointed the gun with both hands. "Your money is quite safe actually. I've come to see you. But first let's get comfortable."

The woman reached into her handbag but this time she pulled out a pair of handcuffs. "Cuff your wrist to that pipe on the wall. Do it," she commanded, tossing the cuffs to Misty and pointing to an old metal pipe about two inches in circumference.

Keeping one eye on the woman, Misty wrapped the cold metal around her wrist, the lock clicking into place. It only took an extra second to lock the cuff around the pipe and she was essentially a prisoner and helpless. So much for making a run for the open door.

Her knees practically knocking together and her skin damp under her arms, Misty faced the woman head on trying not to show any fear.

"Relax," the woman urged, pointing the gun straight at Misty. "We're just going to chat for a few minutes."

"What do you want with me?" Misty demanded. "I don't even know you."

"That's a good question." The woman set her purse down on a table covered with supplies, knocking bottles and boxes onto the floor, her hands trembling. "You haven't figured out who I am have you?"

Misty shook her head, fear making it hard to think. She took in the woman's appearance but it didn't ring any bells of remembrance. The woman was average height with a slim build. Wearing khaki pants with a white blouse, she could have been any number of wives or mothers that inhabited Fielding. Except that this woman was visibly shaking, flushed and sweating. "Should I have? Have we met?"

"We've never met," the woman conceded, her voice hoarse and tortured. "But I know your boyfriend, Sheriff Monroe. I know him well as a matter of fact. And I've come to know quite a bit about you. It seems this town loves to talk about you. I found it all very interesting."

Misty winced at the thought of what might have been said. But the part of knowing Jared stuck out in her mind. "You know Jared? How do you know him?"

If this woman was going to pull some "I've been sleeping with your man and he really loves me" crap, she could forget it. Misty wouldn't buy that for a moment. Especially after the weekend she and Jared had shared. She'd trust him no matter what.

The woman leaned back in her chair, anguish written in every line of her face and the gun still pointed at Misty's heart. "Do you have any idea what I've been through? Jared Monroe has cost me everything I've ever loved. That's why I'm going to take everything he loves from him. Namely you and that baby."

A chill ran up Misty's spine at the cold words, spoken in a tone full of hate, spite, and despair. What this woman didn't realize was that Misty wasn't going to let anything happen to her baby without a fight.

"Who are you?" Misty whispered, her heart clenching in her chest making it hard to breathe. "What are you going to do to me?"

The woman placed the gun on the table and reached into her purse again, pulling out a large mason jar filled with a golden colored liquid and a rag coming out of the top. Misty tugged at the metal cuff wrapped around her wrist but it was tightly locked and wouldn't budge.

The woman picked up the gun. "My name is Lindsey Hicks Jackson. And I already told you what I'm going to do. I'm going to take from Jared Monroe what he took from me. He took everything I loved. He owes me and he's going to pay up. I'm going to set fire to this building and you're going to die in it."

The ex-wife of Boyd Hicks.

Sweat was running down Misty's back and she could hear the blood rushing in her ears. She didn't want to die. She had too much to live for. "You're crazy. None of what happened to you is Jared's fault. He was just doing his job."

"His job?" The gun jerked in Lindsey's hand and Misty stopped breathing for a moment. "His job is to protect people. Where was he when Boyd got me hooked on drugs? Thank God Dale was there to help me. We worked together and got Boyd sent away for a long time. Dale was my lifeline. But then Dale got sent away too and I had nobody to take care of me. And then I lost Tilly. But I met Dave and everything started to be better. I thought everything was going to be okay but then Boyd was let out of jail and Dale told Boyd everything."

"Everything? What did Dale tell your husband?" Misty tried to keep Lindsey talking no matter what. Stall.

"Dale told Boyd about him and me. Boyd was pissed off and he threatened me if I didn't support him seeing Tilly. He threatened to tell the judge about Dale and me."

Lindsey had been having an affair with her husband's brother. It was like a soap opera except that Misty was trapped in it and it was all too real.

"So you killed Boyd? I'm sure you didn't mean to."

"He would have killed me." Lindsey stood and began to pace the room, waving the gun around. "I had no choice. I shot him and then called Dale but he didn't answer. Then I called Dave and he came to help me."

The woman's expression crumpled and tears rolled down her cheeks. "Dave's the only man that has ever truly loved me. When I finally did get through to Dale he just laughed at me. Said I was a great piece of ass and that was it. He just used me for revenge on Boyd. He hated Boyd and tricked me into killing him. Even gave me a gun for protection. For *protection*, he said. He knew I'd end up using it. I fell for it and now everything is falling apart."

Lindsey was also falling to pieces in front of Misty. It was the one glimmer of hope in this dire situation. Keep Lindsey talking until she completely fell apart or Jared came.

"Jared can help you," Misty said urgently. "It sounds like it was self-defense. They won't put you in jail for that and you'll still get your daughter. Nothing has gone too far yet. Jared can help you."

Lindsey stopped and whirled around to face Misty, her eyes wild and her skin pale.

"Where was he when Boyd was threatening me so he could see Tilly? Nowhere. Dave had to take care of Boyd because Jared Monroe wasn't doing his job. Now that Dave's in jail, they've postponed the custody hearing for Tilly. But I know what that really means. It means they're never giving my baby back to me."

Lindsey's voice had gone up several decibels and the words came out in choked sobs. Lindsey's lips trembled while her hand holding the gun shook. Wanting to calm the woman, Misty spoke in a soothing tone.

"A postponement doesn't mean you won't get her back. I'm sure once they see you've changed you'll get your daughter."

Lindsey's features twisted into something ugly, the humanity stripped from her expression. "It's too late for that now. I've lost everything I've ever cared about. Tilly. Dave. Dale. Boyd. Someone has to pay. Jared Monroe doesn't deserve to live happily with you and that baby when he's the reason all these bad things have happened to me. He deserves to suffer. I hope he burns in hell."

Before Misty had a chance to make sense of the woman's words Lindsey Jackson pulled a lighter from the bag and lit the rag hanging out of the mason jar and then tossed it against the wall. The glass shattered, the sound loud in the eerie silence, the liquid a huge blot and dripping down on the flammable paper below it. Orange and yellow flames jumped and danced while the pungent odor of gasoline filled Misty's nostrils.

The strong instinct to survive kicked in and the world seemed to come into sharp focus. She could hear every little breath Lindsey took and see the sweat beaded on her upper lip and forehead. The woman's eyes had gone cold and lifeless, almost like black marbles. Misty's mind ran through scenario after scenario of possible ways to escape and they all ended the same way. Her and Rayne dead in a burned out building.

"Don't do this, Lindsey. I'm pregnant. I'm a mother just like you. I don't think you're the type of person that would kill an innocent child. You're better than that." Misty's voice was filled with desperation that she couldn't hide even as she tugged at her wrist, a futile effort. The flames weren't large at this point but they would grow bigger. The horror of a death by fire was something she couldn't even comprehend. That one human was capable of committing such a grisly act on another was beyond Misty's understanding of the world.

"Maybe once I was better than this. But now I just can't go on anymore and pretend things will get better. They'll only get worse." Lindsey dropped her purse on the floor and pulled a syringe from its depths. "I'm tired. Of everything. This will soon be all over."

With that she wrapped an elastic band around her upper arm and then while Misty watched in horror, Lindsey shot the syringe full of liquid in her veins. She groaned and closed her eyes, her lips turning up slightly at the corners as if savoring the feeling.

"You'll pass out from the smoke before the flames get you."

The words were slurred as Lindsey stumbled to her feet, swaying and unsteady. Her purse dangling from her fingers, she stumbled to the back door, slamming it shut behind her.

The growing yellow and orange flames jumped along the back wall and the smoke was growing thicker.

In desperation Misty frantically pulled open the drawers of the desk next to her looking for something – anything – that would get her out of these cuffs. She wasn't going to die in the building. It was up to her to save herself and her baby.

Her fingers closed tightly around a paperweight, a heavy polished rock Rayne had brought back from one of her many adventures. Misty lifted it high into the air and brought it down on the lock of the cuffs with all the strength she possessed.

She'd batter at the lock until it gave way.

✧ ✧ ✧ ✧

It was a glass of iced tea later when Jared impatiently looked at his watch. Rayne and Misty should have been back a long time ago. She hadn't sent him a text that they'd be awhile so he couldn't think what would be keeping them. He pulled his phone from his pocket and punched a few buttons. Misty's phone rang and rang but only her voicemail picked up.

"That's odd." Jared set the phone on the table in case Misty called him right back.

"What's odd?" Ty replied, pulling his attention from a story their dad was telling them. "Is something wrong? You don't look happy."

"Misty should have been back by now." Jared held up his phone. "And she's not answering her cell. That's not like her."

Ty laughed and shook his head. "She's fine. Man, you worry too much. She and Rayne are probably planning a baby shower or something. It's a man's job to wait for a woman."

Jared had to concede that when Misty and Rayne were together they could talk and lose track of time. If Rayne noticed the engagement ring on Misty's hand they might be starting on the wedding plans right now. And isn't that exactly what Jared wanted? Misty was always telling him he needed to learn patience and there was no time like the present.

Or he could simply take the tongue lashing she'd give him about worrying too much and go down the block and see what was holding them up.

Jared stood pushing back his chair. "I'm going to see what's keeping them. I'll be right back."

"Me too. It's a great day for a walk," Gerald Monroe replied, slapping down his glass on the table.

"It's only two blocks," Jared protested as Ty looked on with amusement. His younger brother obviously had a feeling something was going on and it was more than a simple family lunch.

His father rubbed his upper arm and smiled. "I've been thinking about getting a tattoo. Something to symbolize my life. I've been wanting to talk to Rayne about it. She and I can discuss it on the way back."

His father was thinking about getting a tattoo? What next…a pierced tongue? The staid, serious family patriarch had been acting strangely lately with all the smiling and joking around he'd been doing.

Ty waved them away with a grin. "I'll hold down the fort. Just get back here quick. I'm starving. I'm likely to go ahead and order for all of you and eat every bite."

Typical Ty boast. Jared's brother loved the trash talk more than any of the Monroe boys. "We'll be back in ten minutes tops. Hopefully we'll meet them coming here on our way there."

Back out in the sunshine Jared breathed deeply, enjoying the warm temperature. It had to be a good omen that the day had dawned so beautifully when he and Misty planned to tell their momentous news. He and his father walked down the sidewalk, their long strides eating up the distance quickly. Misty and Rayne were nowhere in sight which gave Jared an unsettled feeling in his stomach. He liked things to run predictably, like clockwork, and when they didn't…? It made him uneasy. Misty could help him change some things about himself but certain traits in him were so ingrained they weren't budging.

"The *Closed* sign is out," Gerald pointed to the large window. "Maybe they already left."

If that were true they would have run into Misty and Rayne on the way here. Jared walked up close to the window and peered inside. The glare of the sun made it difficult to see but he was able to make out Rayne's form slumped on the floor, apparently unconscious.

Jared's heart accelerated and he had to force himself to take a breath as fear coiled in his belly. He couldn't see Misty and he needed to get inside. Now.

He slapped his phone against his father's chest. "Call my deputy Knox and tell him to get to the tattoo shop. I'm going inside."

"I'll be right behind you after I make the call." Gerald Monroe took the phone, his lighthearted expression wiped away. His features were now a tense mask of worry and fear.

"No, you stay out here. I don't want to have to worry about your safety too. There could be someone still in there."

Jared unholstered his service weapon and tried to pull open the front door but it wouldn't budge. With a curse he looked around for something to break the glass.

Gerald was hanging up the phone and pointing to an old truck parked at the curb. "Old Larry always keeps tools in the back. I'm sure he won't mind borrowing for a good cause."

Jared didn't give a shit if Old Larry minded or not. If he was upset Jared would buy the man a dozen new tools. Reaching into the back of the truck Jared pulled out a large sledgehammer.

"Step back, Dad."

A quick appraisal told him that breaking the glass in the door would be safer for Rayne who was slumped in the opposite corner of the shop against a worktable. Jared pulled his hat down low to protect his eyes before swinging the hammer and shattering the glass in the door, shards flying in every direction.

Reaching in the large hole he'd created, he was able to easily reach the lock and flip it open. As soon as he was inside the acrid aroma of gasoline and smoke assailed his nostrils sending his adrenaline into overdrive. His gaze darted around the room but Misty was nowhere to be found. He knelt down beside

Rayne to check her pulse, noting with relief it was good and strong.

"I've got her, son. You go find Misty."

Gerald shouldered his middle son aside and Jared didn't argue. He headed straight for the back room and what appeared to be the source of the smoke. His gaze went first to the leaping flames on the back wall that had eaten into several shelving units but hadn't spread any farther. Yet.

The room was filled with a haze of smoke that made it difficult to see but he could hear coughing in the distance and he prayed it was Misty.

"Misty," he called, praying she could hear him, that she would respond.

"I'm here." He saw something wave through the smoke and bolted straight for her, his heart in his throat. Coughing and choking, he dropped to his knees beside her, his fingers automatically going to the pulse in her neck.

"Rayne?" she asked, the words choked.

"Rayne is fine and with my dad. I'm more worried about you."

"I'm okay but my wrist is cuffed to the pipe on the wall. I've been trying to break the lock with this." She held up a large smooth rock. "So far…no go. I was getting ready to try using the letter opener as a file."

Sirens sounded in the distance and Jared heard the shuffle of boots in the front room. The cavalry had arrived but he was closest to Misty.

"I've got you, honey. I'm going to get you out of here." The words came out so gravelly and constricted he wasn't sure she would understand but she must have as she pressed close to him.

"Lindsey made me cuff myself to the pipe."

Lindsey?

"Lindsey Jackson?"

"Yes, she said you took her husbands and child away from her so she was going to do the same to you."

Lindsey Jackson needed psychiatric help along with a cell next to her husband. Acid born out of anger churned in Jared's stomach. The woman would pay for what she'd done today.

"We've got Rayne out of the building," a voice that sounded an awful lot like Knox rang out. "What do you need, boss?"

"She's cuffed to the pipe." Jared yelled back. "I'm going to try and use my keys but get a saw or an ax just in case."

"On it," the voice replied and Jared heard the clomping of boots in the distance.

Jared cupped Misty's jaw. "Stay with me here. I've got cuff keys in my pocket. I'm going to try those." It felt like knives being thrust into his chest every time he tried to take a breath but he focused solely on freeing Misty from the ever-growing flames that were encroaching, now so close he could feel the heat on his back as the sweat poured off of him.

He fumbled in his back pocket, the darkness making it difficult but not impossible as he pulled the key loose triumphantly.

"I've got it, baby. Hang in there for me."

"I'm scared, Jared. I tried to keep her talking until you came but she left." Her voice shook with fear and it made him want to pull the goddamn pipe from the wall with his bare hands and scream in frustration. But he couldn't give in to any of that. She needed him to keep calm and level-headed so they could both get out alive. She'd counted on him to save her and he couldn't let her down now that he was so close.

"You did real good, honey. Real good. I'm here now and we're going to get you out. Stay still for me."

It took several tries before he found the keyhole but it finally slid in and turned just as he'd hoped, the cuff coming loose.

"Got it." Misty's arms went around him immediately, holding him with a death grip as if afraid he'd disappear. He wrapped his own around her, pulling her close with a sense of relief. Now that she was free he just needed to get her out.

"Sheriff, I've got the ax." Jared couldn't see Knox through the smoke.

"She's free. Let's get her out of here. Lindsey Jackson did this."

"Let's get both of you out of here," another voice said. Someone – perhaps the person who just spoke – pressed an oxygen make over his face and he fought it, wanting it to go to Misty. The baby.

"She's got one too, Sheriff. You're both going to be okay."

Jared refused to let go of Misty even as the fireman helped them both to their feet and escorted them through the building. The fire had grown and now encompassed a full half of the back room.

Jared clutched Misty to his chest as they both fell to their knees on the sidewalk, the sun blindingly bright after the darkness of the building. Rayne was sitting up on a gurney with an oxygen mask, Jared's father and Ty at her side.

He needed to know what the fuck had happened but first Misty needed medical attention. An EMT ran to both of them and Jared pointed at Misty.

"She's pregnant. She needs to go to a hospital and be checked by a doctor." The last words came out as coughs but the minute he'd said the word pregnant they were already loading her into the ambulance. He grabbed Deputy Knox's arm.

"Lindsey Jackson did this. Put out a BOLO. Every man on this. Find her. I have to stay with Misty."

Jared jumped into the back of the ambulance and held Misty's hand. They weren't taking her anywhere without him. The doors slammed shut and the engine roared to life. He had so many questions about what had happened today but the only one that counted at the moment was whether Misty and the baby were healthy.

If they weren't, nothing else mattered.

Chapter Twenty-Eight

Jared stepped into the smoky, dimly lit bar just outside of Hope Lake. The last few days had been hell and he had just one more thing to do to close the Boyd Hicks case.

Now that Misty was home he was back to work. She'd breathed in enough smoke they'd kept her for observation in the hospital but she and the baby were out of danger. Jared of course had been glued to her side which was why it had taken so long to find Dale Hicks.

"Is that him?" Chris nudged Jared's arm and jerked his head toward a dark haired man in his mid-thirties but who looked a decade older from too much hard, fast living.

"That's him. Stay alert. You never know with a Hicks what they're going to do next. He may not come quietly."

Slowly Jared and Chris approached Dale Hicks who was currently drinking whiskey and playing pool. The man Dale was with stiffened when he saw them and it must have tipped Dale off that something was happening.

Hicks whirled around, his hand reaching into his waistband but Jared already had the drop on him. He held the gun steady, pointing it at the man's chest. Chris had already moved toward the friend and was patting him down.

"Got a warrant for your arrest, Dale. Hands on your head."

Dale just threw back his head and laughed, almost dislodging the toothpick that dangled from his teeth.

"A warrant? What for? I didn't do shit."

"Obstruction of justice and accessory to murder," Jared stated, not letting his complete disgust with the man show. "Lindsey spilled the beans. We know the truth."

The man's jaw tightened and the laughter ended abruptly. "Lindsey is a skanky drug whore who wouldn't know the truth if it slapped her in the face. You can't believe anything she says."

"She sounded pretty convincing when she was telling Misty Foster how you provided the gun she used to shoot Boyd Hicks with."

Dale tossed the toothpick away, his eyes narrowing to slits. "So what if I did? Ain't no law against helping a woman protect herself."

"You knew all along that she'd killed Boyd. You covered for her. That makes you an accessory after the fact. You wanted her to kill your brother."

That lazy smile again. "I'm not upset about it. But I don't think you can prove I knew anything. You've got nothing on me and you know it."

Jared had been a cop long enough to know there were no slam dunks in this business. And the evidence they had on Dale Hicks wasn't strong. He'd played the situation perfectly. Making sure his brother knew of Lindsey's infidelities and then exhorting her to "defend" herself. Even supplying the weapon.

But...they did have a few things.

"Telephone records show a call from Lindsey when you were in Cheyenne. Then she called you back a few days after you got out. That call lasted fifteen minutes. Plenty of time to tell you what she did."

"She's a crazy meth head," Dale growled. "You can't believe anything she says. Talk to her again and she'll change her story."

Jared shook his head. "That won't be happening. You see, Lindsey OD'd. I found her in her car on a dirt road on the outskirts of town with a needle in her arm surrounded by pictures of her daughter. She's dead, Dale. I suspect you had something to do with driving her to desperation. You really hung her out to dry. She wrote her entire confession in a letter, including her relationship with you and how you both framed Boyd Hicks. You'll probably do time for that crime too."

They'd had a hell of a time finding Lindsey after she left Misty and Rayne to die. They'd finally received a call from a rancher about a deserted vehicle on the side of the road. Lindsey had been on the run but eventually took her own life.

Dale's mouth hung open and he didn't seem to be able to form words. His skin had turned a waxy pale shade as he worked through the shock of the news. Perhaps he had really cared for Lindsey in his own way.

That kind of care could get you killed.

"I don't believe you."

Jared shrugged, already tired of the back and forth with Dale. "So don't. Doesn't change the facts. You're fucked. You thought you had it all figured out. Revenge on Boyd. Revenge on Lindsey for marrying David Jackson while you were doing time. Hell, you even almost got revenge on me for putting you behind bars. So close but not quite." Jared raised his gun and took a few steps forward. "Now put your hands on top of your head."

Dale didn't move a muscle for a moment and then he slowly raised his hands and placed them on the back of his head.

"I want an attorney. I have a right to remain silent."

Jared wasn't planning to argue. Silence was preferable on the drive back to Fielding. He snapped the cuffs on Dale's wrists while Chris let the other man go.

A cop on either side, they marched Dale out of the bar. He had no idea if any of these charges would stick, but Jared knew as surely as the sun would rise in the morning Dale Hicks was going to break the law again. And when he did Fielding's finest would be right there to arrest him.

✧ ✧ ✧ ✧

"What will happen to Tilly?" Misty asked Jared as they relaxed in the bathtub a week later. The hot water lapped at the sides of the tub as he stroked the soft skin of her arm, grateful that she and the baby were healthy and out of danger. They'd both swallowed a lot of smoke but everything looked okay much to Jared's relief.

"Her foster family is anxious to adopt her, so hopefully there's a happy ending there."

"I just don't understand why Lindsey did what she did. Maybe Dale really did do it."

"She admitted to killing Boyd Hicks and the cigarette came back with her DNA. Add the gun that was found with her is also the gun that shot Boyd Hicks and things look pretty definitive."

"It was probably self-defense," Misty pointed out. She was always trying to see the best in a person. It was one of the reasons he loved her so much. She'd certainly seen something inside of him.

"If she'd called the police at that point she might have had a self-defense argument. But instead she roped her law abiding husband into helping her cover up the crime. Then when he confessed to the murder to keep her out of jail she tried to kill you, and Rayne by default."

And if she'd succeeded... Jared deliberately shook the morbid thoughts away and concentrated instead on the miracle in his arms.

"It's so sad," Misty said softly. Her capacity for forgiveness far greater than his own. "It seems like her life went from one calamity to another."

"What do all those things have in common?" Jared asked, keeping his tone hard. "Her. She made those choices."

"It's still sad. She's dead. Her child is without a mother or father. Her husband is going to jail too as an accessory to murder. It's like she gave up on anything good and decent in her life. I could never do that."

No, Misty was a fighter. A survivor. She wouldn't fold in the face of challenges. She'd rise up and vanquish any demon.

He placed his hand on her belly and felt the growing curve that was their child. Misty was experiencing butterfly wings of movement but he had yet to feel anything.

"I think she gave up a long time ago and what we saw was just a veneer...a mask she wore for the people around her. But you can only keep up a charade so long before the real person comes out."

Misty shrugged. "We'll never know. She was a person full of hate and loathing, mostly for herself. It's such a waste."

The entire situation was tragic. Tilly's parents had made one terrible and selfish decision after another and in the end it had cost her a family. Boyd Hicks was dead by his ex-wife's hand and David was going to do some time. The only person to come out unscathed was Dale Hicks. The district attorney was still debating as to whether there was enough evidence to take the case to trial.

"Dad can't wait until Rayne gets her new shop up and running. He's really excited about getting a tattoo."

Rayne had been a true blue friend before and after Lindsey had tried to kill her. Not knowing who Lindsey was, Rayne had greeted the woman as a potential client. Lindsey had dropped something on the floor and trying to be polite, Rayne had leaned down to help pick it up. That's when Lindsey had slammed the gun into Rayne's temple.

Luckily Rayne didn't have a fractured skull but she did have a nasty concussion. Jared had wanted to help her with all the expenses – medical and business – but she'd steadfastly refused, saying that none of this was his fault.

But it was. He should have followed his instincts and investigated Lindsey more. He'd let his softer side take control because she was a mother trying to get her daughter back.

"Stop it. You're doing it again." Misty sat up in the tub and turned to look him right in the eye. "This isn't your fault. That man confessed. What were you supposed to think?"

Jared rubbed his jaw, his chest tight with emotion. "I was supposed to know."

Misty tapped his chest right over his heart. "No one wanted to believe Lindsey Jackson was capable of something like this. Give yourself a break. You saved the day, handsome. We're all alive and the villains are behind bars. Because of you and your monumental impatience. I wasn't where I was supposed to be and you came to look for me. And thank God you did."

He slid his arms around her so her head nestled in the crook of his shoulder. "So you're not going to give me any more hassle about that?"

She giggled and his heart flipped in his chest. Damn, he loved this woman. "Not for awhile. But eventually? Yes. You can't go around expecting everyone to do everything your way."

Jared chuckled and ran his hands down her slick spine to cup her buttocks. She was always saying that but he wasn't sure he really believed it. His way *usually* was the right way. Most of the time.

Misty slapped at the water to get his attention. "Don't even go there. I swear I can read your thoughts by looking at your expression. And right now you're thinking of reasons I'm wrong. Well, I'm not wrong on this one."

"I'm glad you're here to keep me in line," he said, kissing her damp neck and then nibbling at her ear. "I know you won't let me get away with anything."

"Are you sure about that?" she teased, her hand slipping down to wrap around his cock, hot and hard. "I'm about to let you get away with seducing me."

Jared wasn't one to throw away an opportunity.

✧ ✧ ✧ ✧

Jared had been treating Misty like an invalid all week and she was darn tired of it. True, the first day out of the hospital she'd been overwhelmed by what had happened but a lovely young woman named Jazz, the fiancée of one of Jared's friends had come over to talk to Misty and Rayne about their brush with death. Jazz too had a close encounter with a serial killer the summer before and talking to her had been a great relief. They'd promised to stay in touch and Misty felt like she had found a new friend in Jazz. Someone who really cared and she could talk to.

Misty caressed his cock, feeling it jump in her hand. Jared's breath came out in a hiss and he sat up in the tub, the water sluicing off his yummy naked flesh. Just looking at him sent shivers of pleasure down her spine and her nipples peaked in anticipation of what was to come. Her sexual appetite had only grown since the morning sickness had gone away. Luckily Jared was still not only interested but enthusiastic.

"You're being a naughty girl," Jared warned with a wicked smile although she knew he wasn't going to do anything about it. Despite her pleading he'd laid down the law. No spankings until after the baby was born.

She ran her other hand up his wet chest and dipped her finger into the warm cavern of his mouth. "You've ignored me this week."

Jared laughed and gripped her hips, lifting her so she was sitting astride him. "Only you would say that. I wasn't ignoring you—I was taking care of you. You're so tiny I'm afraid you'll break in two."

She squeezed his cock and a groan fell from his lips. "I'm tougher than I look. I've taken on your whole family, haven't I?"

She'd gone from no family at all to the chaos of the Monroe clan. She and Becky were never going to be close friends that was clear, but Ty, Royce, and Gerald were total sweeties who had gone out of their way this week to cluck over her like mother hens. It felt good to be part of their family.

More at home with his father and brothers, Jared didn't feel the pressure to do every single thing *right* all the time. It made for a happier household and a less stressed sheriff.

Jared cupped her breasts and brushed his thumbs over the sensitive tips until she squirmed above him, her pussy grinding against his cock. He chuckled and pinched her nipples, sending a streak of pleasure straight to her clit.

"Come here, honey. I know what you need." That was Jared. Supremely self-confident to the point of arrogance but that was something she never wanted to change about him.

In the bedroom. She wouldn't have him any other way.

He lifted her up and pressed his cock at her entrance and his fingers gripped her hips. Already wet and ready for him, he slid in easily. She moaned at the pleasure of his cock stretching and filling her. She braced her hands on his chest and swayed her hips forward and back, then side to side.

Slowly at first but she quickened the pace, water sloshing over the sides of the tub and making a mess on the tile floor below. Neither paid it any mind as their arousal built and Misty found herself teetering on the precipice. Pleasure skittered through her from head to curled toes as she ground herself against him with each stroke.

So close, but not quite.

Jared's features were a mask of concentration, his jaw tight and controlled. Misty's fingers gripped his biceps as she slammed down on him, trying to fall over the edge.

"Look at me, Misty." Jared's voice was no more than a growl but their gazes locked as they moved in unison.

He reached between them and ran his thumb over her swollen clit. Misty's body exploded into a million little pieces as the lights danced behind her lids. She heard Jared say her name and then his cock swelled inside of her and heat swept through her veins.

They collapsed together in a heap of arms and legs, breathing ragged and labored, water spilling over the side of the tub. Jared stroked her hair and whispered words of love in her ear. Words she hoped he'd still be saying fifty years from tonight. Or maybe sixty. She wanted to spend her life with him. He'd set a part of her free and she'd never forget that.

"I was thinking," she began, floating to the other end of the tub so she was facing Jared. "I was thinking that maybe we should have that big wedding you talked about. I want everyone to know that I love you. That includes every busybody in this town. What do you think?"

Jared grinned lazily and tucked his hand behind his head as he lounged back. "Honey, you can have any kind of wedding you want. All I want is you. Do you think you can put this thing together before the baby comes?"

"I don't know. I've never planned a wedding."

She'd never even planned a small party before, and she had no idea where to begin.

"Maybe my brothers can help or the wives of my friends. They were really excited about Tanner and Madison's wedding."

Misty knew that look Jared was wearing. It was the take-charge-plan-everything look. But this time she didn't say a word. She was going to need someone like that if they were going to pull off a big fancy wedding.

"We don't have to have a big thing. I'd marry you in the judge's office tomorrow morning if that's what you want."

She meant it. That's how much she loved him. It was hard to believe she'd spent the better part of four months trying not to be with him and now here she was planning their life together.

"You're right. It needs to be big. I want this town to know Jared and Misty are really married. In every way. But there's no reason we have to wait to make vows to each other." Jared sat up in the tub, wrapping his arms behind her knees and pulled her close so they were knee to knee and face to face. "I promise to be the best husband and father I can possibly be and not try and boss you around too much. And I'll love you forever."

She couldn't ask for anything more.

"I promise to be the best wife and mother I can possibly be. I promise not to give into the urges I sometimes have to not talk to people in town. I promise to never let my mother's past influence our lives." She reached up and caressed his stubbled cheek. "And I'll love you forever."

He seemed happy and satisfied. What had started out as an accident had turned into so much more. She'd found passion with the sexiest man in Montana and a family – albeit wonderfully dysfunctional – at long last. Jared had found someone who loved him…imperfections and all. She kept his feet on the ground while he took her to the stars and back.

There would be bumps on the road ahead. They were both strong-willed and had been alone a long time. But there was love to smooth the way and to remind them what was truly important. The family they'd created together.

Epilogue

Big weddings take months to plan.

That's what Jared learned when he and Misty began putting together their special day. Misty was adamant about not waddling down the aisle eight or nine months pregnant so they'd decided to schedule the wedding after the baby was born. They'd ended up renting a large hotel ballroom in Billings for the ceremony and reception and filled it with flowers that Misty had chosen for the occasion.

Gerald Monroe had even managed to keep his thoughts to himself when Jared had announced that the wedding was three months after Misty's due date. He and his father had a new and different relationship now. Jared didn't feel the pressure to *win* at all costs to please his father. Misty's unconditional love had cured him of the need for approval. His father also seemed to have a more casual attitude toward life.

And a new tattoo, courtesy of Rayne, Misty's maid of honor, who was about to open a new shop in Valley Station. She'd worked in a small rental building for awhile but the deal in the nearby town had been too good to pass up. Prime location and low rent.

Jared's gaze caressed his gorgeous wife. Dressed in white satin and lace, she was the vision of an angelic bride. Speaking of angels…

"I'll hold her," Jared offered, holding out his arms and taking the squirming bundle from Misty. He hadn't held his daughter since before the ceremony. Charming, with a smile that lit up a room, everyone wanted to hold the absolutely beautiful Elizabeth Rose Foster Monroe. She had her daddy's dark hair and her mom's violet eyes. She was going to be a heartbreaker, not that Jared intended to let any man near her. Ever.

He didn't care if she spit up on his tux but he knew Misty had talked about saving her wedding dress in case Lizzie Rose wanted to wear it someday. That's when Jared had told Misty that their daughter was never dating.

"You're being bossy again," she'd laughed at him. "I don't think you'll get away with that."

"No dating," Jared whispered in his daughter's tiny ear as Misty floated away to talk with the women huddled on the other side of the dance floor. Jared could see Jazz, Kaylee, Ava, Madison, Presley, and Rayne all laughing and drinking champagne.

Jared sat down at the large round table with all of his sheriff friends. Everyone was there, including DEA Agent Jason Anderson who had been missing for weeks. He'd been kidnapped by a drug cartel but had finally escaped. Jared's friend looked thinner than usual and he now sported a scar on his left cheek, but he still had the same sharp humor and intelligence that had drawn the two men together.

"Thanks for coming here today instead of the roadhouse for a meeting," Jared said as he settled Lizzie Rose into the crook of his arm and gave her a pacifier to suck on.

"Wouldn't have missed this for the world," Reed grinned and slapped Jared on the back. "It's a big day when one of us ties the knot."

Misty and Jared had attended both Reed and Griffin's weddings during the summer. "It's becoming more common, that's for sure. I wonder if Dare or Evan will fall?"

"I heard that," Dare said gruffly, the usual scowl on his face. "I'm not falling anywhere or for anyone. I got too damn much on my plate for that shit."

"Watch your language," Tanner warned him with a smile. "We have innocent ears here."

Red stained Dare's cheeks and he took a gulp of his beer. "Sorry. I'm not around babies much."

Griffin shook his head obviously trying not to laugh. "That's an understatement. Do you even know how they're made?"

Dare's mouth actually twitched into an almost smile. "I have a pretty good idea how it's accomplished."

Logan elbowed Seth in the ribs. "Somebody should tell this guy then because he doesn't seem to know."

Heads whipped around to stare at Seth Reilly who was grinning like an idiot. "Yes, Presley is pregnant again. We're hoping for a girl this time. We wanted the kids to be close together in age. But I swear after this one we're done. She's threatened to come after me with the weed whacker if I knock her up again."

Everyone congratulated Seth and they all made a toast to the baby's health and future. Jared gave Jason a quick glance and the man nodded his head.

"Actually I have some news too." Lizzie Rose had fallen asleep in Jared's arms and he gazed down at his sleeping daughter, feeling his heart squeeze in his chest. Everything he did was for her and Misty. Today was no exception. "Being a part of this group has made me a better lawman. I hope you'll welcome my deputy Knox next month when he becomes the new sheriff of Fielding. I'm stepping down."

There was silence and then everyone seemed to be talking at once. Jared cut them off with a wave of his arm, not wanting them to wake his daughter.

"You're quitting?" Evan asked. He'd been quiet most of the day but then he wasn't a man to speak unless he had something to say. "Is this some kind of a joke?"

"No joke." Jared shook his head. "Misty and I are moving to Seattle. She can be closer to the gallery she works with. Plus there's another in San Francisco that is interested in showing her work."

Jared didn't talk about all the discussions he and Misty had been through the last several months. The back and forth. It wasn't anything they needed to know about. But Jared was sure this was the right thing to do, although Misty had assured him hundreds of times she was happy to stay in Fielding if that's what he wanted. She'd meant it too. All she wanted was for him to be happy.

But Jared couldn't deny the excitement of a brand new challenge. Something he could build from the ground up and be proud of.

"What about your dad?" Reed queried, his brows pulled down. "What will you do there? Be a cop?"

"Dad is coming with us," Jared announced, hiding a smile at how that would have been impossible a year ago. "There are specialists there that can hopefully help slow things down and give him a better quality of life for a longer time. And I won't be a cop. I'm actually going into business with a friend. We're going to become law enforcement consultants. Jason and I."

More uproar as everyone shot questions at Jared and Jason. Jason finally held up his hands in surrender. "Guilty as charged.

I'm stealing Jared away to help me start my company. I've retired from the DEA and hopefully found a niche where we can really do some good. There are so many small town cops that don't have the resources when a big case comes along. That's where we'll come in."

"You'll live in Seattle too?" Griffin asked. "I thought you had family in Montana and North Dakota."

"I do and I'll split my time. Jared is going to be the computer expert. I'll use my government contacts if we need them. And we'll have a man in the field as well."

"I feel sorry for the poor bastard," Reed scoffed. "You're no day at the beach to work for, Jared."

Jared knew that all too well. He also knew that his new partners would kick his ass if he gave them a hard time. Of course he'd have to kick theirs right back.

"He won't work for me. We'll all three be equal partners. And I think Logan is going to do a terrific job."

Griffin slapped the table and laughed. "Okay, this is a joke. No way would Logan Wright leave his sheriff's job."

Logan chuckled and set his beer bottle down on the table, the label half peeled off. "It's not a joke. I've been thinking about it for a long time. I'm a family man now with a wife and two kids. I need to do something less dangerous that gives me a more flexible schedule. When Jason talked about it I knew this was my chance."

Everything was changing and no one seemed to know what to say until Tanner raised his glass in a salute. "Let's toast to your new venture. May it be everything you hope it to be."

The men raised their bottles and glasses and the sound of the clinking made Lizzie Rose screw up her face for a moment. She didn't wake and only wriggled into a more comfortable spot on Jared's shoulder.

The reception began to wind down and Jared found himself standing off into a corner with Tanner. The older man wore a somber expression.

"We're going to miss you, my friend. Fielding is losing one of the best lawmen I know."

"I'm looking forward to new things. I'll miss everyone, but we'll be back often since Ty and Royce will still be here running the ranch and Rayne will have her tattoo shop in Valley Station."

Tanner nodded, his gaze on his wife a few feet away, holding Presley and Seth's son Bennett on her lap. "I'm happy for you. Misty is a wonderful girl. You got lucky." Tanner grinned. "Just like me. In fact, I'm so lucky I think I'm going to take my sexy wife home so we can be alone."

"I guess the honeymoon isn't over," Jared chuckled.

"It will never be over if you don't let it." Tanner slapped Jared on the back. "That's my only marriage advice. Wait—one more thing. Never let her forget that she's the most important thing in the world. Women are forgiving creatures and they'll put up with a whole hell of a lot. As long as they're truly loved and cherished."

Tanner made a beeline for Madison, pulling her out of her chair and twirling her in his arms until she was laughing and giggling, her entire face alight with love.

"Should I be jealous?" Misty's hand on his arm pulled his attention away from Tanner and Madison. "You're watching them awfully intently."

"Tanner just gave me some marriage advice, that's all."

"Are you going to tell me what it is?" she asked, sliding her hands around his waist and resting her head on his chest.

"No, I'm going to show you."

The End

Thank you for reading
The Cowboy Justice Association –
Imperfect Justice.

The hot romance continues in the
Military Moguls series….

Emeralds, Rubies, and Camouflage: Book 4

Myra Burke has lost her faith in men and love. When her ex-fiancé cleans out their bank account she needs a decent job to provide for her four year old daughter and she needs it yesterday.

Holt Winthrop has money, intelligence, and charm. He also has love to give but that isn't an option anymore. Caught in a suicide bombing, he's scarred inside and out. No one would want what he's become.

Against his better judgment, his matchmaking friends convince Holt to hire Myra as his personal assistant. When he finds out she's down on her luck he simply can't say no despite his instant attraction to the curvaceous redhead.

Myra thinks her new boss is not only wonderful but sexy as hell. If she isn't careful she could find herself head over heels for a man like him. Good thing she's knows better. Billionaires don't fall in love with their assistants.

Or do they? As each day passes their mutual attraction turns into a fiery passion that neither can ignore or deny. They'll need all the courage they can find to take a chance on love…just one more time.

About the Author

Olivia Jaymes is a wife, mother, lover of sexy romance, and caffeine addict. She lives with her husband and son in central Florida and spends her days with handsome alpha males and spunky heroines.

She is currently working on a series of full-length novels called The Cowboy Justice Association. It's a contemporary erotic romance series about hunky lawmen in southern Montana who work to keep the peace but can't seem to find it in their own lives. She also has a military/billionaire series and an upcoming contemporary romantic suspense series titled – Danger Incorporated.

Visit Olivia Jaymes at
www.OliviaJaymes.com

Sign up to be notified of Olivia's new releases:
Newsletter Sign Up
http://eepurl.com/Y6aof

<<<<>>>>

10400520R00187

Printed in Great Britain
by Amazon.co.uk, Ltd.,
Marston Gate.